THE DEMON JOKE

OUR SHADOWS WILL REMAIN
BOOK FOUR

ALEC CHARLES

The Demon Joke
Alec Charles

Oxford eBooks

Also In this series:

Big City Secrets
Days of Surrender
Every Open Eye

PROLOGUE

BEFORE...

THERE WERE THREE of us and for a while we were happy. It was me and Lee and we were the live-in lovers of Tiffany Lily. I'd been with her a while; when she was just another ageing actress who couldn't find steady work but could always find the money for some more *surgical improvements*. Tiffany was still getting paid for TV soap operas and dramas she had been in years, sometimes decades earlier. Royalties whenever one or the other was aired in some far off country with a name that's hard to pronounce. The money probably would have been more than enough for someone like you or me to get by on easily enough but Tiffany was always broke - as are most people living it up out in LA. The house, the hired hands, the clothes and the jewellery and the holidays and the restaurants - I don't know, it must have all been on credit or something.

Her star took to rising again right around the time we met Lee. Tiffany bagged a decent role in a soap opera that was going from strength to strength and her popularity started to surge. She started getting so many offers that the TV producers gave her a pay rise alongside a new contract with hundreds of rules about how she could only walk away to star in a movie or another show if certain boxes hidden in the small-print were checked.

Don't ever ask me to explain how, but she was still always making out she was fucking broke. But some people have a different kind of broke to me and you. It's like I said - even before her luck had changed, she had all the luxuries you could imagine and more. The luxuries got noticeably more luxurious but I still used to hear her talking over financial problems with her agent (Mark Chambers, file under A for Asshole). Thing is, I'd never particularly cared and not too long after Lee came and moved in with us, I practically stopped caring. It was Lee. Lee was a good guy. Sure, his morals were questionable but he was better than a brother to me. He brought a little light into the darkness I'd locked myself away to make amends for past sins. He had me believe that the cosmos might have thought my debt was almost paid and things were only going to improve because of it.

PART 1

MUSIC FOR THE MORNING AFTER

1

It was Tiffany shouting, "Where is he?" that woke me up. She was just screaming the same question over and over, taking steps that sounded far too heavy to be her own as she stormed down the landing opening and slamming the same doors. "Where is he?" she screamed on coming into the bedroom. She wasn't asking anybody in particular.

"What's going on?" I groaned, nose feeling packed from the coke I'd taken late in the night and then again early in the morning. "What the fuck is this?" I sighed, rolling onto my back.

"He's gone," she screamed, disappearing inside the walk-in wardrobe. Clothes were flung out on their hangers. Boxes filled with whatever and neatly placed in a row along the floor were kicked. "He's gone," she screamed again.

"Jesus fucking Christ!" I hissed, making a fist and bringing it to the wall directly over my head.

The doorbell sounded. Tiffany stopped her assault on the contents of the wardrobe and came rushing out of it as silently as she could manage. "That's him," she said, "it has to be!"

I sighed. I hadn't heard Tiffany making her way downstairs but when I heard the front door open and close soon after, I sighed again and sat upright - dropping my legs over the side of the bed. It had gone quiet. I still wasn't capable of thinking properly; couldn't sense any urgency or take any guesses at what was happening. In fact, I had already come to the conclusion that whatever problem Tiffany had been experiencing was already over. So I just sat there, making fists with my feet, right up until she came into the room and stopped at the foot of the bed.

"One of the guards at the gate handed this over to Mark," she said, tossing something onto the bed. I turned around to take a look at it. It was the card you needed to get in and out of our gated community without any hassle. Every home had one. "I hope you're proud of yourself," she said, "but you did it. Whatever you said to him was enough to chase him away."

I rubbed at my head. More than anything in the world, I needed a cigarette. "Mark's gone?" I asked her.

"Sure," she said, "play the innocent. You know full well what I'm talking about."

I shrugged. Mark going would be no big deal. In fact, the only disappointment I'd feel on never seeing him again would all be down to not being able to poke fun at him anymore.

But then the missing piece became clear to me.

"Wait a minute," I said, "where's Lee?"

"Oh," she laughed, "you're good. You're very good. Take a round of applause," she said, clapping sarcastically as a single tear rolled down her cheek.

"Lee's gone? When?" I asked, "Did he say anything?"

"I know the two of you were talking about something early this morning," she said, heading to the door, "and if I find out you said something to him and that's the reason he isn't here, there'll be trouble."

2

I STAYED SITTING there on the bed for over an hour, then I heard the front door close so I looked out of the window and saw Tiffany and Mark were leaving. They climbed inside of his car and drove away without a word.

"The fuck is going on?" I muttered to myself.

First thing I did was take a good look inside of the walk-in wardrobe. I wasn't expecting to find Lee hiding in there or anything - I just needed to see for myself that his things had gone and they had. Well, practically everything had gone. I didn't need to perform a detailed search or anything like that... The second I saw his stained and stinking rucksack had been taken, I knew for sure that he had no intention of returning and I had no idea whether I should be cheering him on or hating him for it.

"Bummer," I sighed. Without slipping into anything more than a bathrobe I made my way to the bathroom before heading downstairs. The air was too thick with the smell of cigarette smoke. Tiffany must have been smoking one after another without a moment's break in between and Mark, being the kind of person that he is, would have taken in alongside her for some phony show of solidarity and support. There was an open packet of cigarettes in the left pocket of the bathrobe I was wearing - Lee's funnily enough, like a parting gift for me to find. I took a smoke from the pack, lifted a box of matches from the kitchen worktop on passing and went straight out of the patio doors and into the back. The sun was high and bright; just another day like nothing whatsoever was out of the ordinary. I'd been standing out here with Lee just a couple of hours earlier. Had he seemed down? No more than he could be from time to time. Hadn't said anything that gave me reason to think he would be walking out on us. I thought it over in detail, trying to look over every word for some hidden meaning while I looked to the swimming pool despite the sun's blinding reflection hovering over the still water.

Nothing. Absolutely nothing.

I sighed, lit a cigarette and tossed the burning match into the water. It was too hot and I was too beat to enjoy it but I took a pull on the cigarette and held the smoke inside my lungs until my chest was just about ready to burst.

"So long, Lee," I said, coughing gently.

3

TIFFANY AND MARK returned to the house after close to four hours. I was out back, relaxing on a sun lounger with a single vodka and orange when I heard them coming into the kitchen. "All I'm saying is," Mark was explaining as he wiped his horn-rimmed spectacles across his trousers, "is the police aren't going to be interested until he's been gone twenty four hours."

"So you're still here?" Tiffany spat out at stopping beside me, intentionally blocking the sun. Before I could even think of how best to reply to that, she had turned back to Mark and was lighting a cigarette. "So what do you expect me to do, Mark? What do you expect me to do?"

He sighed, sat in the vacant lounger between Tiffany and myself and eased his foot out of his right loafer. Mark always looked a little damp and a little too pink, like he was slowly being roasted alive. Whenever he was more stressed than normal, like he was right now, his pristine-white shirt became transparent with sweat and clung to his chest like it was a second skin.

"Hello," Tiffany growled, "Earth to Mark! Is there anybody home?"

"I'm thinking," he said, looking inside of his shoe before shaking a small pebble out from it.

"You," Tiffany said as she turned her attention back on me, "you know Doyle - where the fuck would he be right now?"

"We looked everywhere for him," Mark said to me with a weary-sounding sigh, "and I mean everywhere."

"So *now* he can talk," Tiffany snapped, turning back to him. "Well," she asked him, "what's the next big idea, Mr Genius?"

Mark slipped his foot back inside of the loafer. "All we have to remember," he said, "is that Lee signed a contract and you have nothing at all to worry about."

Even I knew that was the stupidest fucking thing he could have said at that moment.

"Oh," Tiffany laughed, "the contract, of course! You hear that," she asked me, "we have nothing to worry about. Except," she screamed at him, "Lee has gone missing!"

"I don't know what to say," he said, "it's not like we're talking about a small boy or a puppy! Lee's a grown man and if he's decided to move on then we should let him go and move on with him. It's not like he emptied the safe or took any of your jewellery."

"Oh," Tiffany shouted, "oh!" and then she marched right back into the house and slammed the patio doors shut so hard behind her that it's a miracle the house didn't come falling down around them.

Mark sighed. He wanted me to say something – anything - right there but I'd always enjoyed leaving him hanging or poking fun whenever the opportunity arose so I took my time, drinking a little vodka and orange and taking the cigarettes and matches from the floor beside me as slowly as I could manage. "Boy," he said, admitting defeat, "I really should learn when to keep my mouth shut - am I right?"

"You really found no sign of him?"

"No." Mark asked hopefully, "Do you have an idea where he might be?"

"Wish I did," I said, lighting a cigarette, "but I'm kind of glad I don't."

"I hear you," Mark said with one more sigh, "I hear you." We were silent for a little while but then he went and asked me, "Did you really have no idea he was planning on leaving?"

"Who said he planned it? Maybe he just woke up and decided it was time to be someplace else."

"Maybe you're right," Mark said, "I just don't know what to think right now."

I turned my head to face him and said, "You got your car keys in your pocket?"

"My keys? No," he said, "I put them down by the front door. What makes you ask?"

"Haven't heard Tiffany for a while," I said, "and I sure as hell wouldn't want her behind the wheel of my car right now."

Mark sat there for a second or two, trying to make sense of what I was saying, and then he jumped up onto his feet and ran inside the house calling Tiffany's name.

4

Two, MAYBE THREE days went by and no word came from Lee. Tiffany had her P.A. - a beautiful young thing named Samantha - call the general hospitals to see if anybody matching his description had been brought in but all she got in return was a couple of false alarms. Chambers somehow prevented Tiffany from doing anything too drastic. If it was down to her, she probably would have had a *Missing* poster on every streetlight come the end of the first day. It was funny for me because I wanted Lee back myself but I knew it was purely down to my own selfish reasons so I didn't offer to help out at all, I just kept my ears open to what the others were talking about and silently wished him all the luck he could possibly need. Tiffany didn't really talk to me at all - not unless she really had to - which she practically didn't. I just took it easy beside the pool; had a few light drinks during the day and some blow to keep me up until the early hours of the morning so she wouldn't wake up when I finally crawled into bed because I sure as hell didn't want to be ordered onto the couch. She was missing filming - calling in to say she was coping with a personal crisis of some kind - and I was petrified that some debt collectors would turn up out of the blue and toss us out onto the street because she wasn't getting paid.

And then one morning, it all changed again.

She was sitting at the dining table, all dolled-up and trying to look like someone who doesn't have a care in the world. Samantha was beside her, a vision of genuine fucking beauty. Tiffany's skin looked all the more like plastic because of it.

"Good morning," Tiffany said to me with a smile, flicking ash from her cigarette into a clean bowl while Samantha continued to work away on her laptop. "There are some waffles going spare if you would like some."

All I could do was hope, *pray* that Samantha wouldn't look up to greet me and see me standing there in my open bathrobe and fading y-fronts.

"That'd be nice," I said, reaching for the cigarettes and box of matches inside one of the few pockets I had at my disposal.

"Maybe have them in a little while," Tiffany beamed, "because there is someone here to see you."

"Cole," he said, entering the room like the villain of a stage-play, "so good to see you."

Dr Pink. A man who was nothing but sharp angles when you saw him one month and then as round as a fucking globe when you saw him the next. Only the fingers never seemed to change. They always looked like stripped bones.

"Doc," I said with a polite nod, "it's been a while."

"Hasn't it?" he said, stopping right in front of me. His eyes looked into mine. I could smell tuna and cucumber on his breath. "Cigarette?" he asked, pulling an open pack from out of nowhere. I'd forgotten all about mine even though I was holding them. And you want to know something important about Dr Pink? The man didn't smoke but he always carried a pack with him. I don't think you can ever trust somebody like that, not ever. Someone always out to gain favour, I mean.

"I've got my own," I smiled at him and then I looked over his shoulder to ask Tiffany, "should I be concerned?"

"Nonsense," Pink laughed, dropping a hand on my shoulder. "I'm here for a simple check-up, nothing more."

"I need you at my side tonight," Tiffany said, "very important business. I just need to know you're fit and healthy. Last thing I need is you passing on a cold and making me look bad because of it."

"I'm intrigued already," I smiled, bypassing Pink to reach the dining table. "Are you going to give me any more details or is it all going to be a surprise?"

"The new producer starts in the next few weeks," she said, "and he wants to speak with me."

I'd heard a few things about the guy stepping into the role of producer for the soap opera she was working on and not a single bit of it was good. People in the industry had decided to give him the moniker of 'The Axe Man' because he tended to get rid of a lot of people once he joined a show. Names meant nothing to him. People like that are dangerous. And they said he was a devoted Scientologist. That made him that little bit more dangerous.

"You want me there? Wouldn't it be better if it was just you and Mark?"

"Don't be silly," she smiled, crushing her cigarette at the bottom of the bowl, "this isn't business - it's pleasure."

"If you're sure."

"I'm sure," she said, getting to her feet. "Samantha - let's give the men a little privacy."

Samantha rose to her feet, acknowledged my presence for the first time and walked out of the room at Tiffany's heels. Things hadn't sat right between the two of us since I'd told her I was in love with her. And I wasn't, if you're interested. But I'm not one of those guys who'll tell a girl that just to try and bed her. At times I was convinced I was in love with her but then I'd masturbate and realise I wasn't actually in love with her once I'd added some fluid of my own to the toilet water. The only thing I never once doubted was how soft the hair around her pussy must be.

"Well," Pink said to bring my attention back on him, "let's go and get the party started."

5

PINK WATCHED ME slip out of my bathrobe and underwear as he pulled the latex gloves over his hands. "Dinner with Mr Pate," he said, "you must be very excited."

"That's his name," I said - standing before him, "Pate?"

"Scott Pate," he smiled, stepping towards me, "I know a few people that have worked with him."

"I'm sure you do. They tell you anything interesting?"

"This and that," Pink said, kneeling before me and gently taking my left testicle between finger and thumb. "I'm afraid it wouldn't be proper for me to discuss what I have been told."

"Yeah," I said, "I bet it wouldn't."

Pink turned his attention to the right testicle. "Do these get regular use?"

"A gentleman never tells."

"Of course," he smirked. "And Miss Lily is your only sexual partner?" he asked, first tilting his head to look underneath my floppy before he took it in the open palm of his hand to examine it up top.

"Well," I said with a sigh, "I guess she is now."

He had my Jap's eye open wide by pinching the end of my dick. I was worried he was about to take a swab but he seemed happy enough to just squint an eye of his own and peer down there. "Of course," he said, "Lee... How have you been feeling since he decided to move on?"

"I don't know," I shrugged. "I miss having someone to talk to."

"Of course, of course. Please turn around and touch your toes."

I did what was asked. Pink spread my ass cheeks to take a good look at my hole. I felt more than a little sorry I didn't have it in me to break wind.

"Well," he said as he gently patted my ass, "everything looks okay here. You can straighten up and slip back into your underwear."

I straightened up, slipping into my underwear. The packet of cigarettes he'd presented me were within reaching distance so I took a smoke and lit up. "Picture of health, right?"

"It's far too early to tell. Tell me," he asked, "how many are you smoking each day?"

"Ten, sometimes fifteen," I lied.

"And you're exercising and eating right?"

"Like a soldier."

"That's good," he said, "that's good. Now if you can just follow me into the next room, I'll be able to take a blood sample."

"Haven't taken one of those in a while."

"You'll be fine," he said with a smile, "I'm sure your veins are still working. You are still capable of getting an erection, aren't you?"

"Jesus," I said, "where are you planning on getting the sample from?"

"Ha!" He said, "That's funny! I'll have to remember that one."

6

Tiffany's favourite restaurant was a place named Knewman's. It was expensive, the staff treated her like royalty and she got to patronize people she introduced to the place by telling them that the K is silent on the way in.

Pate had booked a table at another restaurant. More expensive. One that didn't give a shit to who she was - they simply wouldn't allow her to smoke in there. Tiffany hated the place, never ventured there because of it. I had to wonder if this was all coincidence or whether Pate had really done his research and chose this place because of it.

The chauffeur-driven limo we'd arrived in pulled to a stop. Larsen, Tiffany's favourite driver, didn't even have to climb out to open the door for us; someone manning the door of the restaurant hurried over with dignified steps. "You're not going to faint on me, are you?" she asked before the door was opened for us. I'd only given my blood sample to Pink early that morning.

"I'll be fine," I told her.

The door was held open for her. As usual, I climbed out first and offered her my hand. It was a display that usually got her noticed. Here, nobody seemed to care. Even the paparazzi waiting nearby didn't want to waste their batteries on a TV star when Hollywood names could be arriving at any minute. She didn't notice. She was too busy lighting a cigarette - a hit of nicotine to last her until whenever.

"This place is far too expensive," she said loud enough for the employee to hear, "and I've waited far too long for meals."

"You think we'll be here long?" I asked, chaperoning her to the entrance. She walked fast, knowing the guy who had opened the car door for us would have to try and reach the entrance before us.

"I certainly hope not," she said as he went by us as quickly as he could without it almost turning into a run, "the steaks taste like they could have been brought over from McDonald's."

The door was held open for us. Tiffany waltzed on in without acknowledging the effort the guy had gone to just to get there before us. I gave him a brief nod and a slightly embarrassed smile and then the head boy standing beyond the entrance greeted us from his podium and asked whether we had made a reservation. "In a way," Tiffany said, fanning herself down. "It's too hot in here," she observed before asking me, "do you think it's too hot in here? I think it's too hot. The air conditioning mustn't be working properly."

"It's probably just cold outside," I shrugged.

"We're here to have dinner with Mr Pate," Tiffany said, turning back to the man. "Table for four."

Four of us. It was possible that Pate had brought a date of his own but it was more likely to be Chambers. Earlier that morning Tiffany had allowed me to think Chambers wouldn't be here. If he was here now then it would be clear she was just keeping me out of the loop for whatever reason - her blaming me for Lee's absence being the most likely - and was wanting to keep me on my toes.

"Mr Pate," the man nodded, smiling as he signalled a young waiter over with a hand movement so subtle it was hard to register. "Let us guide you to your table, madam."

We fell in behind him, made our way through a sea of tables claimed by guests who didn't look twice at Tiffany. As a matter of fact, I made a double take or two of my own at some of the faces. They were forgotten about easily enough because once I saw Pate - sitting alongside Chambers, who I'd been under the impression wouldn't even be here - I only had eyes for him. It's not that he was attractive or anything, just his face looked like it could start melting if the candle on the table was moved a little too close. Him and Tiffany would have our table look like a *House of Wax* reunion.

"Tiffany," Chambers grinned, getting to his feet once we were close enough for him to stop pretending he hadn't noticed us, "you're right on time - as usual!"

Pate looked right by us and said to the waiter from behind a frozen smile, "Go get us some menus, would you? And don't forget the drinks ones," he added with a dry laugh. The waiter nodded and moved on without first offering to sit Tiffany. Chambers was up in a flash, graciously easing her chair out from under the table as I dropped myself down and took a deep breath.

"You," Pate said to me without the slightest change of emotion on his face, "you look familiar. You acted before?"

"Cole?" Tiffany laughed, pressing her hand atop of mine for Pate to see. "Cole has enough difficulty telling the pizza delivery guy where to come - he could never be an actor!"

Pate took a deep breath, held it as he shrugged and finally let it out. "I don't know," he said, "I just say it how I see it. You ever thought of going into acting?"

"No," I said, "I can't say I like actors too much."

"Ha!" Pate said, "We have something in common already! What's your issue with them?"

"I wouldn't say it's an issue," I said as Tiffany squeezed at my hand to try and encourage me to fall silent, "it's just they get a lot of credit for all the hard work others have put into the same thing."

Pate brought the palms of his hands together, placed his elbows down on the table and rested his chin upon his knuckles. I thought that any minute now, his face would start to drip off of his chin for sitting too close to the flame.

"And now I see why you caught my eye the moment you arrived," he said. "What is it, Cole, are you an undiscovered writer or director?"

"Cole used to write," Tiffany said in as proud a tone as she could manage. "I always tried to encourage him but he's too lazy. Dropped out of college, didn't you?"

"It's not for everybody," Pate said with a wave of the hand before I had the chance to answer for myself. "I quit college, started right at the bottom of the industry and worked my way up. You can't walk down the street without knocking into an actor. Actors will undercut one another and perform all manner of deeds to get their parts; but writers," Pate beamed, "writers have the real struggle. You want to know what I think? I think some of the best writers in the country are begging on street corners."

A waiter arrived with a selection of menus and spread them out across the table like a blackjack dealer cutting a deck. Pate smiled to the waiter, glanced down at the menus and then back to the man who'd brought them. "Thank you," he said. "If you don't mind my asking- are you Chinese or Japanese?"

The waiter gave him a quizzical look and for a second it felt like he had no intention of answering the question - at least not politely. "Korean," he said.

"Ah," Pate said with relief, "good for you, son. We'll call you over once we're about ready to order."

The waiter nodded and walked away. Pate smiled, opened a menu in front of him and explained his interaction with the restaurant employee. "I lived in China for a number of years," he said, "and the people there are the most unhygienic you could possibly imagine. I'm absolutely serious. The youngsters were up to nothing but bed-hopping and sexual orgies; apartments where the cockroaches went unnoticed, there was that much garbage on the floor. And the smell," he said with disgust, "the smell of those people! No wonder they always seem to be wearing those plastic masks. But anyway," he said, "that's enough of that. Cole - what did you used to write?"

"This and that," I shrugged on pulling a menu toward me. "I just enjoyed telling stories."

"Isn't that great... What made you give it all up?"

"Personal problems," I said, "not enough money to keep me going."

"He was pretty good," Tiffany said, "I'm not saying his work was perfect but I've seen a lot worse."

"I don't suppose you have anything I could take a look at?"

"I don't know," I said, "I'd have to go and dig around to find something."

"Would you?"

"How about Tiffany?" Mark interrupted. "If you want to

talk writing," he said with a smile, "maybe you should ask the bestseller sitting at the table."

"Mark," Tiffany said with faux embarrassment, "I'm sure Scott knows everything he needs to know about my writing."

"You could say that," Pate said in agreement - eyes scanning the open menu before him, "I had lunch with your ghost-writer not two days ago."

It took everything in me not to laugh.

Pate looked up at me to ask, "Do you miss it? The writing, I mean."

"I don't know... For a while I felt guilty whenever a day ended and I hadn't even tried sitting down to write; then when I tried writing it was impossible for me to put a decent paragraph together."

"Scripts could be your calling," he said. "A couple of sentences to set the scene in a script could take a couple of pages in manuscript. Dialogue is a hell of a lot easier to put down. Trust me," he smiled, "I became successful once I made the switch."

"Please," Tiffany purred, "I've seen your early work and it was miles ahead of what Cole could ever do."

"I was working with good people," he said to her before turning his eyes back on me. "My, my, my - how you have not found fame and fortune out here already is a complete mystery."

Tiffany was in good spirits during the ride back home. She talked about nothing other than how Pate had told her "big stories" concerning her character were being discussed and Chambers only encouraged her thinking that she was safe. Me, I was 50-50. I can discuss a lot of things but it doesn't mean any of it is ever going to happen. So I left them to it and just sat back, smoking in silence. Chambers was looking at me from time to time in a way he never had done before. He looked like he wanted to say something but didn't know how to start.

7

I woke up because I'd heard somebody calling my name. The bedside clock said it was nine in the morning. The sun was already illuminating the bedroom and the air was heavy. Tiffany's side of the bed was empty, cold.

My name was called again, much more audible this time around. It was Tiffany who was calling me and it didn't sound like she was in the house. Confused, I pulled myself out of the bed and went over to the open window that looked out onto the street. Chambers was at the kerb, sat behind the wheel of his cherry red hummer, and Tiffany was standing at the open passenger door. The outfit she was wearing belonged on somebody twenty years or more her junior.

"Cole," she waved, just in case there was any chance of my somehow missing her. "I'm going away for a couple of days," she said, "I'll call you when I get back."

"Where're you going?"

"I can't hear you," she claimed, climbing inside of the vehicle, "wish me luck," and with that she slammed the door shut and Chambers hit the horn just once before moving on. Bewildered by such unexpected developments I opted not to return to bed but instead slipped on Tiffany's freshly washed robe and made my way downstairs in search of clues to what was happening. I found nothing but the stale smell of cigarette smoke and a half-eaten bagel. Still, the bitch had been kind enough to leave one of the Platinum cards behind...

8

I ALWAYS TOOK a good look at the swimming pool before jumping in because I was terrified of an alligator or crocodile finding its way there. I'd never have admitted that to Tiffany, not even to Lee when he was around, but it was a true concern of mine. People wouldn't understand it even after the sightings of Reggie in South Bay in such recent history or if you pointed out to them how some people will illegally keep 'gators and crocs as pets. But you know something? Even I felt a little stupid taking such precautions but it was a phobia and a phobia is nothing but an irrational fear. You can't escape it, can't reason with it, so I took a good look into the clear water before jumping right in. The water was cooler than I'd been expecting but I took myself right under, hearing the whine of a mosquito near my ear. Despite my discomfort around the water, I've always felt something close to bliss on being fully submerged. I don't know - it's just the feeling of weightlessness or how every sound apart from that of your own heartbeat is muffled.

Closing my eyes, I eased myself close down to the floor and felt at the tiles with my fingertips. Lee came to mind. Lee and his fear of moths. Mottephobia... we Googled it one night. My heartbeat remained calm and steady.

9

It would have been no trouble for me whatsoever to take the car but I opted to walk out; out of our gated little neighbourhood and onto one bus for a while, then another and finally a third. There isn't a single place out in the City of Angels I particularly dig but I rode on out into the real badlands... To buildings with barred windows that had been long abandoned and then reclaimed by those confident they were tough enough to hold onto them. I hopped off the bus once the driver finally pulled up a good twenty or so yards from the stop - the man clearly in no rush to welcome others aboard - and took to walking again. It was starting to rain. A kid that looked a lot like young Lou Reed was walking along the sidewalk with an electric guitar. It wasn't even in a bag - he was wearing it like he had just stepped off the stage. He caught me looking at him and lowered his gaze. He must have thought I was planning on asking how much it would cost for the guitar.

Matt was standing out on the stoop when I arrived. He was a giant of a motherfucker with a tattoo of the Confederate Flag on the left side of his shaved head. On his right arm he had a tattoo of a smiling naked woman removing a Ku Klux Klan hood from her head; an assault rifle of some kind over her shoulder, strap resting between her perky tits. He turned on hearing my footsteps and smiled, recognising me. "Cole," he said as a gorilla paw wrapped tight around my slender hand, "what brings you out here?"

"Social call," I told him. "He in?"

"Sure," Matt said, "nigger's in. Go on up."

"I won't be disturbing him?"

"Who'd give a fuck?" he laughed. "Go on," he said, "you got a hall pass."

We bumped fists in understanding and I walked on into the building, the door falling shut behind me. A girl came walking down from one of the floors above. She was around sixteen or seventeen, strung-out and wearing nothing but a grey t-shirt with an image on it that appeared instantly recognisable to me; the open left eye of a female and the carefully trimmed eyebrow above. The cover of the one and only LP released by The La's - it fucking had to be - and what were the odds of me seeing it so unexpectedly after Lee had gone from my life?

Doyle had loved that band when I first knew him a long time ago. He'd claimed the frontman, Lee (that *would* have to be his name, wouldn't it?) Mavers was a genius whose name and talent should have been as respected as that of Mark E. Smith. Doyle had particularly rated a song of theirs called *Looking Glass* and he always used to be playing it on the acoustic guitar he would eventually break over the head of a drug dealer with plans of cutting my face to shit.

I remembered the kid I'd seen out on the street, the Lou Reed lookalike, and remembered how Reed had hung out with Bowie who had inspired Ian Curtis who Doyle had also admired more than a country of old had their king.

Trying to shake myself free from the clutches of old times I stepped forward and took a hold of the girl's shoulders as her bare feet landed on the hallway. "Sweetheart," I said but she managed to break free without any real effort, without even realising I was there, and continued for the door. "I don't think you want to go out like that," I called after her and then she was gone. I stood looking at the door a little while, waiting for Matt to come escort her back inside, but he didn't.

I took a deep breath and reminded myself of why I was even here, made my way up the stairs without giving the girl and the danger she could be placing herself in a moment's thought.

10

YOU COULD HEAR some generic rap-shit playing far too loud on the other side of the door so I banged the side of my first hard against it to try and make sure somebody heard. Some skinny guy I'd seen dozens of times but couldn't name opened up. His eyes were bloodshot. He looked more than a little dazed. The smell of burning dope was more than enough to explain such an appearance. "Cole, man," he said, stepping aside to welcome me on in, "been a fucking while, son."

Two black dudes with cornrows and loose-fitting clothes were hogging up the couch, playing a PS game on the widescreen TV. If they had heard the knocking at the door, they clearly didn't give a shit. I walked in without offering any or either of these assholes a word. I just scanned my immediate surroundings, making my way to the kitchen because that's where Albert would be hanging if he wasn't out here. Albert was a kike; the son of a stockbroker who'd told his parents he was living out here with classmates while he studied Law. He'd told me he dropped out of college the week he'd attended his introductory seminar - said he'd only enrolled so he could move out of the family mansion without his parents busting his balls too much. His plan was to make a big enough success of himself that, come the time he should have been graduating, he would be able to reveal his true career choice to his parents and have them be proud of him.

He was in the kitchen, just as I'd knew he would be, wearing skinny jeans and a NWA t-shirt that looked three or four times too big for his stick-like frame. Guy looked like he could have been fresh out of Dachau. He didn't notice me straight away, he was too busy talking to a girl snorting lines from the kitchen worktop. She looked cute from behind and he was just talking without any breaks, like what he was saying was just one really long word until he finally caught sight of me from the corner of his eye and then he was stepping forward like a TV show host with a glint in his eye and a welcoming smile on his face.

"Cole," he said, "have I got something amazing to show you! Nikki," he asked the girl, "show my friend Cole your amazing gift."

She turned and moved toward me like she hadn't fully noticed me. Rubbing at her nostril and simply staring at a part of my body that I couldn't yet confirm, she could have been sleepwalking. When she took a hold of my hand I almost jumped in surprise, her own was that cold. But I didn't. I let her turn my hand palm-up and look at it for a split second before she had released it and was turning back for another line of coke already. "S.N." was all she said.

"Isn't she," Albert laughed, "isn't she fucking great?"

"Sure," I shrugged, "she's the best. But what's S.N.?"

"Only the initials of the girl you're going to marry." He grinned, looked back over his shoulder at her and then back to me. "Isn't she great?" he asked. "Nikki has a talent."

"I'd always hoped I was going to marry Laura Dern," I sighed. Dern reminded me of Lee because he liked her. I'd gone and said her name aloud just to remind myself of him - just to hurt myself a little - because that's exactly the kind of person I can be.

"You can't argue with destiny," Albert said, grinning as he placed a hand on my shoulder. "But what can I do you for? You look a little down, is there anything wrong? Nikki-baby, doesn't Cole here look a little down?"

11

It was two in the afternoon when I finally woke up *properly*. I'd woken a lot earlier - drank a glass of water, used the bathroom and gone back to bed - but at two I knew right away I wouldn't be able to get comfortable enough to sleep for another couple of hours so I got up and headed downstairs in Tiffany's bathrobe. There was a smell in the air - cooking fat. I thought nothing of it, just assumed either Tiffany was back already or Samantha or somebody else had come over to take care of some business.

I was wrong.

The patio doors were wide open and he was relaxing in one of the sun loungers - had his back to me like he owned the place or something. All I could make out of him was a head of brown hair, a white shirt with grey trousers and brown loafers. His grey jacket had been carefully folded over the free lounger.

"The fuck is this?" I muttered.

Son of a bitch even had a tall glass of orange juice resting underneath the chair.

I lit a cigarette and walked for the patio doors, legs trembling and my heart beating so wildly it made me a little dizzy. It seemed too late for me to head back upstairs and grab a gun or even a baseball bat and grabbing a knife or a fork on the way out would be no fucking use to me if the man was packing, so I just tossed my fate to the winds and went for it - death or fucking glory.

He was up the second he heard me, one quick and fluid motion and he was standing there looking at me with his glass in his hand. He looked a little younger than me; had a neatly trimmed goatee beard that looked like it wouldn't particularly thicken no matter how long he left it. Sweat stains beneath his armpits.

"Cole," he said. "You're Cole, right?"

I stopped at the patio doors like a confident son of a bitch and asked him, "Who are you and what the fuck are you doing here?"

"I'm sorry," he smiled, "my name's Hollis Silverdale. I'm working for Miss Lily."

"Right," I said, starting to relax already. All I could think about was how dumb his chosen stage-name was. "She ain't here," I said, turning my back on him to take a bottle of fresh orange juice from the refrigerator.

I'd no idea just how dehydrated I must have been until I started drinking the chilled orange juice and found it next to impossible to stop. He was just standing there, watching me, when I turned back around. The second my eyes were on him again, a friendly smile jumped up onto his face, like he was feeling a little embarrassed or something. "I'm sorry," he said, "I should have told you I knew she wouldn't be here. Heck," he laughed, "I wasn't even sure *you* were here up until I checked the bedroom!"

"You watched me sleeping?" I asked him, feeling more than a little weirded-out.

"Ha," he said, "I wouldn't go putting it like that. I just took a look around the bedroom door a little earlier and saw you there. I didn't want to disturb you so I thought it might be a good idea to wait by the pool."

"You said you worked for Tiffany."

"That's right," he nodded, "I do."

"Well what the fuck do you need me for?"

He laughed, looked to the floor a second and then back at me. "Here," he said as he took his jacket from the back of the free lounger, "take a seat and talk with me."

"You a Scientologist?" I asked, heading fully out into the afternoon sun. "You're acting pretty strange."

"No," he laughed, "I'm catholic," and he waited for me to be sitting down before he got back in the lounger he had claimed during my absence. "You want a smoke?" he asked, taking an open pack of Marlboros and a light from his jacket.

"You having one?"

"I'm trying to cut down he grinned," and I pulled my hand

back the second he said it. Another asshole like Pink, carrying cigarettes on him not out of habit but to try and put you at ease so you slip up in front of him.

"Same here," I lied. "Are you going to tell me what you're doing here or not?"

"I'm sorry," he blushed, "I'm a little distracted by my surroundings. But like I said," he smiled, "my name is Hollis Silverdale and I'm a private investigator."

I was still convinced he was an actor because his name sounded like it had been penned by somebody lacking in imagination. I reasoned he must have been about to start acting alongside Tiffany on the show and she'd told him to come over here and test out his acting muscles on me so I just nodded and said, "Sure... You have any I.D.?"

"Pardon me," he said - still smiling as he dug inside of his leather wallet until he was holding out a plastic card which looked like it could have been ordered online or from the back of a crime magazine. "You want to know the difference between a private investigator and a stalker?" He joked while I checked it out. "*That* card!"

"Cute," I sighed, handing it back to him. "So, are you ever going to tell me what you're doing here?"

"I understand a close friend of yours and Miss Lily's has recently gone missing without any explanation," he said and right away I knew he wasn't here to prepare for an acting gig. Tiffany wouldn't use something like Lee's disappearance for something like that - not when it was still so painful for her. Well, maybe more embarrassing than painful.

"Her representative," he continued, "called by my office and asked if I would be interested in trying to work out just what the heck is going on exactly."

"Well," I told him, "I don't think I have any information that would help you out."

"You never know," he grinned, "sometimes it's the little things that shine the brightest light. So, would you be willing to answer a couple of questions I might have?"

"Sure," I told him and right away he was taking a Dictaphone from his breast pocket. I hadn't seen one of those in years. They'd gotten a lot smaller; a lot shinier.

"This really won't take too long. It can't," he laughed, "this only records up to twenty minutes at a time."

"Your case solved in twenty minutes or less," I said, "you should put that somewhere on your card."

"Ha," he smiled, "maybe I will. Are you ready to start?" he asked and thumbed down the record button without first waiting for a response.

12

His first question was, "Did you like Lee?"

"I like Lee," I said with a nod. "He was somebody I could talk to out here."

"What did you talk about?"

"This and that," I shrugged. "I was trying to get him into the music I'm into but movies were more his thing. Movies and women from England."

"He had a number of relationships with English women?" Silverdale asked. He was excited, certain he had picked something up at record speed.

"No," I grinned. "Lee just loved famous women from England for whatever reason - especially the porn stars. And he was *obsessed* with vintage pussy. We'd be watching one of the old music channels and Abba or someone like that would come on and Lee would go, 'Can you imagine how hairy her cunt must have been here?' Seriously," I laughed, "he'd say it whenever it was just the two of us watching something. You know," I added just to eat away at the recording space, "Lee was obsessed about the past, too. He used to talk about how you remember an old teacher or something like that, never ageing in your mind when they could be in an old folks' home or something... Maybe even disfigured or killed in a road accident the day after you'd last seen them."

"So you think there's a chance that Lee has gone back to revisit his past?"

"I don't know," I said, "he always struck me as the kind of guy who's forever heading forward... The past interests him because he knows there's no way back there."

Silverdale nodded. "One name in particular I was told to look into," he said, "is Father Doyle."

"Lee won't be with him."

"What makes you so sure? They're cousins, right?"

"Right," I laughed, knowing full well even Tiffany would've known the two weren't actually related. "You want to set yourself the impossible task of finding Doyle, you got the whole of Los Angeles to find him," I said, "but I'd recommend starting with the down and outs. I'm telling you this for free," I said, "Lee won't be with him."

"You're sure of that?"

"I'm sure of that," I laughed. "Doyle holds a grudge like no other and Lee left his side for Tiffany."

Silverdale nodded once again. "Just like you did," he said.

"That's right," I agreed, "just like I did."

Silverdale looked over to the pool and drummed his fingertips along his chin a while. "Did Lee ever talk about moving on? From *here*, I mean."

"No," I said. "First I knew about it was Tiffany screaming one morning and blaming me - not that she had any reason to."

"Strange," Silverdale said, "strange, strange, strange. He never mention any other family?"

"An older brother," I shrugged, "once or twice. Had no idea where he was. Brother had got up and left one night without saying much."

"He left the family home? You have an address?"

"Afraid not," I told him. "Doyle might."

"Doyle might," Silverdale repeated and he looked back over at the pool. "You think I'll maybe find Lee if I look around south L.A.?"

"I don't know," I laughed, "I suppose it's as good a place to start as any."

He turned his head slowly back around to look at me, making the smile on his face impossible not to notice. "I don't know," he said, "I have a good feeling about one place in particular. Has a man with a Confederate Flag tattoo on his head, a lot of people coming and going at all hours to visit some Jew-kid..."

The prick had already been tailing me.

"Trust me," I grinned, "you don't want to go there."

"You sure about that? You sure I won't find Lee relaxing there, maybe waiting for Tiffany Lily to put a reward up for information?"

"Straight up and down," I warned, "you don't want to go looking around there at all. People won't respond well to your questions or line of work."

"Okay," he said like he was without a care, "thanks for your assistance," he added, slipping the Dictaphone back inside his breast pocket as he got up on his feet. "If it's no bother, I'll come and speak with you again soon. This first meeting was just to try and coax the memories back up to the surface."

"Right," I said.

"Before I go," he said, taking a sealed manila envelope from another pocket and holding it out for me to take. "Makes interesting reading," he said once I accepted it.

"I'll take a look once I find the time."

He laughed at that and said, "I can see myself out."

13

You want to know what was in that sealed envelope? The envelope I ripped open less than five minutes after the gumshoe had left? Dr Pink's latest report on me, that's what.

"Son of a," I said, "bitch."

As far as my sexual health was concerned, I didn't even have a mild dose to my name but that was to be expected so there was no real cause for celebration. Then there was the list of what had been found in my blood.

Cocaine, pot, ingredients from the prescription essentials including antidepressants, painkillers and slimming pills of Tiffany's, even a little MDMA.

"She fucking gave him the results to look at," I said and I crumpled them up into a ball and tossed it into the trash. The cigarette I'd lit was doing so little that I'd as good as forgotten all about it.

Tiffany had hired a private investigator to find Lee and she hadn't just set him loose on me but give him whatever she believed could be useful to him. It was more than a slap on the dick, it was a kicking while I was out cold in the fucking gutter. To say I was feeling irate would be a huge understatement.

"Fucking assholes!"

I dialled her cellphone and it went straight to voicemail. I called Chambers' and it did the same.

"Motherfuckers!"

I called Chambers' office and a woman claiming to be called Velma answered the call (secretaries working in acting agencies tend to work under a number of names not only to make the place look a lot bigger than it is but to make it easier to avoid people whenever necessary). "Velma," I said, "I've been trying to get in touch with Mark Chambers on his cellular but it's going straight to voicemail."

"One moment," she said.

"Wait," I yelled but it was too late, the bitch had put me on hold. I paced the floor in circles, pulling deep on my cigarette as I waited for her to come back on the line. The worst part about it was she hadn't even asked for my name or my reason for calling and that, more than likely, meant she had just placed me on hold and went back to whatever magazine she had open in front of her. She could have been rereading the daily horoscopes she now knew word for word.

"I'm sorry," she said on returning, "I'm unable to connect you to Mark Chambers at the moment."

"Velma," I said, "listen to me- I know he is with Tiffany Lily right now because the two of them left my place together, do you understand? I am close to Tiffany Lily and it is fucking important that I get hold of her or Mark right now."

"I'm sorry but I have another call coming through - do you mind holding the line?"

"Velma," I said, "if you put me back on hold, I swear I'm going to_"

She put me back on hold. I was sure I was going to scream a curse or something similar but nothing came out apart from a loud, meaningless noise.

I busted two knuckles open punching the nearest wall, tossed the telephone receiver I was holding into the pool and headed back inside without waiting to see it sink all the way to the bottom.

I headed out after I'd taken a shower and asked the guys manning the gates if they could remember letting somebody through to see Tiffany. "You mean Hollis?" one of them asked and the way he knew his name worried me a little.

"Yeah," I said, "that's the one. Listen, you don't let him in anymore- you understand?"

"Miss Lily said we're to let him in whenever he wants."

"Well she isn't here now, is she?"

"I'm sorry," he said, "but she said let him in and that means we have to let him in."

"Tell you what," I said, "I'll give you a hundred just to keep him out until she gets back, how's that sound?"

"You'd have to give us all a hundred," he smiled, "otherwise he'd be back in as soon as my shift was over."

"Forget it," I said, "don't push your fucking luck."

14

Samantha was understandably surprised to find me standing outside her building. She looked cute; hair tied back, white training vest with blue shorts and white sneakers, a sports bag over her shoulder. And she walked fast. It was difficult to keep alongside her.

"Cole," she asked, "what are you doing here?"

"I was in the neighbourhood," I said. "Listen, do you know where Tiffany is?"

"No," she said, "she gave me the week off."

"You haven't heard from her?" I asked, struggling all the more to keep up with her as I went through the difficulty of lighting a cigarette on the move.

"No," she said. "Is something wrong?"

"Maybe," I said. "Listen, did she mention Hollis Silverdale to you?"

"Silverdale? I don't know the name."

"You sure? She ever mention getting a private eye in front of you?"

My ribs were stabbing into my sides like blunt knives, my insides tightly pressed on the inside of them.

"No," she said and I thanked the lord for the fact we had to stop because of moving traffic. "Is that what she's done... Got a private investigator to look for Lee?"

"Sure has," I said. "But she never mentioned it to you? I thought it would have been your job to find her a list of names."

"Not this time," she said and a red light meant we could start walking again.

"You can tell me the truth," I said, "I won't let her know you told me and I won't have a problem with you for keeping it from me."

"I never found his name and I didn't know she was getting an investigator," she insisted. "This must be down to Mark."

My chest was on fire and my mouth was too dry. The pain in my side had me wondering how much worse it could possibly get.

"Sure," I said, "I can believe that. So what're you doing with your vacation?"

"Not a lot," she said, "catching up with a few old friends, visiting family. The usual stuff."

"Where you going now?"

"Yoga class."

"Yoga," I said back to her, "so you're pretty flexible."

"I guess. Oh," she said, "here's my bus! I'll see you soon!" and she raced off to catch her bus. Feeling confident she wouldn't be looking back, I stopped and doubled over with my hands on my knees to try and shake the pain away from my body. Samantha boarded her bus and was gone and although I was glad she hadn't seen me like this, I was sad she hadn't paused getting aboard and looked back to see if I was still there. She had rejected me once before but I still clung on to the hope she did like me, it's just she couldn't do anything about it with working for Tiffany. More usual than not, all signs pointed to her not being attracted to me in the slightest but I liked to tell myself that something would happen between us if just one little thing were to change.

15

THERE WAS A message on the answering machine when I finally got home and more than anything, I hoped that it was from Tiffany.

"Tiffany," a man's recorded voice said, "this is Scott Pate. I'm calling because there are a few things concerning the upcoming amnesia plot that I'd like to run by you. I'll be working at home for most of the day, so you can contact me at_"

He left his number. I dialled it there and then, hoping he'd be able to give me just a little information on Tiffany's whereabouts.

"Scott Pate," he casually answered, "who's calling?"

"Mr Pate," I said far too quickly, "this is Cole; I was Tiffany Lily's guest when you met her for dinner recently?"

"Cole," he said - sounding truly surprised to hear from me, "what a pleasure this is! How are you doing?"

"Concerned," I answered truthfully, "I haven't been able to reach Tiffany."

"Ah," he said, "I remember now!"

"You know where she is?"

"Yes," he said, "yes, of course. She's having a little minor surgery taken care of. I okayed it, of course. I'd forgotten all about it until now."

"Surgery?" I asked, "What kind of surgery?"

"I'm not too sure," he admitted, "she promised me it wouldn't alter her appearance so I agreed to her request for time off."

"Well do you know where she is?"

"I don't know," he said, "my assistant might but I'm sure it's nothing for you to worry about."

"Sure," I lied, "you're probably right."

"Anyway," he said, "while I have you on the phone - how's the writing coming along?"

"Oh," I said, "you know how it is... I'm just trying to settle into something at the moment."

"That," he said, "is music to my ears. Did Tiffany tell you we just lost an apprentice writer on the show?"

"No," I told him, "she didn't."

"Really? She must have forgot - I personally asked her to let you know. You know how this industry works? You get as many friends and likeminded people together as you can, and you place them all in the same room and have them work on the same project."

"I didn't know that," I said, too dumb to realise why he was dragging this conversation on any longer.

"Cole," he said, "you're young and you have life experience and that, to me, is rarer than gold. How would you like to meet-up and we'll have a chat about you getting your writing muscles back into shape on the show?"

"You're shitting me?"

"Ha!" he laughed. "How about we meet at seven? You bring some samples of your writing and we'll see where it goes. But I have to warn you," he said, "even if you get the chance to come aboard, the money I'll be offering you won't be life-changing."

"This sounds like a fantastic opportunity," I said breathlessly, "I'd love to discuss this with you."

"Wonderful," he said. "There's a bar close to the restaurant we ate at..."

Dressed in my finest suit and with some samples of my work in the leather satchel over my shoulder, I got to the bar Pate had suggested at five minutes to seven and joined the queue of people waiting to get in. At seven o'clock there was no doubt in my mind that the line hadn't moved; at five minutes after seven I gathered the courage to march my way to the front. The bouncer looked at me with the same curiosity in his eyes as those I'd walked in front of, his giant arms folded over his oak barrel chest. He finally opened his mouth to tell me, "There's a line."

"I'm meeting somebody in here and I'm running late because the line hasn't moved since I got here."

"Who're you supposed to be meeting?"

"Scott Pate," I told him.

"Hold on," he said and he stepped inside the doorway, pressed a finger to the piece in his ear and turned his back on me so I wouldn't be able to see what he was saying. He turned back around soon enough and pulled the velvet rope aside for me to enter. "Go right in," he said, "sorry for the inconvenience."

"Forget about it," I said and I patted him on the arm as I walked inside. It was all signed pictures of famous faces and long red drapes against the walls, round tables with pristine white cloths reaching to the floor. There was a band playing on the stage, middle-aged black guys in powder-blue suits. The bartenders were all male, all clean shaven, and wearing waistcoats. Pate was sitting alone at a table venturing close to the shadows, dressed in a black or navy blue suit with aviator sunglasses and a cherry red baseball cap pulled low. The cap and glasses had him stand out like a sore thumb compared to the few others, all in their finest clothes, all laughing respectably and facing the stage. Whether it was for my benefit or his own, I never asked. I was a little preoccupied because, making my way over to him, my palms got sweaty and I saw myself for the fraud I was. The writing in my possession was nothing new, nothing particularly exciting. It was work that I'd never fully got into the hang of, never dedicated myself to. Words spoiling a page when I was bored or unable to sleep. I was about to stop and turn, to race for the exit before he had even seen me, when he turned his head real slow and stopped once he was facing me. He smiled, raised a hand in friendly greeting. I swallowed, smiled and held my own hand in the air. Legs of lead carried me over to his table.

16

"Cole! So glad you could make it! What do you think of the band?"

He had said practically all of this before I'd even managed to fully get my ass onto the chair beside him.

"My baby cousin is their manager," he said. "Of course, I was the one to get them the regular gig here. What do you drink?" he asked, raising a finger into the air to attract the attention of a cute member of staff in a frilly pink blouse and a tight miniskirt. "You like vodka? Rum?"

The girl was at his side before I had the opportunity to answer him.

"Ellie," he said to her, "I'd say you look fantastic but you always do! Two vodka Martinis - shaken, not stirred - and don't forget the lemon peel."

"Right away, Mr Pate." She turned to walk away, thought better of it and turned around to face him again. "Mr Pate," she said, "do you know a guy called Jimmy Milne?"

The name clearly amused him.

"Jimmy Milne?" he laughed. "I know him, but nowhere near as well as the clap-clinic does," Pate said, "they have a file on him bigger than the telephone book! But why," he said, "are you asking about that particular lowlife?"

The girl's eyes moved to the side for a moment. She pulled a face that made it easy to see how she was wrestling with the decision of showing her hand or keeping it close to her chest. "Well," she decided, "he said he'd secure me a call-back for a role I auditioned for and I got it, but now he's saying I have to do something else for him if I want to get the role."

"That sounds like Jimmy," he sighed, now serious and seeing no humour in what was being discussed at the table. "The proof of the matter is," he said, "you got that call-back on your own talents, Ellie, it was nothing to do with Jimmy Milne. Jimmy

Milne doesn't know the right people and the people he knows don't have much time for him."

"So he can't help me out?" she asked, looking more than a tad disappointed.

"I'm afraid he can't," Pate said, "but trust me - it's a blessing."

"Thanks," she said, "I'll go get your drinks."

"I'm known for making great TV shows and TV movies," Pate said to me once she was out of earshot, "but I'm just as famous for my straight morals and conservative views. People know they can come to Scott Pate for the truth and out in Los Angeles, you have more chance of tripping over an extraterrestrial than you have of hearing the truth."

"It's a good trait to have," I nodded.

"TV movies," he said like doing so would leave the taste of stale jizz in his mouth. "Hate that term," he said, "it's like they're saying they aren't good enough for the theatres, but have you seen half the crap they put on the big screen now? The only problem with a lot of TV now is the damn commercials. Jews got their fingers into Hollywood, then they got into advertising. Their money goes back and forth, back and forth - it's a never-ending cycle. You circumcised?"

"No," I smirked, taken aback at the unexpectedness of his question.

"Rarity in our country," he said, "Jews go wherever the money flows and that means they got into the medical business a long time ago, too. Made their routines everybody's routine. I still remember the first uncircumcised dick I ever saw," he told me with a shake of his head, "getting ready to play college football and I glanced over at my team mate and saw it. You believe that? Whole thing was new to me."

Ellie brought our drinks over to the table. She waited for Pate to have thanked her before finally asking, "So this audition I have... Do you think you would be able to put in a word? *Please*?"

"Ellie," he smiled, "I'm an incredibly selfish man and if you left this place, I'd never be able to get a drink as good as you can make them."

"You could drop by the studio and I'd make you a drink just

the way you like them."

Pate smiled at that, moved and squirmed like a bad actor trying to come across as uncomfortable. "Okay," he said like she had successfully twisted his arm, "you have a name I can go to - casting director or somebody like that? The name of the production will help a little if you don't."

"I'm not sure what the show's called," she said, "they're keeping that under wraps, but I auditioned for Andrew Braise and Linda Compari."

"I know them," he smiled, taking hold of his drink, "but if I do you this favour - you live up to your end of the deal. Can you do that for me, sweetheart?"

"You're the best, Mr Pate," Ellie said and she bent down to embrace him and kiss him firmly upon the cheek.

"Easy," he said, "easy! A public display like this could land me in all kind of trouble with the gossip writers!"

Ellie laughed and as good as skipped away from the table, comfortable with the idea that her time working bad hours for lousy pay would soon come to an end and she'd have a glittering career with all kinds of big-money contracts with famous makeup brands and clothing lines. Pate took a sip from his drink, laughed and leaned in real close. "I had to do something," he said, "that girl couldn't make a decent drink if her life depended on it. You like that?" he grinned seeing how I laughed. "It's true," he said, "taste of her drinks will turn the drunkest man sober. You see the singer?" he said, abruptly changing the subject on looking back at the performers holding the stage, "His brother is a she-male, or claiming to be one anyway. Has started using a girl's name and dressing as a woman, is on medication to grow tits but has said he won't go full-op, meaning he's fully intending to keep hold of the family jewels. Does that make any sense to you?"

"Not really," I grinned and I took a mouthful of my drink. It tasted like any other glass of cold vodka would. "I don't get how you can identify with being a woman when you're wearing a man's biological attire," I added just for the sake of it.

"Biological attire," he repeated back to me with a grin, "I like that one. You use phrases like that a lot in your writing?"

"Only if it comes naturally," I shrugged.

"Bingo. That's exactly how it should be. Too many writers lose sleep, trying to write something that sounds good over something that sounds believable. Most of the conversations I have during work hours," he paused to take a little more of his drink and grimaced with dissatisfaction before continuing, "are just the same thing repeated over and over again but put a little differently. It's what we do as a species," he finished, "we just spout the same garbage over and over again."

"What'd you just say?"

"Ha! You're funny," he said, getting to his feet with his hands already dropping to his belt. "Finish your drink - I'm nipping to the restroom and then we're getting out of here."

"Where we going?"

"You'll see," he said, grinning from ear to ear as he walked away from the table. He held his right hand up to one of the men working the bar and stuck out his thumb and pinkie. I thought he was making devil horns but the barman understood and turned to the telephone behind him. I allowed myself to relax a little now that I was alone and took a long gulp of my drink, the alcohol burning my throat and chest over giving it a warm glow.

And that was when I noticed Hollis Silverdale sitting at the bar.

17

He'd removed his jacket and covered the empty stool beside him with it like he was claiming the seat for someone and he was just sitting there, seemingly admiring the bottles on display behind the bar. He had a drink in front of him - scotch or bourbon. I don't know which but it was something I *knew* he would have been happy to order 'on the rocks'.

And I just went storming over and kicked at the legs of his stool with all my might.

Silverdale did something of a mixture of a fall and a spring in the air, managed to land on his feet but stumbled back a couple of paces before securing his balance. The boys tending the bar stopped what they were doing and looked at us, wondering whose job it would be to split us up if we started fighting. The band went on playing. I didn't bother turning to see if any of the other drinkers had noticed the commotion from their tables because I only had eyes for the gumshoe. He wanted to go at me - the look was right there, right behind the eyes.

"The fuck," he finally said, "do you think you are doing?"

"No," I said, "not me, you. What the fuck do you think *you* are doing?"

And that look... That look was still there, right there for me to see.

"What's the matter with you? I'm just having a damn drink!"

"Here?" I laughed. "Now? What are the chances of that?"

"Fuck you," he said, "do you think your missing friend is the only one I'm even working right now? You think every waking thought is consumed by the mystery of what the fuck happened to fucking Lee? Get the fuck out of here," he warned, "before I lose my fucking temper with you already."

"You didn't follow me here?"

"Fuck you," he said, "I know the guy who runs this place."

"Yeah? So what's his name?"

"Fuck you."

"Well point him out to me. Can you do that? Can you point your friend out to me?"

"You want me to point him out to you? Well go find yourself a seat and stick around, because he's running five minutes late."

"Ha!" I said, "Isn't that convenient?"

I had no idea where this was headed. Dropping my hands to my hips I glanced around to be sure none of the boys working security were coming over and realised Pate was standing almost right behind me, grinning like crazy as he watched on. I looked back to Silverdale and saw him just as he was, almost frozen solid by the anger he was feeling.

"You know who this is?" I asked him, throwing my thumb over my shoulder.

"Him?" he said after looking to Pate for a single beat. "I'm guessing he's the guy flying you back home."

"Funny," I said, "he's Scott Pate - can you remember that? You tell Tiffany I was here with Scott Pate and we weren't happy at how you came in and started hassling us."

"I'll tell her."

"You do that," I said before turning to Pate and saying, "you ready to get out of here?" a lot more forcefully than I'd been intending to.

"You don't have to finish this on my account," the old man laughed.

"Fuck this," I huffed and I stormed toward the exit without even giving a shit whether either one of them was following. The air outside felt a lot colder than it should have been for that time of year. I took my cigarettes from my jacket and fumbled around for my light. Pate stepped forth with a gold-plated Zippo before I could find it and presented himself to me as a modern day Prometheus. "Well that was a memorable display," he laughed.

"Yeah," I said wearily. "I'm sorry about that."

"Please," he grinned, "I'm more than aware of how Hollis Silverdale can get under the skin."

I looked to him and said, "I thought you two didn't know each other?" and because of those damned aviator glasses I saw just how clueless I looked saying it.

"We've never met," Pate said, snapping his lighter shut, "but I know people that have used his services or found themselves being followed by him - some within the industry, others being members of religious organisations he's trying to gather dirt on. From all accounts," he concluded, "he's persistent."

"Good to know," I sighed. "He come here often?"

"Here?" Pate nodded. "I've seen him here a couple of times."

"Shit," I said.

"What's done is done, and here," he said as a black Mercedes came steadily heading toward us, "is the cab I ordered," he held an open hand up as confirmation for the driver.

"I'm sorry," I said, "but I don't think I'm in the mood to stay out after that."

"Don't be absurd," Pate insisted as he put an arm around my shoulder, "we've still got much to discuss and I've so many things to show you!"

18

THE DRIVER WAS a world away from Larsen, Tiffany's chauffeur of choice. Larsen looked human. You could imagine him returning home to his empty apartment, feeding his cat and sitting down in front of the TV while he waited for his microwave meal for one to be ready. *This* driver was tight skin and prominent bones of sharp angles. You could imagine him working the catwalk in designer clothes or modelling tight briefs in black and white photographs.

"You remember what I told you about the singer's brother?" Pate asked me.

"Sure," I said, "self-made hermaphrodite."

Pate smiled and nodded. "Friend of mine," he said, "his teenage son fascinates me. You look at his Facebook page and his Myspace profile, he's supporting one cause or another almost every day. Boy's always writing about what's upsetting him, what has him weeping, what fight is worth fighting," he smirked, "seems happiest when he's recognising himself as being bisexual. It wasn't like that when I was growing up," he said, "nothing like that at all. It's this world," he sighed, "it's changing in a way people like me could never imagine or understand, and I witnessed the sixties and, then later, the Aids explosion."

"Every movement confuses the generation that came before it," I said only because I couldn't think of anything else at that moment in time.

"This movement," he seemed to agree, "of open feelings and a man being proud of favouring dick, is something people on my side of the lot can't tap into. It's the counter-culture revolution all over again," he said, "the auteur is coming up with something fresh for the public when us stiffs over at the studio can think of nothing more than to get another Elvis picture out."

"It's hard," I said, "I completely understand where you are coming from."

"But you're the outsider," he said as he excitedly threw an open hand down onto my knee, "you haven't been boxed-in by the studio men. You can still adapt for any scene, am I right? You just examine something and then you can put it down on the page for others to relate to... People I could never represent."

Pate sure was putting a lot of praise on me considering he hadn't even glanced over any of my work.

"I want to gather some people," he said, "and I want them to pull in the pink viewing figures. Cole," he asked, "are you willing to help me?"

I swallowed before confessing, "I don't know if I can."

"Don't be so hard on yourself," he laughed, "you'll take to the water like a professional. I want the sexuality, the politics," he said, "and I want the falling rain to wear innocence down not just for sensationalism but for believability. After all," he grinned, "who better to write on strong sexuality and the removal of innocence than somebody like yourself?"

I loosened the collar of my shirt. "I'm not sure I understand," I told him.

"Please," he said, "anyone and everyone over at the office knew about you and Tiffany and Lee and now Lee is gone, Tiffany is trying to keep herself from having a complete breakdown and you're left picking up the pieces. Don't look so surprised," he said before he turned to stare out of the window, "Los Angeles has always had stories like yours - it's just you never get offered the golden contract to write the story yourself."

I'd started biting my thumbnail. It was a dirty habit I'd kicked a long time ago.

"I must confess," Pate said with a sigh, "I'm not happy with Tiffany's success. I'd never heard good things about her and she threw a project I was a part of into development hell a number of years ago. All someone like Tiffany Lily is really good for," he said, "is taking advantage of more talented people and furthering their own career despite their minimal talents and I would like nothing more than to bring that to an end. I want to bring on the true age of the admired writer," he smiled, "and I want you to be one of my advancing troops."

"Have you heard anything? Do you know if she's looking to throw me out with the trash?"

Pate took a deep breath and pulled a disinterested face on answering my question.

"For the moment," he said, "I have to keep her close because she's popular with the viewers for a reason I'm unable to understand but that doesn't mean I have to like her or the way she is... The way she keeps people like you completely dependent on her. But if I could just help one person she has tried to break," he said, "tried to convince is without meaning or importance and have her look on as they become more and more influential, then I will know I have taken something from her she could never reclaim and my world would become that little bit cheerier."

19

It was a big house... A *lot* bigger than Tiffany's and a whole world more expensive. You could probably count the number of brick walls on one hand; most of the structure looked to be glass and the place seemed to open up and become one with the picture postcard perfect garden and tropical swimming pool beyond because of it.

"I know exactly what you're thinking," Pate said as he pushed the door open, "it's cold and it's sterile and I agree with you one hundred and ten per cent. This place is strictly for business; the family home is a couple of miles east from here."

The driver brought the engine to a standstill, deciding we would be here for a while and all you could hear was the sound of invisible crickets.

"Actually," I said, "I think this place is incredible."

"Maybe," Pate said leading the way to an open kitchen of black marble surfaces and sparkling silver, "I'm not an architect in the traditional meaning of the word. You want a soda?" he asked, opening the refrigerator.

"Sure," I said and he tossed me a chilled can.

"Look at that fruit bowl," he smiled, opening his own Pepsi-Cola as he closed the refrigerator door using his ass. "Take a look," he said. "What's missing?"

Oranges. Pears. Grapes. Kiwis. Pineapple.

"Bananas," I said, panicking a little for fear of getting the answer wrong.

"Sure," he laughed, "there are no bananas. But there are no apples, you see? Don't you think it would be a bit of a cliché," he laughed, "the producer offering young talent the bite of an apple?"

"I guess."

He pulled two large glasses from a high cupboard and placed one directly in front of me. "The kid I want to be your inspiration," he said pouring his drink, "has something of a biblical name. Ezekiel, but he isn't one of those negroids if you believe it or not." He stopped pouring the contents of his Pepsi can into the glass to look me in the eye. "I should make this crystal clear," he told me, "under no circumstances are you or the people you may be working with to reveal that Ezekiel was an inspiration for the end product - understand?"

"Sure," I said, "I understand."

"I just had to be sure," he said, returning to the task of pouring his drink. "The boy's father would *not* be pleased if he was to find that out and taking me to the courts for a creator's credit and a slice of the profits wouldn't be enough for him, he's such an opportunist cunt. Pardon my French," he smiled.

"What would he do," I asked, "would he eliminate the competition and go out to make sure you never worked again?"

"He probably would," Pate agreed. "But he could use the attention to land his precious Ezekiel a pop or modelling career and you know how I feel about people lacking in talent being big successes. You want a slice of lemon? Lime?"

"I'm good," I told him and being reminded of the drink I was holding, I popped the ring pull and emptied the contents into my own glass. Pate looked to the contents of his own glass like the answers to all of life's mysteries had been written across the surface of it. "I should warn you," he said, "if you think Tiffany is giving you a hard time over her missing boy, you have no idea how hard she'll make it if she finds out you're collaborating with me."

"You're kidding," I said, "you own her ass, right?"

"Right," he laughed, finding my own naivety to be hilarious. "I'm the new producer on a show that's already proved to be more than successful, and a lot of that is down to her," he said. "My past and recent successes mean next to nothing right now; the studio would side with her over me in a heartbeat - it's just that she doesn't know it or wouldn't risk it. As much as I hate to say it - I can't target her until I've proven the show is more successful under my control than it ever was before."

"You really have it in for her, don't you?"

"This is Los Angeles," he said, "you need to hold a grudge to keep yourself going. You have to play the long game," he continued, turning around to look out at the sparkling night sky. "You never know," he sighed, "she could get addicted to surgery and the public will fall out of love with her once the jokes start coming."

I went to take a sip of my drink but held it once the thought popped into my head.

"This surgery she's having," I asked, "did you give her the idea?"

"If it was my idea," he said, turning back around to face me, "she'd be having work done on her bitter personality. Anyway," he grinned, "come on up to my office and I'll introduce you to the online presence of Ezekiel Noah Bircham."

"You mind if I smoke?" I asked before following.

"In here," he replied, "absolutely. Go have your cigarette outside and meet me upstairs, okay?"

"Not a problem."

20

THE MYSPACE PAGE was the first thing we looked at together. The profile picture showed a youngster sitting in a tall red chair with a window behind him. He was pale, his hair the lightest shade of rusted-brown you could imagine, and his face held sporadic clumps of hair in the first misguided attempt at growing a beard. He wasn't smiling but I could never imagine why a boy in a flowery shirt and lime green jeans would have reason to look so smug. "That him?" I asked Pate just to have the kid's identity confirmed.

"That's our boy," Pate said with a nod. "I've written down his Myspace and Facebook addresses for you, so don't worry about not being able to find them once you're gone."

"Nineteen years of age," I mumbled, scanning the prominent information available. He'd refused to provide any inquisitive souls with his sexuality but most of the comments he had posted would make it clear for a blind man to see where he was positioning himself. I mean, sure, he had somehow come to the conclusion that comments including "Just bought a new blender and you know what? As long as you include ONE banana, you can blend ANYTHING and it tastes great! (Nom! Nom!)" just *had* to be shared with the world but even those were buried amongst the numerous posts on gay rights and struggles, an admiration for his misunderstanding of feminism and his moist-eyed wonderings on why all races just can't get along.

"Nineteen years," Pate said back to me, "and his grammar and punctuation would be embarrassing in a kindergarten. I mean - just look at that! You wouldn't believe how much his parents have forked out on private tutors and schooling. The latest excuse is that he's dyslexic," he sneered. "I'm not trying to be unkind here, I do believe there are people with dyslexia, but it's now just an excuse for ignorance. Like the other one - ADHD?

Every spoiled asshole has that now."

"Does he have many photos?"

"Hundreds of them," Pate laughed, moving the cursor and there they were, all kept in his online photo albums. "Where do you want to look first?"

"There," I said, pointing to the collection titled *Krazy Nights Out* because obviously, no night is truly crazy unless it's spelled with a fucking K. "Let me have a look at where he goes and the kind of people he goes with."

Underneath every picture we looked at, our boy Ezekiel had posted the name of the bar or club where it was taken along with names of his friends and a failed attempt at a humorous description. It had only taken a few clicks of the mouse to give me an idea to where he would be on a certain night and I felt that the job at hand would be piss-easy because of it. I even thought I could become a private investigator myself if this didn't work out.

I noticed his friends had posted comments of their own under his pictures and reading them started to give me a headache. The whole bunch of them just came across as so spoiled and stupid, so annoying, so phony-liberal, that my first feeling of how easy this would be started to be replaced with the notion of how challenging it would be, making jokers like these likeable or at least interesting.

"What do you think?" Pate said, "You want to look at any of the other albums?"

"Actually," I told him, "I'm just going to head outside for another smoke."

"Another?" He laughed and turned his face back around to the monitor. "You be careful - those things will age the skin."

Standing in the brilliant moonlight, I smoked my cigarette in no time whatsoever because of how excited I was.

It was the ideas... They just kept coming.

Ezekiel was at college age and he was determined to be seen as this right-on feminist. It had me remember my time at college, to my second semester when I picked a course focusing on feminist literature because I'd foolishly assumed the class would be filled with open-minded, sexually liberal babes. So as you have probably guessed already, it wasn't quite like that and the whole semester was a waste of my time. Well, it was until now, anyway.

Even now I can still remember that morning all of a sudden. Out of the blue it just leaps to the front of my mind and I see it like it's happening there and then, right in front of me. The morning we turned up for our lecture to see someone had found a way into the room at some point over the weekend and wrote across the front wall in giant green letters:

ERICA JONG IS ONE BORING STUPID CUNT

The lecturer had taken one look and dropped her cup of coffee, then all of her papers, and stood there with both hands to her open mouth. She was, obviously, an aged feminist with hair down to her ass and clothes that were both collected from goodwill stores or homemade. To have somebody who had clearly played a significant role in how her own beliefs and opinions were formed described not only as boring but also stupid *and* a cunt was too much for her to deal with so early on a Monday morning. Class was dismissed, we got the morning off.

Laughing to myself beneath the moon, staring to the clear waters of Pate's pool, I knew that I could use that memory. I tried to imagine the forced anger a character like Ezekiel would feel on witnessing something he would like to genuinely believe was a great injustice and if he couldn't genuinely believe it, well, he could always try convincing those around him that he believed it.

I sighed and dragged in the last pull of my cigarette alongside some of the cool night air. The lecturer - it just seems so wrong referring to her as a professor, even if she did have the qualifications that earned her the title - had been named Sam. Her family name long escaped me. But some of my classmates had said she lived out on some free-love hippy commune while others had said she lived in a tent in a public park because her husband had kicked her out of the home and moved his secretary in.

Flicking what was left of my cigarette into the bushes, I turned to head back inside of the house.

21

I MUST'VE STAYED at Pate's place for a good few hours, the two of us talking excitedly about this idea he'd had that I was to play a role in moulding. We laughed and we drank and he told me to just *go* for it, to approach my writing like it was a script for a pilot guaranteed a full season already. He told me to go into it without worrying, because it could always be reshaped once he introduced me to the other people he was busy choosing from. He told me to think My So Called Life and Party of Five made for the Sex And The City audience and when it finally came for me to leave I had the guy in the Mercedes take me home - heading right in through the gates so the boys running security would know how Tiffany wasn't the only big-shot I knew.

I was over the moon, drunkenly singing to myself while I dug the keys to the front door from my jacket pocket.

A car engine came to life and headlights struck me. A little too confident because of the alcohol I'd downed, I turned to give the newbie on the scene my most confrontational of looks. The car crawled in my direction, the driver nothing but a black blur until he dimmed the headlights right before he passed so I could get a good look at him.

It was Hollis Silverdale and he gave me one major fucking grin.

The way Silverdale had made a point of me seeing him left me more than a little pissed but I managed to sleep easily enough. I was just as irritated when I woke the next morning but I resisted the urge to call Tiffany right away and instead made a couple of laps of the pool before showering and eating breakfast. *Then* I called Tiffany.

Her cellphone was switched off. I tried Chambers but his just rang out; the cocksucker had even turned off his voicemail service.

"Fuck 'em," I said, lighting a cigarette and I took the plastic

Tiffany had left behind and made my way out with it in my back pocket. I even headed out in the BMW, hoping the sight of me behind the wheel would easily do more than piss off the security boys at the gates because they would never be able to take possession of such a majestic ride.

PART 2

DAY I FORGOT

1

I COULD HAVE easily bought a brand new laptop but instead I went to a fairly reputable pawn shop and purchased a used one. The cashier tried to talk me into buying all kinds of add-ons and security features but all I needed was something to write on. There was a computer back at Tiffany's place I could use for going online and looking up porn, but this was to be my writing computer and nothing else. Sure, it didn't come in the box or anything like that but I felt proud to have it in my possession as I left the store and got back inside the car. Lighting a cigarette and smiling to myself, I got the engine running and started the journey to a Starbucks I knew nearby. Letting the place have one writer bound for success working away in there at long last was my free gift to them.

Fantasies came to mind; dreams of being a recognised talent known for appearing in that same Starbucks like clockwork to get his work done. I thought of the young women desperate enough for a starting role to hang around, desperate for me to notice them and just as desperate to please me.

I didn't fight them.

The girl who made my coffee had a good face and great tits but she did her best to avoid making any small-talk and had me sitting at a table in no time at all because of it. I shrugged it off. A couple of years and a few magazine covers and worthier talent than her would surely be eating out of my hand or - better yet - eating out of my new jeans.

There was a guy at another table with a laptop open in front of him. He waited for me to catch his gaze before giving a foolish grin and raising his drink in silent toast. I looked down at my own computer and shook my head enough for him to be left with no doubt that I didn't want anything to do with him. He kept looking at me for a while. I was just sat there, waiting for my laptop to fully come to life, and I could see him looking at me all sad from the corner of my eye.

And within minutes I regretted not buying any of the internet security or whatever at the pawn shop.

The Starbucks I was in had Wi-Fi but I didn't want to risk going online to check out Ezekiel's online presence and pick up a virus because of it. A message kept popping up in the corner of the screen to let me know it was possible for me to go online and every time I closed it down, it would reappear in no time at all. Feeling more than a little annoyed at this, I took a deep breath and opened a new Word document - wrote **Episode One** in bold letters and leaned back in my chair.

This is where my life would truly begin...

They say that one page is one minute of screen-time when you're working on a script and I had five pages done without breaking a sweat before my coffee was gone. Five golden pages if I say so myself. The as-yet-unnamed character based on Ezekiel Bircham was in a panic; he was desperately searching for a place to use as a toilet because, on a night out, he had taken too many poppers and was struggling to keep his shit from spilling out from his ass. I've heard that can happen. You take poppers one too many times and you suddenly lose something you've had control of for as long as you can remember. What I had written may not have been a realistic depiction but it would capture the attention of the viewer real easy.

Five minutes down in no time at all. Five entertaining minutes at that.

I threw the other supposed writer a confident grin before heading out of the door, the idea being to race back to Tiffany's place and reward myself with something of an online porn-binge. You know something, I'm just going to come out and admit it - I got hard during the ride back because I was that pleased with myself. Thoughts were battling for control. Ideas were coming to mind for the script; where it should go next, snappy lines of dialogue. They were going up against the names of porn stars my fingertips were longing to begin an online search for the moment I got back. It's like my mind had been split into two; the professional half and the half that simply wanted a little fun.

2

I CHECKED THE answering machine the second I was back. There wasn't a message waiting for me but I can't say I was particularly surprised. Tiffany wanted me to be worried, to be pacing the floor, but it wasn't happening. She had no idea her leaving had coincided with everything improving for me so I just shrugged it off, smiled and stood smoking a cigarette at the patio doors. I had a champion boner at the idea of jerking off to some free porn but I made myself wait; teased myself as my own playful lover.

It's just that after the tension had been released, I felt more than sad. I felt well and truly depressed.

Lee had kept coming to my mind and I couldn't drown out my concern for him. The flesh made visible via free online porn sites hadn't been enough to fully push him out of my mind; I was hoping he was enjoying himself somewhere and not stuck in a cell or fighting for space under a bridge or something... I even went to the categories section of the site I was on and selected *British* as if it would somehow let him know that I was thinking of him and believe me, it took me a long time to finally make the crumpled tissues in the palm of my hand heavy and wet. I'm not boasting - far from it. My boner kept losing its proud stance over my worrying about him. I even felt more than a little guilty when I finally came, wondering what kind of a friend I was - jerking off while he could have been in some serious trouble somewhere.

"Fuck it," I muttered to myself.

Tiffany, she had a room *filled* with everything she had appeared in on VHS and DVD. It was a temple of vanity; a huge TV on the wall her altar, the spacious couch the pew for all worshippers. There was a wastepaper basket hidden to one side of the couch and it wasn't uncommon for Tiffany to go rummaging in there when she was looking for something she had misplaced or proof that I'd helped myself to some of her pills without asking... You know, empty bottles or wrappers?

I dropped the hot and moist bundle of tissue right into that wastepaper basket knowing full well she could end up coming across it in a matter of days. Doing that just made me smile to myself. Lighting a cigarette I closed the door shut behind me, made my way downstairs and outside - claiming my otherwise unwanted spot beside the pool. The temperature in the air was dropping and it wasn't the most enjoyable cigarette I'd ever smoked - it wasn't even particularly enjoyable to tell you the truth - but I just stood there and encouraged my mind to go blank in a desperate attempt to hit Zen. All kinds of stupid thoughts come to mind when you do shit like that.

This was L.A., the home of hardcore pornography and I'd just watched a limey get fucked a number of miles and even years away to get my kicks.

Did Lee ever let me in on his secret to why he was practically obsessed with British pussy? If he did, I couldn't remember his reason.

How much coke did I have left? Would I have to be paying Albert a visit sooner than I thought and would it be an idea to tell him about Silverdale and his investigation into Lee?

What fucking surgery was Tiffany having?

Why are there so few rock n roll bands worth listening to these days?

Et cetera, et cetera.

I set myself to work just to settle on something, telling myself there would be the reward of more masturbation once I was happy I'd done enough research. Research... You have to laugh. I was looking into Ezekiel as you can probably guess and I'll tell you this for free; social media had gone and made the P.I. licence that Silverdale carried around with him well and truly redundant. The kid made as good as everything available for the public to know of (and to be honest, a lot of it wasn't even worth knowing). Why the fuck would anybody need to hang around outside his home when they could see he had posted a message saying what time he had gotten out of bed, what he had for breakfast, where he was heading after a shower? Stalkers must have it so easy these days, I'm telling you.

"Yeah, I *could* stand outside your home in the rain for hours on end - or I could just sit here by the radiator with a fresh pot of coffee and a new record on..."

But Christ, the boy was annoying and the majority of his friends were just as bad. And I only say majority because a couple of them were cute, but I'm getting off point here.

The whole bunch of them wished it was the sixties or something. All wanting somebody else to pat them on the back approvingly for saying something about sexism being wrong or racism being wrong. They wanted to believe they were part of a movement out to convince the world of its evils and they'd supposedly get all upset at their given examples of how nobody was listening. Fuckers were constantly claiming to have wept or to be in a rage over something somebody had said on the news.

And then there was his spelling and grammar - it was easy to see why Pate had taken offense at it!

If you long to expose the masses to their own ignorance, you should learn the differences between *to* and *too*; *their* and *they're* and my own favourite of a bad bunch - *whether* and *weather*.

Here's a crazy idea while we're at it - don't just throw apostrophes and commas all over the place like you're trying to spend all of them before they lose their value.

The fucking idiot was enough to make you light another cigarette and just stare at the monitor blankly, trying to work out just how the American education system got to be this bad. I had to take a break from reading his supposedly 'out-there, right-on' views and look into his good-looking jailbait friends for a while, just to calm myself down. But calm and semi-aroused I eventually returned to his pages and glanced at the updates, excitement taking hold of me on seeing his new posts.

Posts about how he was going out that night, to a bar I fucking knew...

3

I WENT FOR navy blue jeans with black Converse All Stars, an open flannel shirt with a Brian Jonestown Massacre t-shirt underneath and a dab of cologne behind each ear so Ezekiel would get a nice scent if he leaned in to make sure I could hear him over the music (it'd be easier to see him often and without question if he were to kid himself into believing he was falling in love with me - if only so he could later play the heartbroken man). Tiffany wasn't around to say it so I told myself how good I looked, made a couple of last checks on various social media pages and headed out in the BMW. There was no doubt in my mind that the kid would probably be travelling in a friend's much better car but the one I was in still added a little class.

"Cole," one of the boys manning the gate said before letting me through. "How're you tonight?"

"Great," I said.

"Have you heard anything from Miss Lily?"

"Get out of here," I spat, "what do you take me for, her fucking keeper?"

"I didn't mean to offend."

"Fuck you," I said and with that I was free to go wherever I wanted, and where I wanted happened to be Albert's place because I had given myself enough time to pick up a couple of supplies and chill out before hopefully running into Ezekiel and his friends. Matt was acting security on the stoop, just as you'd expect him to be. I watched him hitting on a couple of girls walking by while I was parking the car; fucking black girls and he has a Confederate Flag tattoo on his head and he's asking if they'd like him to show them a good time, it's fucking ludicrous.

"Matt," I said on approaching, "how's it going?"

"Cole," he said, shaking my hand, "I'm good; you?"

"No complaints."

"You look good," he told me.

"Thanks," I said, "I'm going out tonight."

"Date?"

"Nah," I said, "just meeting a few friends. He in?"

"Yeah," Matt said with a nod, "he's upstairs. Might not be too happy to see you."

"Me? The fuck have I done?"

"Jew's got his panties in a twist," the big gorilla said, eyes following a gang of three adolescents making their way along the opposite side of the street. "Ex-cop came by here asking questions. Guy called Hollis Silverdale."

"Shit," I said, "I fucking told him not to come here. It's all on Lee," I told him, "this guy's been hired to find him."

"Albert told me as much," Matt said, "but he certainly isn't happy to be involved."

"Fuck," I said, "leave it to me, I'll sort it all out. Will he be okay with me turning up?"

"Sure," Matt said on stepping aside, "I was just letting you know he might be a little pissy."

"I appreciate it," I said, "I really do. He have an audience up there with him?" I asked, stopping at the door.

"Couple of stoners but no tail."

"Well that's something," I sighed. "And thanks for letting me know - I mean it."

"No problem."

Fucking Silverdale coming around here was something I just didn't need. He would find nothing at all of interest concerning Lee here but he could make things more than a little inconvenient for me. Albert could cut ties with me and leave me without a reliable supplier and believe me, Albert was one of the best suppliers you could find out in LA. Once he got to know you it was easy for him to see you as a friend. He saw you as his friend and you were charged less, you could collect on tab and he wouldn't give you product mixed with talc or baking soda. I found myself growing increasingly angry walking up the stairs to his apartment and I hoped it would show. Let Albert see how offended I was at that little prick minus a badge turning up here, poking his nose where it had no purpose being; get a show of real solidarity going. It's just that when Albert himself opened the door in a baggy pair of sweatpants and rolled his eyes at me, there was no doubt at all he was going to be pissy.

"Oh," he said - making room for me to walk in, "look who's showed up! Feds didn't follow you here, did they?"

I could've smacked him square in the mouth for saying that; there was two fucking black guys sat together, two real gang members, both bleary-eyed and looking super-fucked and he's saying shit about being followed by the law as I walk in? There was no need for that. He could have even gotten himself killed with that shit. Man had muscle on the door but if people pull guns and take to firing up here, all that muscle isn't going to be worth a dime.

"Relax," I said, "there's nothing for you to worry about."

"Nothing for me to worry about?" he said back to me, pressing his hands tight against his ears as if he was preventing his head from exploding. He turned to face the two black guys, dropped his hands and gave an exaggerated shake of the head on saying, "There's nothing for me to worry about, you hear that?" to them. When you've been out in Los Angeles as long as me, watched as many scenes being filmed as me, you get used to this kind of amateur shit but it doesn't get any easier to watch.

"So tell me," Albert said, turning back to face me, "who is going to worry about it, huh? Are you gonna worry about it for me? You planning on taking care of it?"

"Albert," I sighed, reaching for my cigarettes, "Hollis Silverdale is just a private investigator. What are you so worried about? I told you he might come sniffing around."

"You told me?"

"Yeah," I said and I placed a cigarette between my lips before carefully placing one between Albert's as a show of friendship and trust. "I fucking told you he might waste his time coming here, ask a question or two about Lee."

"You told me he might come over here?"

"Sure I told you," I said and I lit my cigarette before asking him, "don't you remember?"

Albert yanked the cigarette I'd given him from his lips, angrily threw it down on the floor and jumped onto it like a bawling two-year old might. "I think," he yelled, "I'd fucking remember you telling me an ex-cop might come pay me a fucking visit!"

The black boys were pretty wasted so they started laughing at this display we were putting on for them, but I was still aware how all this talk of ex-cops coming by might get them nervous and nervous people are stupider than usual when they're high. I stepped forward and pressed my hands down on Albert's shoulders just to keep him on the spot. Veins were standing out around his temple, his neck; his face was dark red and he was breathing real heavy... I started to wonder how to react if he was having a heart attack.

"Albert," I said, "chill the fuck out and listen to me, will you? I told you about the private investigator - I looked into him myself. You know what he is? He's just a star-fucker," I smirked, "gets his money from degenerate stars for getting the dirt on the other degenerates. Tiffany heard he was good and has got him looking for Lee so he came here. He won't be back."

Albert swallowed, patted my hands with his own and looked down... For a second I was sure he was going to start crying. "You swear," he said to me, "that there is nothing to worry about here?"

I smiled and said, "You watch too many movies when you're stoned, you know that? They get you thinking that straight cops turn away from a corrupt police force to try and make a difference, but it's never been like that. Dumb cops leave a cushy job and a decent pension because they think there's more money in private investigating."

Albert smirked, nodded and headed over to a reclining chair. "You're right," he laughed. "Of course you are. But that son of a bitch turned up here," he said, "and he finishes asking me about Lee and starts trying to get info on me. Can you fucking believe that? Son of a bitch was trying to get me to give him my back story - like I need a son of a bitch like him running back to my parents!"

"Forget about him," I said. "How'd he even manage to get up here when you've got a tank standing at the front door?"

"Ah," Albert sighed, taking a packet of cigarettes and a green plastic lighter from the floor, "he came over first thing... Matt was at his place, fast asleep. No one's to blame here."

"I don't know," I said, "maybe this is the wakeup call you've been needing... You could maybe have Matt come live here."

"Are you kidding?" he laughed, lighting his cigarette, blue smoke soon spilling from his mouth. "You want us to set up shop like we're a bunch of queers or something?" The black boys started laughing. Albert, always one craving approval, turned to them in search for a little more. "The Neo-Nazi and the Yid! You believe that? Would you, I don't know," he laughed, "would you watch that on Comedy Central? I can get it written up," he laughed harder, "I could have your whole season ready come the end of the day if you think it'll sell."

"Albert," I said, "I'm sorry but I don't have the time to hang around here tonight; I got places to go, business to take care of..."

"Right," he said, grinning from ear to ear as he got back on his feet. "What's her name?" he asked.

"I told you already - it's not like that," I smiled, "not tonight. I'm out as a professional right now - got to do some research for a TV producer I'm about to start working with."

"Shit, that's impressive. That's real impressive," Albert said, "it really is. I'm happy for you, man," and with that he pulled me tight and hugged me. He was sobbing heavily into my shoulder in no time at all.

4

I PARKED THE car in the nearest available space that I could find and started my walk to the club. The girls working the streets were high quality given the area. There was one in bright pink stockings I noticed a mile off and probably would have gone home with if she had approached me but she was heading in the opposite direction and didn't even glance at me. The bums were the same level of bum you can find anywhere in Los Angeles; they'll come over and say they need just one dollar to get someplace for the night before walking the block, telling their next victim how they need just one dollar. Others, fucked on paint-stripper or bath salts, aggressively explored their own worlds without truly noting those around them or were unconscious in the alleyways with their faces in a pillow of cooling vomit.

People were smoking outside the club. It gave the impression of a queue from the distance; had you think that *this* had to be the place to stop in. Most of them - especially the girls in tight dresses or ripped jeans - were most probably on the payroll. Two black guys, quarter-backs in trouser-press-fresh suits, were standing nearby. Both wore earpieces and shades. One of them gave me the most fleeting of glances as I made my way down concrete steps leading to the entrance, heading underground like a misplaced Morlock. Music was spilling out already; distorted guitars with feedback. It was a live recording but not a live act on the premises. It was a trick that would work on the office workers from the banks and insurance companies but not people like me.

I walked in, tried to remember how long it had been since I'd last came in here. It didn't look to have changed a bit; you walked in and found yourself on a large dancefloor, the bar area facing you from the other side of the room. A doorway on the left wall took you onto a short corridor that turned once or twice and put you squarely in a sitting area where a DJ played softer sounds. You could play pool there; stare at TV screens high on the wall but never hear them.

The dancefloor was relatively empty, as was the bar area. Three extremely fuck-able barmaids, each desperate for somebody to serve just so they would have something to do if even for a moment. I was surprised at how quiet the place was. It was reasonably late, the place should have been quite busy. Had I fallen so behind? Had I really lost an understanding of how the nights worked these days? Would it have been a better idea for me to have only headed out in another hour or so?

I made my way to the brunette barmaid, reason being I'd have less competition for her attention if Ezekiel and his friends weren't to show (the other barmaids included a blonde and another with black hair holding a cherry red streak. Every drunken guy would try and get an invite home from one of these over the underrated brunette as far as I was concerned). She stepped forward to serve me. Under bright lights strategically placed to deter disagreements over how much money you had handed over, you could see her complexion was completely flawless. The bright lighting only acted to make her all the more stunning and I began to wonder just how much competition I could have to face for her.

"Hi," I said, "bottle of beer and a single whisky," I told her, "and take one for yourself," I added, reaching for my wallet. She thanked me, turned around and set to work collecting my drinks. I glanced around while I was waiting and failed to spot any security inside. The coke I'd bought from Albert was in a small fold of cardboard in my back pocket- a fucking fold like I was sixteen again or something. Up until recently I'd had a cute little vial on a necklace, something that would make you look spiritual or something when really it was a way to carry cocaine on you that would never be found during a routine stop-and-search.

It had disappeared. I'd looked everywhere for it but had no success. Either Tiffany had hidden it out of spite over Lee's disappearance or it had snapped free from my neck at some point and I had been too loaded to notice at the time. You ask me, it was most likely Tiffany had taken it.

The barmaid returned with my drinks. She'd decided to take the money for her own instead of the drink. I handed the money over without complaint regardless and when she placed the change in my hand she leaned over and asked, "Didn't you used to go to The Henbury?"

The Henbury; talk about a fucking blast from the past... A club I was visiting before I was to meet Doyle, that's how long ago it was. "Wow," I laughed, "now there's a place I haven't thought of for a long time!"

"I thought I recognised you from somewhere," she grinned. "I used to go there every Thursday night."

She recognised me. She recognised me so there was a chance she had always wanted to screw me.

"I didn't embarrass myself too much, did I?" I laughed. "Constantly showering you with flowers and sonnets every Thursday? I've always thought that's how I'd react on meeting somebody like you."

Flattery - the guaranteed top spot in Cole's patented *How to Seduce Women* technique. "I've always thought that's how I'd react on meeting somebody like you" was a fucking good one to use. Let them think you see them as this rare, never-before encountered specimen. Let them think they are the girl you have been waiting for all of your life. Every girl wants a man to look at her, get to know her, and hear nothing but The Beatles' *In My Life* every time he thinks about her or looks into her eyes. Flattery gets you everywhere and everything.

She blushed but her eyes moved to the side for the skip of a heartbeat as she noticed somebody take place at the bar to order a drink. She knew she had to go and serve him but wanted to stay here with me a little while longer, it was clear as day to see. "What's your name?" I asked her.

"Gemma."

"I'm Cole," I said with a smile, "I'll see you a little later," I promised before turning away. It's a cliché but it's also true - always leave them wanting more.

5

THE WALK THROUGH the corridor leading into the smaller room was brief yet memorable... guys with their backs against the wall, necking a girl who was happy to grind up against him; small groups trying to take a quick snort of cocaine before staff came passing through. One guy was standing all alone, eyes fixed on another guy and girl too busy locking tongues to notice. I wondered if the voyeur knew either of them; was he waiting for his friend to come up for air or was he wondering how his favourite girl could do that to him? Either way it was something I could use in my script, no doubt about it.

They'd changed the layout of the chill-out room - knocked a wall down and rebuilt it a little farther back to add more space for sitting; added a small bar and a couple of old arcade machines. The place was as empty as the dancefloor on the other side of the corridor, maybe even quieter. I glanced over at the talent working the bar and decided Gemma was the best option to go for before sitting down alone to try and enjoy my drink over sounds somebody like me just couldn't relate to. This place was entirely out of my zone nowadays, I had moved on without caring to admit it. Bored, I took to going through each and every contact on my cell to see if an urge came to text somebody I hadn't spoken to in a while took hold. Eventually I settled on messaging Pate, telling him the screenplay was going great. I'd just finished sending it when a dumpy girl wearing something modelled on a bullet belt, only it was loaded with plastic shots, came and stood at my side. "Want to buy one?" she asked with a smile.

"I don't know," I said, "what is it?"

"Flavoured tequila," she said before dropping a finger on each individually coloured lid of the containers. "Bubblegum, chocolate-mint, banana, sour apple and cherry."

"Give me a sour apple," I said, opening my wallet.

"That'll be ten dollars," she said, pulling a shot free.

My fingers temporarily froze on hearing the price. Ten dollars for a shot of tequila? Talk about steep. I fished a ten free anyway and handed it over, refusing to offer a tip. She kept the smile regardless, handed me my warm container and was gone before I'd even opened it. I downed the contents, shuddered at the taste and tossed the disposable shot-glass over my shoulder. I doubted very much it would be her responsibility to sweep the floors come the end of the night but at ten dollars a drink, you expect somebody to come tidy up for you.

The room began to attract more people as the night progressed. Yuppies appearing fresh out of Wall Street like it was the 1980s, desperately tried to grab the attention of a group of girls without making it too obvious; the guys had their shirts completely unbuttoned to show flat stomachs but flabby hips as they laughed obnoxiously, desperate for the girls to head over in their direction for a good time and thankfully, they didn't. And I didn't hit the bottle hard. It wouldn't have been a good idea because of the car I'd arrived in. Sure, I was drinking, but I made regular trips to the bathroom to counteract the alcohol and sharpen my senses with a little blow.

Cocaine in a fold of cardboard, now stashed in one of my socks in case a bouncer forced his way into the stall where I was pretending to take a crap... The fucking indignity of it all.

The dancefloor had gotten busy during my time away; people dancing in small groups, girls dancing around their bags... Dancing is just a mating ritual when you stop and think about it and if you stop and think about it on a dancefloor then you're reminded of King Louie and his people in the animated Jungle Book movie.

Gemma must have been taking a break because she was standing on the other side of the bar, laughing with a man she was standing close to. I felt the great weight of disappointment land on my heart and tried to block it out by remembering why I was here in the first place... I wasn't here for her, I was here for Ezekiel Bircham and he could have arrived long ago for all I knew.

"Hey," some guy said, taking a hold of my elbow with his pupils with whatever drugs he had taken, "do you know what song this is? This song is fucking lit!"

"No idea," I told him, walking on, allowing him to fade out into the background. Determined to find my designated muse I looked at every nearby face for a moment longer than necessary, constantly moving. There was no sign of him. A couple of people caught my attention - I was sure they were friends of his online - so I hung around them as discreetly as I could but he didn't appear, no matter how hard I willed him to do so. Eventually I had to admit defeat. I looked back at Gemma one last time, saw her working the bar again and busy with a customer, and walked out into the cold night air. Pate had replied to the message I'd sent him. He said he was looking forward to seeing what I had written.

6

I woke up on the comedown of all comedowns. I would have killed to have Tiffany back and if not Tiffany then at least some of her hired hands... I'd even take Chambers, so long as he was willing to bring me hot soup with a freshly toasted roll and a promise this feeling wouldn't last.

There was a dull, steady ache right in the centre of my skull; a packet of cigarettes beside a bottle of vodka and a glass on the bedside table because late last night, it had seemed a good idea. Forcing myself into a sitting position, the dull ache moved like the bubble in a spirit level. Feelings like this are a young man's game - they can deal with it, even if it means sleeping until it's all over. Feelings like this have me want to quit drinking altogether. Lee used to joke that I was a sucker for punishment. Even Doyle used to say this feeling was God's way of reminding us of the drunken promises we had made.

I groaned on pulling myself to my feet and recognised the sound I had made. My dad used to make it every weeknight, when he woke after taking a nap in his chair and dragged himself up to do whatever it was he had to do. I've read somewhere how children miss a generation; your children won't be like you but like your own parents. I don't know what research proved that to be the case because I've never been interested enough to look into it.

First thing I did was slip into Tiffany's bathrobe, leaving it unfastened because it was already a little hot, then I went into the next room and used the computer to get online - paying that Ezekiel bitch's Myspace page a visit.

Fucking posts and comments from the early hours of the morning onwards. It took me less than a minute to see they'd chosen some other bar over the place I'd lost a night to; they even put jokes you'd only get if you were there with them up for all to see. And the pictures... There was just so many pictures of them all, every son of a bitch had uploaded photographs and tagged every son of a bitch they'd caught in the frame. Stupid poses and people acting like they were having a much better time than they really were. And nobody posted a bad picture of themselves. Not intentionally, anyway. But Ezekiel... Ezekiel was wearing a pale blue shirt with swirling patterns all over it with a deep red jacket on top, obviously going for some kind of dandy look. And he'd had his hair cut; short back and sides but the length kept on top so he could push it back. It did him no favours. His nose looked a little fat, his cheeks were puffy and it was there for all to see that his hairline was receding.

"Vain, posing bastards," I sighed while lighting a cigarette. I felt like opening my own page just so I could bombard them with abuse - first insisting they shouldn't decide they'll be going someplace else last minute, then asking if they had any idea how pathetic they fucking looked.

The telephone started ringing and stopped me from putting this plan into action. At first I was going to just ignore it but then I realised it could be Tiffany so I ran for the phone, convinced it was going to stop dead the moment my hand took hold of the receiver.

It didn't.

"Lily residence," I croaked. "Cole speaking," I added once I'd had the time to clear my throat.

"Cole," he seemed to yell back at me, "it's Scott Pate. How are you doing?"

"I'm good," I lied. "You?"

"Left blowing in the wind," he laughed. "Friend of mine cancelled our tennis game, so I was wondering if you're free to meet for coffee and a talk?"

"When're you thinking?" I asked.

"Now," he said. "I'm driving over to your place to pick you up right now. That is," he said, "unless you have any other plans?"

"No," I said, "no plans. It's just that I've been writing all morning," I claimed, "haven't had a minute to take a shower or get dressed."

"That's what I like to hear! Tell you what - you start getting ready and I'll wait for you outside. I'm around fifteen minutes away, give or take the state of traffic; it's worse than usual right now."

"That should be enough time," I said, "I'll see you soon."

"Don't forget to clean behind your ears!"

My heart started beating like a wild animal trapped inside of me. The ache in my head pounded against my skull as I raced to the bathroom to take a proper look at my appearance. The stubble was fine - a lot of creative types had stubble. The bloodshot eyes and dilated pupils were an altogether different beast. Sure, a lot of creative types wear those too but I had no idea how Pate looked upon casual drug use.

"Shit," I said, raiding the medicine cabinet behind the mirror. Tiffany had left her eye-drops behind. The instructions said one drop into each eye first thing at morning and last thing at night but I put a drop in each eye knowing they'd get a second once I was done in the shower. Sniffing my underarms got me nothing in return but an odour not too different to onions. "Son of a bitch," I said, hoping the time I had at my disposal would be enough for me to head out smelling of roses and if not roses then at least something finer in the manure than fucking onions.

7

THE MERCEDES WAS waiting outside when I came out of the shower. The needlessly handsome driver was standing beside it, a little too casual to be professional, with one arm resting against the roof. He belonged on a billboard or in the pages of a magazine specialising in the needs and interests of people with money to burn. I'd have fucking bought the car from him myself if I had the money.

But I got dressed as quickly as I could without looking like a bum, intentionally going for a casual slacker look of my beaten white Converse All Stars, grey corduroy trousers, black t-shirt and a grey hooded jacket left open. It worked with the messy hair and stubble but my eyes were still looking worse for wear. The second dose of eye-drops only made me want to blink more than usual.

"Let's get this done," I muttered to myself before heading out of the door. The driver saw me coming, threw me a barely noticeable nod of the head and opened the door for me. Man looked like he should have tossed a cigarette into the gutter to finish the look good and proper. I thanked him without giving him my advice and climbed in beside Pate. The man gently closed the door behind him and made his way to the front.

"Cole," Pate said with a smile that revealed almost all of his blindingly white teeth, "good to see you. I didn't wake you, did I?" he asked right as the driver got us rolling.

"I'm a little fucked," I answered truthfully. "I went out last night and -"

"Hold on *one* second," Pate insisted, taking a bottle of aspirin from an inside jacket pocket and reaching down to the side of him to grab a bottle of mineral water. "Excuse me," he said, shaking an aspirin or two free, "migraines - bane of my existence. I always know when one is coming," he continued, "because it feels like toothache - always one of the same teeth, up and right at the back. Then it spreads to my eye and it feels like somebody is handling my eyeball with dirty hands," he concluded, throwing back the tablets and chasing them with a mouthful of water. "I've begged my dentist to remove the offending teeth but he swears it won't make a difference."

It was just a whole lot of information that seemed worthless to me but I played interested and asked him, "You always suffered from them?"

"I started having them a couple of times a year from my late thirties," he said, "now I'm having them every couple of months. My wife is the same," he added, "only she'll take something for them and lock herself away in a darkened room, try and sleep it off. She says when she's having a migraine," he said as if he admired her for it, "it's like she's seeing everything in heat vision."

We'd gone right through security without my noticing so whether the boys at the gates took much interest in us, I can't tell you. But they were probably panicking, I'm confident of that much. The queen was missing and the young prince was receiving powerful visitors in her absence. Visitors who were getting through without passes. I smiled, thought about tearing into security over it when I had the chance.

"Anyway," Pate smiled, "what was it you were saying - you went out last night? You're young," he shrugged, "I get it... Go out and chase skirt while you still can."

"It was more business," I said, "or an attempt at it. I was looking at that Bircham-kid's Myspace page and he was talking about going out with his friends. I went where they had said they were going," I sighed, "was hoping to start making my way into their little circle for research purposes."

"Did it work?"

"Afraid not," I said. "I gave up on them and came back home. They ended up going someplace else in the end."

"You had a good idea," Pate said, "and I'll be happy to reimburse you for money spent."

"Don't worry about it," I said although if he offered me the money again, it would be graciously accepted.

"No," Pate said, "I insist. You showed more initiative than most of the other supposed writers I'm surrounded by and you should definitely try it again. Just be sure," he insisted, "Ezekiel is *never* made aware of the fact you are working for me... Can't even find out you know me for the moment. Same goes for his friends."

"I understand," I said.

"That's my boy," he said and he grinned as he patted me on the knee. "Don't tell me the night was a total waste. You speak with any pretty faces?"

"There was one," I told him, "barmaid recognised me from a place I used to hang out in when I was younger."

"So you made an impression? Good man," he smiled.

"Nah," I said, "she was just fishing for a tip and she got it. And this place I was in last night? They had a girl selling shots of flavoured tequila, right? Selling a shot in a disposable cup for ten bucks."

"Ten dollars for a shot? Did she dip her titties in it for you? I'm sorry," he laughed, "the vulgarity in me," he said, "sometimes it just rolls off the tongue before I can stop it."

"You don't have to hold back in front of me," I laughed, "you're not the guy I'm researching."

"Ha! It's this town," he said, "this industry... Everybody wants it to look so clean and respectable all of a sudden, but it was built on blood-stained money, corruption and sexual favours. I'm not saying *everybody* was like that or we should have kept that business model but most of these alleged do-gooders are worse than the powers of old. Me," he shrugged, "I just have the mouth I needed to get somewhere. I'm all talk. I like being polite and honest to myself and others," he said, "but sometimes when you're talking business - especially if it's with a team of young guys - you slip into old habits and feel the need to swing your dick around and bang on your chest to have them know you're king of the mountain."

We stopped at Knewman's, which was a surprise to me because I'd thought Pate didn't like the place but I didn't ask him about it. Didn't ask him if he'd heard from Tiffany or Chambers, either. It was a bit funny, sitting there, to begin with; you could see the people out on the street from where I was sitting and I began to wonder about how I would react if Doyle walked by in the company of Lee. Despite the potential importance of this little meeting, I found myself wishing they would. I'd even settle for Doyle on his own, because it would give me the opportunity of asking somebody who might know Lee's current whereabouts.

"I'm really happy with the team I'm getting together for this project. There's an attractive young woman I would very much like you to meet," Pate said to secure my attention. An abruption of unexpected laughter from a nearby table burst his bubble - those responsible being a party of six Indians or Pakistanis; I'm not sure which, it was one or the other and I guess they were dressed in their traditional clothing.

"George Harrison," Pate said, "has a *lot* to answer for."

"Excuse me?" I smirked.

"Beatle; gave the world this idea of mysticism and divinity out in India but it isn't like that at all and I should know," he said, "I've known people that have worked there and I read a lot. Rape attacks are through the roof," he continued, "men throwing acid in the face of women who have rejected them... Did you know," he ended, "that a husband in parts of India can bury his wife *alive* if he has reason to believe she has been unfaithful?"

"Are you serious?"

"Deadly," Pate said, "India or Pakistan; I forget which but there isn't any real difference between the two of them."

And I wondered if this was how every meal with Pate would be - Scott Pate's personal knowledge and opinions on the races of the world.

"But this girl," Pate smiled, "she's younger than you but she's worked in radio for a few years. Her scripts are funny, grab your attention and really pull you along for the ride. I told her to get out of radio while she can, gave her a bit of information on the project to tease her with and it worked. I think the two of you will get on like a house on fire," he said.

"She not worried about the idea of working with somebody

so inexperienced?" I asked.

"No," Pate laughed. "She's very open-minded... A friend of mine told me she's bisexual. I have to say," he smiled, "if I was a lot younger and unmarried, I'd be the first to try and straighten her out."

"I look forward to meeting her."

"I look forward to you both meeting," he said as our drinks arrived. "How's the script coming along?"

"Good," I told him.

"You have my personal email, don't you? You feel comfortable sending me what you have in the next couple of days?"

I swallowed, panicked inside at the idea of how much writing I would have to see done in the next few days to try and convince him how good an idea it would be to keep me on the team and not on the bench.

"Sure," I said, "that shouldn't be a problem."

"That's good. And I want you to know," he said, "a problem of yours is a problem of mine, now that the two of us are working together."

"I appreciate it."

"I'm being serious," he said. "Is Tom Selleck being any bother?"

"Tom Selleck?"

"Magnum," he grinned and he grinned even harder once my face made it clear for him to see I wasn't following. "Private investigator!" he laughed. "Is Hollis Silverdale still harassing you?"

"Well," I sighed, "he isn't here with us right now but he's still interested... He's been looking into places I'm not comfortable with."

"I'm not proud to admit it but I know guys," Pate said before stopping to sample his drink, "that would pay somebody to beat him up a little and I know guys who would go through the courts to have him stand down."

"Which of the two would you recommend?"

"Neither, because he's costing Tiffany Lily money. That doesn't mean I wouldn't have some fun while he was around. Take him places that'll make him feel uncomfortable or bore the shit out of him. You see him waiting outside," Pate said, "you invite him in for a drink and sit back watching garbage all day or reading a book.

"Tiffany will drop him," he finished, "once she sees he isn't bringing home any results. Stop him from getting results, stop him from finding work."

The front door was open when I arrived back home but I thought nothing of it; this wasn't the kind of place for burglars to get into easy, so the most likely answer at the time was that I'd left it open and not realised. I noticed the smell of fresh coffee was in the air as I walked inside. Tiffany back? Unlikely. She'd want to announce her return with French horns and fireworks. Could Chambers or even Samantha have been sent to collect something on her behalf? Again, unlikely. She'd be sure she had absolutely everything she needed, hoping it would lead to me dropping down at her feet come the time she returned.

You guessed it - Silverdale was sitting out back; his ass in a sun-lounger and a cup of fresh coffee in his hand. "Cole," he said with such a cocky grin I wanted to feed my entire fist into it, "you have a productive lunch? There's fresh coffee in the pot, why don't you sit down and tell me all about it?"

8

I TOOK PLENTY of time pouring myself a coffee and coolly said, "I could shoot you right now for trespassing," as I did so.

"Nah," he said, "you'd never get away with it but we'll agree to disagree to keep the conversation progressing. Scott Pate, huh? Things I could tell you about him..."

"Funny - the man's never heard of you," I bluffed, making my way to the free sun-lounger. The coffee was a little weak for my liking. "You heard from Tiffany?" I asked.

"I'm in regular contact," he said. "You heard from Lee?"

"No," I said, looking across the swimming pool.

"I could tell you some things about him, too," he grinned.

"That's wonderful," I sighed.

Silverdale took a notepad from his pocket, opened it and started to move along the pages as he spoke but I didn't believe for one minute he had written any of this down. "Lee is cautious to the state of being paranoid," he claimed. "Let's say he has something about *John* to get off his chest, and he decides to unload this on *Bob*; Lee would be a little worried that Bob knows John, so he'd change John's name for the story. John's name during Lee's account would be inspired by somebody from a movie or a magazine article... Anything he'd been paying attention to in his recent past."

Lighting a cigarette gave him the impression I was taking in what he had said - that I was weighing it up for accuracy. Finally, I looked to him and said, "Who the fuck are John and Bob?"

"I'm not at liberty to answer that question," he smiled. "But what about that description of Lee," he asked, "you have anything to say to that?"

I shook my head. "Can't say so."

"What about you," he said, "you ever wonder what he said your name was to others?"

"I don't know," I sighed, "Handsome McWonderful if he was

in a flattering mood."

"Right," he grinned and he glanced over his notes again for dramatic effect. "Lee also told stories," he said. "Sometimes exaggerations of things he had experienced, sometimes just outright lies, but usually to make himself or the people he knew appear more interesting. You think you ever fell for any of his stories?

"He ever tell you how you could both take some of Miss Lily's money and move on together?"

"Jesus," I laughed, "whatever you're getting paid for this, it's too much."

"I'm just trying to see the whole picture," he shrugged, returning the notepad to his pocket. "You think I'm looking at it wrong, you can easily straighten the angle I'm viewing it from."

I nodded and said, "You got absolutely nothing from Albert, did you? I told you it would be a waste of time. You could have gotten yourself in trouble by going there."

"Ha! You think some rich Jew-kid is something for me to worry about? You might be impressed by the gang members he has selling out on the streets for him but me," he said, "no, not me. These gang members he's using are dumb as fuck! These gang members or the hick he has standing outside of a night will be busted and Albert will be right behind them. He ever tell you how his old man plays squash with Senator Rhea?"

"No," I said, "we have more interesting things to talk about."

"Oh," Silverdale said, "from my perspective, this is interesting. If your friend is ever facing charges, he'll walk and all the arrests will be on his little gang members and regular buyers. You'll walk out with whatever you're smoking one day and head straight into handcuffs."

"I thought you were looking into Lee? All this," I said, "all this sounds like you're worrying about me."

"No," he smiled, "I'm not worried about you at all. To be frank," he said, "you mean next to nothing but you could just have information that would be useful to my investigation. And I know people," he added, "that could prove useful, should you ever be arrested for possession."

"Get out of here," I laughed. "You threaten me with talk of senators backing stings and you expect me to believe you could help me out if it happened? You?" I laughed. "You're fucking nothing," I told him. "You're a small man with a slip of paper from the courts allowing you to root through my garbage."

Silverdale grinned, nodded, finished his coffee and finally got to his feet. "You ever feel the need to talk," he said, "I'm only a phone call away. You could find out all kinds of interesting things about the people you're hanging out with through me."

"Right," I called out to his retreating figure, "just you remember that I'm the only person that could ever tell you anything worth knowing about Lee!"

He left the house. I stood up and overturned the lounger he'd been sitting in. "Motherfucker," I yelled. He probably heard it out front so I called it again, louder. More than a little pissed off and back inside the house, I made the call to Pate's office. His secretary disappeared from the line but returned quickly enough to tell me she was connecting us.

"Cole," he said, "I wasn't expecting to hear from you so soon. Is anything wrong?"

"Silverdale," I said, "I need to know if you can have his fucking legs broken!"

"What's happened?"

"He was waiting for me when I got back," I said, "and he's out to do nothing more than get under my skin."

"Cole," Pate said, "take a couple of deep breaths and relax. Listen to me - people like Silverdale always appear once you're going up in the world; grubby little people from the shadows looking to improve their own lives at your benefit and you know what you do? The only thing you *can*... You shine a light on them."

"I have no idea how you're trying to help me out here," I snapped. "Are you going to give me a number or not?"

"No," Pate said, "because it'll only do more harm than good and in the end you won't thank me for it. Just sit back, put your feet up and think of your work. You're a creative and a creative levels the playing field in his own way. If you need to, call me when you're in better spirits and we'll discuss the issue together, *sensibly.*"

So I was rightly pissed over what happened but I had nobody to vent my frustration on. Tiffany and Chambers? Their phones just went unanswered, just like the line for Chambers' office did because they must have been told to ignore my number. I almost called Sam but decided not to, realising she was probably as much in the dark as me and shouting at her would only make me feel bad. With so few options at my disposal I decided to run it off but only managed to get a couple of doors down the street before my legs were burning and my sides were hurting like you would not believe. In the end I took a shower and headed out, catching a bus into the city just to keep myself distracted.

I had no idea what I was looking for so when I finally found it, it felt like destiny.

I'd strolled into a supermarket, headed straight for the back wall where the magazines were on display and just took to looking until the publication focusing on real crimes and major cases solved by private eyes appeared to leap out at me. I took it in my excited hands and headed straight for the back inside cover where private investigators paid for their adverts to be printed. Well, most of them did... A piece of white cardboard slipped out from the back and landed at my feet; when I picked it up and turned it around, the first thing I noticed was the badly stencilled magnifying glass over an eye in the top left corner. The text in the centre of the card had clearly been placed there using an old manual typewriter. It read:


```
B. DEXTER, PRIVATE INVESTIGATOR
RESULTS AND VALUE FOR MONEY!
```


The number beneath was a landline. Smiling, I pocketed the card and returned the magazine once I'd carefully taken hold of the copy behind it. Once again, B. Dexter had slipped his card into the back for free advertising. With a twenty dollar bill in my possession, I bought a pack of ten Marlboros just to make change for the payphone out on the street.

9

THE VOICE THAT answered my call didn't belong to the moment, it was the sound of somebody having been pulled away from something else entirely and was now struggling to blend in. I wondered if B. Dexter could be a lot better in his line of work than his advertising methods had led me to believe... I pictured a grizzled man on a stakeout, so engrossed in his work that it had taken him a while to notice the ringing of his cellphone. Then I remembered it was a landline that I had called and unless the guy just happened to be on a stakeout in his office, he must have just been asleep.

"Hey," I said, "am I speaking with B. Dexter?"

"You are," he said, "how can I help you?"

"Well," I told him, "I found your card and would like to hire your services. It's a simple enough job," I said, "probably won't go longer than a couple of weeks."

I heard him light a cigarette on the other end before speaking again. "I'm available to meet and discuss this for the rest of the afternoon," he said. "You want to make your way over to my office so you can tell me all about it?"

"That'd be great," I said, "where can I find you?"

His office was above a Chinese supermarket. I was pacing the street looking for the door when a shop worker coming out on his smoke break finally noticed me and asked, "Need help?"

"If you can," I smiled, "I'm looking for 183A-"

"It's around the back," he said, striking the match with his thumbnail to bring a virgin flame into the world. "Ring the doorbell and take two steps back," he advised, "that way he can see who it is and he'll buzz you in. He can't see," he finished with a laugh, "he'll think it's debt collectors and hide."

"Okay," I smiled, "thanks for the tip."

Dexter buzzed me in almost right away and I closed the door shut behind me to prevent any debt collectors from interrupting our little meeting. The carpet on the stairs was a faded green colour and the air was musky. The door at the top of the stairs opened up into a large room with a decent-sized leather couch and a couple of matching arm chairs. They were in decent shape but looked like they could have been found in a goodwill store or even a street corner. The only other door in the room swung open and Dexter revealed himself as theatrically as possible; white vest with black trousers and braces tight against his shoulders. Three day stubble and hair that would have started the week looking tidy but was now adopting a greasy shine and had him look like he could have just got out of bed. The baseball bat in his hand was a nice touch, if not there only until he was sure the debt enforcers hadn't figured a way in.

"Mr Dexter? My name's Cole," I said, "I called you a little earlier to discuss a job you may be interested in?"

He waited somewhere between two and three seconds before nodding - then he made his way toward me. He got so close you couldn't help but see how the whites of his eyes were almost red and the bags beneath them belonged in a grocery store. "Bill Dexter," he said, offering his hand, "private investigator. Pleasure to meet you, Cole."

"And you," I said. "I'm sorry but I've never done anything like this before... Do we just talk about it here or do we go to a bar or something like that?"

"Nice idea," he grinned, "but I never drink during the discussion - keeps the mind sharp," he said. "How about you follow me into my office and give me the general thread of whatever your problem is?"

His office was slightly bigger than one of Tiffany's walk-in wardrobes; spotless walls and a smell of paint too heavy to make its way out of the single tiny window and into the world beyond. I've no idea how he managed to get a table in there but he had and he had to squeeze past it to get in the uncomfortable chair with its back against the wall while I claimed the matching one with the door not quite at my back but to the side of me. "You can smoke if you like," he said, taking a glass ashtray with a layer of solidified ash covering its insides and placing it down in the centre of the table. "A lot of people find it easier to talk if they're smoking."

"I'm good," I told him, "just finished one."

He nodded at that. "So what is it?" he asked. "You think your girlfriend is cheating on you? Maybe your kids aren't yours? I'm not implying anything - not trying to put any ideas in your head," he said, "it's just that's the common complaint for guys around your age. That or needing somebody to scare off their baby sister's boyfriend," he smirked.

"I want you to follow somebody," I told him, "not necessarily discreetly."

His smile broadened. "So somebody does need scaring? That's fine by me," he said, "I've got scaring down to a fine art."

"Maybe more annoyed than scared," I shrugged. "You might have a problem doing it," I sighed, "professional courtesy or something - I don't know - because the man's in the same line of work as you."

Dexter laughed at that. His throat moved up and down his neck like a child's bouncing ball as he did so. "You want me to harass a private eye?"

"Yes," I said with a nod and not a trace of a smile. "My girl is worried about a mutual friend of ours," I sighed, "he made tracks without letting us know and that doesn't bother me because what he's gone and done must be what he decided is best for him. But she's worried," I said, "and nothing is making her feel better. So she got this private investigator to try and find him."

Dexter nodded, lifted a pen and an office notepad from the same desk drawer he'd taken the ash tray and prepared to make his first notes. "This friend of yours," he said, "you didn't scare him off, did you? Didn't give him a warning or anything for getting too close to your woman?"

"No," I laughed, "not at all. Look," I said, "he's a grown man and it should be down to him whether he ever comes back or not."

Dexter nodded and scribbled something illegible. "Last thing I need is to take this job and then find out how your friend has been found on a slab somewhere," he said, "and believe me, it'll come out in the end if that's the case."

"Come on," I said, "he was more my friend than hers... I loved him like a brother."

"You never threatened him? You promise me you never confronted him over something and things got a little out of hand?"

"None of the above," I said, "straight up and down."

"Between you and me," Dexter said, writing something else, "I wouldn't care if you did as long as I wasn't working the case... Some men have it coming."

"Not Lee," I said, "and he doesn't need someone looking for him when he mightn't want to be found." I wanted a cigarette but fought back against the urge in case he assumed lighting up was a sure-fire sign that I was guilty of something.

Dexter nodded and said, "To be clear - I am not to look for your friend... I'm doing nothing more than following the guy sent to look for him?"

"Feel free to piss him off as much as he is me," I said. "I meet a friend for a drink and he's there. I go for a walk and he's there."

"I need to ask," Dexter said, "are you worried to what he'll see you doing? Are you cheating on your girlfriend or participating in illegal activities?"

"I have a couple of friends making a little extra money on the side through selling drugs," I told him, "but I do not take part in that."

"You take drugs?"

"I dabble a little," I shrugged, "you're going to if your friends are dealing, right? But my girlfriend knows about this and it isn't an issue."

"Understanding girl," he smiled. "Look," he said, "if you're short-changing me on anything here, I'll walk away. If you give me a big enough reason, I might even tell this other investigator what I've seen or heard - do you understand?"

"Absolutely."

Dexter kept his eyes on me a moment, finally blinked and said, "Okay," before looking back down at his notepad. "I don't suppose you know the name of this private investigator?"

"I do," I said. "Hollis Silverdale."

"Hollis," Dexter said, writing it down, "Silverdale."

"You know him?"

"No," he said, "not yet." He placed the pen down on the table and looked at me again. "I'm ready to start right now," he said, "all I need is for you to agree to my terms. They're not to your liking," he shrugged, "I wish you all the best and you walk back out of that door and find somebody else."

"Throw it on me."

"My price is one hundred and fifty dollars per week," he said, "and I'm entitled to thirty dollars per day expenses for food plus gas money. I provide you with receipts and the total is added on to the following week's pay."

"That sounds reasonable," I said. "Is there an ATM nearby? I can go get you three weeks' pay right now."

His eyes lit up on hearing that. Poor guy was probably wishing he'd tried two hundred. I would have given him that - it's not like it was coming out of my own wallet. "There is," he said, "post office down the street... You can't miss it."

"You do this well enough," I said, "this'll be over and done with in two but I'll let you keep the extra as a bonus."

10

I was in the mood to celebrate - that's how confident I was that Dexter would rid me of Silverdale - so I made my way downtown to Albert's place. It was too early for Matt to be manning the stoop, he was probably sleeping off a long night at home, and his absence was all the more noticeable on stepping into the building. Two guys were at the side of the stairs, one huffing on a crack pipe as the other - a legless man of around sixty years old - waited his turn from the comfort of his wheelchair. Neither one of the pair offered me the slightest bit of attention.

Heading upstairs, I heard two guys in conversation heading down from the floor below. Two black youths, both falling silent the moment they spotted me. "How's it going, boys?" I asked.

"Whatever," one of the two replied.

Albert opened the door to me in a pair of something too short to be referred to as *shorts*; I was fucking terrified his circumcised dick or even his balls were about to break free at any given moment. "Cole," he smiled, "come in."

There was a girl of high school age on his couch, strung out and probably oblivious to her surroundings, and two young guys sat on the floor - both pretty stoned and staring at whatever show was on TV at that time of the day. There was one huge, family-sized bong on the floor between them and the smell of grass was heavy in the air. A credit card waited beside a small mound of coke on the nearest table littered with spilled tobacco, cigarette papers and a couple of pre-prepared roaches.

"Everybody," Albert announced, throwing his arm around me, "this is Cole."

One of the two guys looked at me before getting a fit of the giggles he couldn't even break free of when it started to hurt, the other just looked at me from his pink glass eyes and muttered a greeting only a dog could have heard without any difficulty.

"Cole's a writer out in Hollywood," Albert added with a grin, "so be careful what you say around him! How's it going, buddy?" he asked, pulling me closer. "You here for a social call or are you here to make a purchase?"

"To celebrate," I told him, "because the private eye who came bothering you will be chased away in a couple of days, never to return."

I'd already withdrawn the money to make a purchase but hoped a large discount would be made available with such a reveal.

"You are a fucking gem in a mountain of garbage - you know that?" he asked while patting my cheeks. "I fucking love you," he declared, pulling me close, "I fucking love this guy like he was my own brother. Now let's get fucked," he screamed, "let's get fucked!"

The other three guests were already too fucked to excitedly cheer, regardless of how much Albert had wanted them to. One of them was still giggling uncontrollably, curled up in the foetal position with tears running down his crimson face. A part of me hoped that I was about to watch a man laugh himself to death.

11

It came down to Albert and me.

Out of the two guys, the one who had nearly laughed himself to death, fell into a deep sleep. His friend, seeing how Albert and I were taking turns cutting up lines, decided to come join our way of killing time and regularly handed loose bills on over to Albert to guarantee his place at the table.

His friend eventually woke up - pale and with a long scratch down the side of his face that nobody could explain - and hid himself away in the bathroom until he had nothing left in his stomach to bring up. He shuffled back into the living room, thanked Albert for a good time but said it was time to leave. His buddy left alongside him. I wanted to tell them they were forgetting the girl but no words would come until they had left the apartment and closed the door behind them.

"Al," I said when they must have been halfway down to the first floor already, "they left *her*."

"Her?" Albert repeated back to me, momentarily oblivious to who it was exactly I was talking about before his eyes landed on her. "Oh," he said, "don't worry about it - she's not involved with them," and he cut two more lines and helped himself to the first.

The girl's features had changed since I had first seen her. She was reminding me of somebody I'd long tried to forget and it was making me feel uncomfortable. The TV was too loud all of a sudden. It was so loud it was impossible to make any sense of what was being said; it was just a constant, all-devouring noise and the girl looked so much like somebody I knew once - looked so lifeless and beyond help - it terrified me.

I repeated a mantra in my head, telling myself over and over that everything was going to be okay.

"I hate it when people watch shit here," Albert said, muting the TV as he headed over to his sound system. "Let's put a little music on... Any requests?"

"You're the man of the house," I said behind a forced smile to present myself as a man without a single fracture or shadow spoiling his soul, "surprise me."

Albert may as well have walked to the sound system in slow motion, it took him so long to get there. I closed my eyes and tried to steady my breathing; it was too deep, too loud - a miracle my friend the dealer hadn't noticed it already. But having my eyes closed only acted to make it worse... I could feel the heat of the fire on my face, could still hear the impact of metal on metal in my ears, feel the resistance of the girl's chest as my palms pressed down on it to try and get her breathing again...

I opened my eyes wide, gasped and pulled a hand down over my face. Albert was pressing down a button on the sound system, the unknown girl was still in a state all of her own on the couch. She didn't look too familiar anymore. Music finally started to play. I didn't recognise the song or the artist. I was back here, now.

12

WE'D STOPPED SNORTING, stopped smoking, stopped talking because we were just that fucked. The music sounded familiar. It could have been playing on a loop, maybe a part of my brain was just registering it a fraction of a second quicker than my own sense of awareness. And it had started to grow cold. Cold and dark. The girl was still with us.

Matt came into the apartment looking so healthy he was absolutely glowing. The take-out food he had in a bag smelled good but made me want to barf. He looked at the two of us and laughed. "Look at you two sorry-ass motherfuckers," he said. "I bet you've both been sitting here all day, doing nothing more than tricking yourselves into thinking you feel good - am I right? That shit wears off! I went running when I got up, worked the weights at the gym. I got so many fucking natural chemicals in me right now from doing all that shit, I feel like fucking God."

Albert swallowed and slowly pointed towards the take-out bag. "You get that from the tofu place? It smells good," he said, "can I have some of that?"

"Get your own!" Matt laughed and then he turned to me and said, "That's the real reason why all the yids are so fucking rich - always getting whatever they can for free!"

The muscle turned and left, off to claim his place on the stoop, and I was so out of it that I temporarily gained superhuman powers. I heard every step he took to get back down onto the first floor - heard him offer a greeting of sorts to somebody making their way up the stairs. No, two guys were coming up, I was sure of it until my powers left me just as unexpectedly as they had came and all I could hear was the sound of my own breathing and the slow traffic out on the street. When nobody else entered the apartment after a while, I figured the whole thing had been an effect of my drug-induced imagination...

Then they came in, like they had waited outside just to make a dramatic arrival.

Three of them, Filipinos but I mistook them for Mexicans to start with. One of them was around seventy and with salt-and-peppered hair. Dressed in what looked to be an expensive suit that almost made the others look like two random guys in the habit of following a stranger around town. They were young and dressed identical, like Bruce Springsteen in the eighties with their blue denim and white t-shirt. One of them was wearing sneakers with high soles in a bid to look taller than he really was.

"Reyes," Albert said, "it time already?"

The old guy didn't take his eyes off of us. The two behind him just sneered, awaiting a response and when the old guy finally gave it, it was in Spanish. The younger two didn't need telling twice; they each took an end of the girl on the couch and lifted her up, heading toward the door like removal men carrying furniture. The old boy finally took a leather wallet from his pocket, but he still kept his eyes on us - freed a generous amount of large bills from a giant wad and tossed them in Albert's direction like confetti before turning to make his way back out. "Nice doing business with you," Albert croaked but the figure, the girl and his flunkies were already gone.

"What was all that about?" I asked.

"Just topping up my allowance while helping a brother out," was all Albert was willing to give away. He took a deep breath, moved closer to the coffee table and started rolling a cigarette. "You don't know how good you got it," he said. Maybe he said it to me, maybe to himself.

13

Pure electricity was running through me when I returned home - I was aware of everything, particularly the fact it would be a long time before sleep would finally come for me. I went online to browse Ezekiel Bircham's latest thoughts and dilemmas and found little more than bad grammar and punctuation; a grasp of the English language that would make a newly arrived Martian blush and what looked to be a new insistence of calling people 'bro'. He had also taken on a new yet already over-used habit of encouraging people to hug their 'GLB brothers and sisters' in a supposed act of solidarity and support when, in reality, he clearly just wanted to make a big deal of how much he liked dick in a bid to shock.

The boy would be impossible to make likeable on the screen. I went to work regardless, rushing through a number of scenes in a drug-induced burst of motivation; writing even though I had an idea it would be bad come the clarity of a new day.

And the birds had started singing come the time I finally started to feel tired. I got into bed as the sun was rising but got up soon after, convinced I would die if I were to sleep so soon - all because of a documentary on drug use I had once watched with Lee (the presenter had said drugs increase the heart rate but when you're going to sleep the heart rate naturally drops so drug use before bed was a pretty bad idea if you wanted to wake up again). Cursing my own paranoia and telling myself yet again how all this abuse could do with a knock on the head, I made my way outside and got comfortable in a sun lounger with a glass of orange juice - just to shoot the breeze until it seemed safe to go back upstairs. Tiffany came to mind as the light on the surface of the pool became too much to look at. I couldn't help but think about how well I was doing without her and how it would probably make no difference if she never returned.

14

IT SOUNDED A lot like an alarm clock. The drone attributes ingrained deep down inside of me took control of my muscles and limbs, had me toss the blanket aside and reposition myself so that I was sitting - waiting for clarity to come in an impending moment... Once I remembered *why* I had set the alarm, I could go about getting ready.

It wasn't an alarm clock, it was the ringing of the telephone.

It rang until the answering machine kicked in but no message was left; the caller waited a second and called back immediately. It looked to be important. I got myself up and answered the telephone before the answering machine took charge for a second time.

"Cole," Pate asked down a crackling and wind-heavy line, "it's Scott. How are you doing?"

"Tired," I answered with honesty.

"Late night? Business or pleasure?"

"All business," I said. "Where are you? The line isn't too good."

"Driving out into Hollywood. Listen," he said, "I'm meeting with somebody involved with the show I've got you working on and I think you should come along and meet them."

I remembered how Pate had told me there was somebody else writing for him, a girl. I wondered just what the chances of her being beautiful and available were. It was enough for me to decide it a good idea to struggle through the comedown just to get a look at her and hope for the best.

"What time and where?"

"I knew you wouldn't let me down! Do you have a pen?"

Somebody told me a long, long time ago that drinking either cranberry juice or pineapple juice will get cocaine out of your system in no time. You'd have thought Tiffany would have provided an endless supply of the juices, what with her distaste at me snorting, but you couldn't be further from the truth. The refrigerator always had a number of bottled juices. Juices you'd never have fucking heard of otherwise but never, *never* cranberry or pineapple. It's like a part of her wanted to keep me under its effects or something... But it didn't matter to me. I hit the cartons of orange juice, downing them even after I could feel my stomach expanding due to the excess liquid that was gathering. There was every chance I'd lose all control of my bowels on the way to or during the little meeting but I was desperate and when you're desperate you're willing to try anything that might help.

15

Being a man who never learns, I opted for eye drops and sunglasses to try and resemble something close to the average human. The sun was bright, the air baking everything it came close to, and the smart but casual clothes weren't enough to stop me from sweating like a stuffed pig. I wondered just how many important deals had been made out here by people feeling like this.

The bar had an outdoor seating area; I saw Pate immediately and felt my expectations disappear on realising his companion - who I could only see the back of - wasn't female. Pate noticed me as I approached, smiled and waved as if there was a chance I was yet to spot him. The guy he was sitting with turned to take a look at me. His skin had been pulled so tight he looked about as smooth as a store mannequin; his hair was most likely the result of an implant... It looked a lot like toothbrush bristles.

"Cole," Pate smiled, coming forward to embrace me, "it's good to see you! This is Nate Leonardi," he said to introduce us, "one of my nearest, dearest and oldest friends."

"Cole," Leonardi said, getting to his feet so he could shake my hand, "glad to have you onboard. Scott has told me a lot of good things about you."

"Not good enough," Pate insisted, patting me on the shoulder while simultaneously placing me in the free seat at their table. "Look at you," he said, "you're so tense! Doesn't he look tense? At least he isn't one of those juice-heads who live their lives at the gym! You were up writing all night, am I right?"

"I got a couple of hours sleep," I said, taking the cigarettes and lighter from my jacket. "Either of you mind if I smoke?"

"Go right ahead," Leonardi said and he delved a hand into his own pocket to unearth his own packet; Winstons or another similar-named brand I'd never heard of. "I always enjoy it more when I've somebody to smoke with."

"Two black-lung bastards if ever I saw them," Pate grinned. "I'm going to get us a couple of drinks, leave the two of you to get to know one another..."

"Bring out a pitcher while you're at it," Leonardi suggested, "it'll mean us going back in there a lot less. My," he said - turning to me once Pate was gone, "is your body in withdrawal hell or what?"

I looked back at him and said, "What do you mean?" despite knowing exactly what he was talking about.

"Come on," he smiled, "you can't kid somebody who has been in the game as long as I have! You have the cocaine blues, am I right?" He didn't give me time to respond. He had his cigarette burning with the quickest glimpse of a flame and spoke as fresh smoke crept through the narrow gaps between his whiter than white teeth. "Scott have you thinking it wouldn't be a good idea to take stuff like that - at least not to let him know you are? Scott used to be one of the worst when it came to coke," he said, "but was always real funny about it... He could never go into a stall and take a line, he was always petrified of a bouncer coming in and tossing him out, so he used to only do it in the alleyways outside or in the back of a car taking him from one place to the next!"

I swallowed and asked, "So you have no issue with people using it?"

"Are you kidding?" he laughed. "It'd blow your mind if you knew just how many deals had been made out here by people high on cocaine. All you have to remember," he advised, "is to go over whatever you put down on paper when you were high... More so than usual."

I took a drag on my cigarette, leaned back in my chair and slowly released it. "I'll keep it in mind," I said.

Leonardi nodded and looked over at a waiter clearing an empty table. "Scott's excited about having you onboard," he said. "Your writing and experiences, combined with the others he's picked, has him convinced he's working on the next big thing."

"And what do *you* think?" I asked.

"I trust Scott," he said. "Always have. Where he sees potential,

I make it my job to see it before it's been fully revealed to me. But anyway," he continued, turning to look at me, "how's Tiffany?"

"You know her?"

"From days gone by. We shared a surgeon for a while."

"Tiffany has fallen off the map," I sighed, "at least where I'm concerned."

"Then don't be concerned," he said.

I nodded, took another pull on my cigarette and decided to ask, "You have a problem with her or is it only Scott?"

"I don't have any issue with her," he said, "only a problem with people *like* her. This business is held together by the real talent, the quiet writers and producers and directors... Even an editor worth his salt is rare to come across. But the cast," he grinned, "the people seen as the stars of the show? They're a dime a dozen and they're screwed once people realise that. They need us, we feed them, and still they look down on us all. I'll let you in on a little secret - you know people like Tiffany... the names demanding the big salary? They make it near impossible for people like you to make it into the business. Money can't be spared on nurturing fresh talent like your own and to me, that's just fucking awful - it really is."

Pate came heading back out, carrying a tray holding three bottles of beer and three tall glasses. A young Mexican waiter was close behind with a pitcher filled with something bright and yellow, flower petals floating within the whirlpool of its bowels. "It's their new cocktail," Pate was all too happy to announce, "the barman said it tastes like a dream but gets you loaded," and he placed the tray down in the centre of the table before reclaiming his seat.

"The barman *would* say that!" Leonardi laughed before turning his attention on the young waiter preparing to place the pitcher down before us. "Poncho," he said, "how have you been?"

"Mr Leonardi," the waiter replied, "things have been going smoothly."

"Cole," Leonardi said, "this is Pedro, a dear friend of ours, but those close to him know him as Poncho."

"Right," I said with a smile, "how's it going?"

"Nice to meet you," he said, shaking my hand. "If you'll excuse me," he asked of the table, "things are picking up inside, so I'd best get back in there."

"Do what needs to be done," Pate told him, slowly filling the empty glasses with the brightly coloured cocktail as he did so. "But what did I miss?" He asked, "What were you two guys talking about?"

"This and that," Leonardi said, leaning back in his chair before adding any more. "I was just telling Cole how difficult it can be to find new writers."

"Finding them is easy," Pate claimed, "it's keeping them that's difficult. Cole," he said to me, "new writers can be seen as a risk if they haven't got so many years chalked up in the business, you know that? So when a studio has to add a couple more zeroes onto the salary of a star, they'll toss out the new writer as a cost-cutting exercise because the older writers are happy working without a raise for the foreseeable."

Leonardi gave me a knowing look, a "*What did I tell you?*" if ever I saw one while bringing a bottle of beer to his lips. "Then there are the cancelled shows," he said.

"Don't even get me started on those!" Pate exclaimed. "Talented writers get a pilot written up, people like us get the pilot made, and then some scrotum in a tie pulls the plug because he'd rather take a safe bet for the ratings by giving some media sweetheart yet another pay rise! We need a revolving door for the supposed acting talent," Pate concluded, "and golden escalators for the writers, that's what this industry needs!"

16

From the stall you could hear the music shaking the dance floor beyond the restroom. Pate had called it a night before sunset but Leonardi had wanted to stay out, saying he hadn't let loose for a good while and business commitments to begin in the next couple of days would prevent him from doing so in a hurry - once they were underway. Leonardi was what I wanted to become out here. The cocaine he had on him would no doubt do exactly what he had claimed it would and that was to wake the dead. He lost a lot in a casino, won a little but had a good time throughout - the staff and other gamblers treating him like a king. The strip club he took us to was one I'd never been to before, the women were all angels and he had paid for the two of us to venture into the VIP room where girls poured expensive champagne across their tits and demanded you lap it up. When we were leaving he had handed his business card to one of the girls - a stunner named Michelle or Rochelle, I can't recall which - and she had slipped the card beneath the buckle on her left cowboy boot and not into a purse fit to burst for the number of cards she had accepted but would never look at again.

The rock club we had stumbled into was, according to Leonardi, owned by a number of Hollywood A-listers who didn't want it known simply because they had no desire to be accused of imitating Johnny Depp. The clientele dressed like they didn't have a dime to their name but the price of drinks proved otherwise.

And I have to say it again - the cocaine Leonardi provided was fucking unbelievable. He had given the usual talk I'd heard out here so many times before I'd long lost count; talk on how coke wasn't as pure as it used to be, how you were paying for chemical cocktails put together to mimic the effect, yadda-yadda-yadda, but *his* stuff was of the variety not sampled by many for years because he *knew* people.

Brother, that first toot made me a believer... The man *knew* people.

So, when he recommended we head to the restroom for another line I practically led the way. Being a gentleman, I let him pick the stall to use and bolt the door. There wasn't even any spilled piss on the floor, no damp toilet roll or a brown submarine breaking the surface. Even the fucking air held traces of jasmine.

He tapped a couple of small clumps of white on the skin beside my thumb and I took it back after providing him with the briefest of thanks in return. My sinuses were clear. My throat long dead already, heavy with a taste not too different from ear wax left baking in the sun. Leonardi took his time getting his own ready - I'd already started to wonder if he had OCD or something because he had to follow routines and keep everything in order. And already wondering if another line was to be made available so soon or if we would be making our way back to the bar, I checked my cell just to have something to do to keep me from noticeably fidgeting.

"Waiting on a call?" he asked, finally moving an open nostril across the back of his hand.

"Just," I lied, "checking to see if Tiffany has tried getting in touch."

Leonardi nodded, leaned back against the nearest partition wall and took a deep breath of air through greeted teeth. "Let me ask you something," he said, "you and Tiffany... The two of you close? And I don't mean in the *biblical* sense," he clarified, "I just want to know if you depend on one another."

I thought about it and nodded. "We depend on each other," I said. "She keeps me in a life I couldn't have had otherwise and I bang her brains out from time to time."

"But you have no loyalty to her? No real sense of owing her or looking out for her best interests? You should tell me now if you have," he said, "because it will all come out eventually."

"I'm not a good person," I admitted, "but maybe I'm finally seeing the signs that I don't deserve to be punished anymore?

Hand on heart," I told him, "my best interests are my interests."

Leonardi smiled, nodded in complete and true understanding. "This isn't just crossroads you're approaching," he said with a grin, "it's the intersection of the fucking cosmos! You can either take the risk and help us carry some of the burden to welcome the new dawn of the writer or you can sit back, have Tiffany keep you on a leash until she tires of you and watch as the only writing gig in the business is freelance and poor-paying.

"Don't disturb the woodlice beneath the rocks you turn on looking for your muse," he spoke, "but stand tall as the icon for every generation of writer that follows."

"Hallelujah," I said because I was digging his script.

"Hallelujah," he repeated back to me before pulling me close so that he could talk in but a whisper. "Tiffany Lily will be the first to fall in a just war," he said, "and at first, no one will see the significance in what has happened - no one will see what is coming. But the *names*," he grinned, "the names will become illegible and the stars will never shine as bright again because *we* are the makers and breakers of this town! Now tell me," he asked, "can I get an *Amen*?"

"Amen," I said and he hugged me, unlocked the door of the stall and walked out into the restroom. There was a guy washing his hands and he looked up into the mirror to take a look at whoever was coming out of the stall and was clearly surprised to see two men coming out together. Leonardi dropped a hand on the man's shoulder and gleefully said, "Best suck-job *ever*," and then he was gone, making his way back out onto the dance floor. I stopped to wash my hands in an available sink, feeling the gaze of the other man on me. He wanted to say something but decided against it, walked on out of there without saying a word.

17

Leonardi had walked out onto the main bar area and dancefloor all of five or so seconds before me but I couldn't see him. The place wasn't particularly spacious or crowded but I couldn't see him amongst the small groups of people claiming an area as their own or the flashing lights and artificial smoke.

Like a lot of places out in California, the regulars wore clothes to make you wonder how they could even afford a drink in a place like this. Jeans made with tears already in them to hint at life experience. All I could see was fraudulent.

It was during my slow walk to try and find Leonardi that I spotted Gemma, the barmaid who had remembered me from the Henbury. She was with three friends, all of them standing out because of their beauty, all of them holding cola mixed with something in a plastic cup. I tried to contain my excitement and headed by them - acting a little more drunk than I really was. Once I was directly in front of them I paused, turned and pointed at Gemma as if I was trying to remember just how it was I knew her exactly while I waited for her to notice. She did. Her and her friends looked right at me. After a second I made out it had just dawned on me *how* I knew her... And she recognised me, smiled and stepped forward to embrace me. Her signature scent was fabric softener and reasonably priced perfume. It was nice.

She said something into my ear but it was impossible to know what exactly because of how close her lips were mixed with the ridiculous volume of the music being played. It didn't matter because the warmth coming from having her body positioned so close to my own made everything else feel irrelevant at that moment in time. She stepped back smiling and said something. I smiled, acting a little embarrassed to the fact I hadn't heard her. She laughed, pulled her friends closer one-by-one and loudly said a name as she pointed at each one in turn. I didn't give a fuck but I smiled regardless, shook each hand made available during the introductions. Once it was over and done with I leaned in close to Gemma and asked, "You want me to buy you a drink?" This time she pulled a face that made it obvious she couldn't hear me. I stepped closer, brushed a little hair behind her ear and asked her for a second time if she would like a drink. She shook her head, stepped close and told me she was in a round with her friends. You do hear the news you don't want to hear, don't you?

"Let me know if you change your mind," I nodded, backing away without caring whether she could hear me or not anymore. "I have to find my friend."

I spent a good thirty to forty minutes searching for Leonardi... I looked in the darkest of corners, slowly moved across the dancefloor, asked bar staff if they had seen who I was describing to them, returned to the restroom, looked outside and came back in - over and over again before finally admitting he was gone. Despite it all I still wasn't comfortable with the idea of leaving; I was scared of receiving a call from an irate Pate the next morning, screaming down the line about my abandoning his friend and insisting our deal was off because of it... Off before it had truly began.

I can't tell you what made me notice him, whether my madness-detector had kicked in or whether it was something else, but I did. I watched the young metal head walk right out onto the dancefloor with a crazy grin on his face; watched people around him laugh yet back away from him as he unfastened his belt. In an instant his pants were around his ankles and he stood there with his cock in his hand, pissing clean all over the floor. You mightn't believe it but the smell of spilled piss claimed the room in an instant. Two bouncers rushed over, took a hold of him and dragged him - still grinning as he struggled to pull his jeans back up - towards the fire exit while screaming at him, probably letting him know how bad a beating he could expect in response to his actions. Despite the pain about to be inflicted on him, he never lost his smile.

18

I ASKED THE guy manning the door to call me a cab and he give me a look and said something about how it wasn't the Ritz so I just started walking, wondering if I'd manage to hail a cab at all or if there would be a bus to catch that would carry me at least some of the way back home. Some of the girls standing on the street corners looked like the Country and Western pop starlets who had successfully made the transition over to pop music and given the opportunity, I would have gladly taken any one of them back home with me. Then you had the others, standing beneath an unforgiving streetlight despite the scabs against their lips or the black eye from a demanding pimp or the man who had turned a trick on a trick.

Los Angeles is the banquet for a man in search of a vice but eventually you have to admit you can't live off one alone.

19

MY HAIR WAS tightly taken hold of, my neck twisted with the flick of my attacker's wrist before my face was forced deep into the pillow and I couldn't breathe.

It was a very expensive pillow... A simple boy like me would never dream of dying so close to the kind.

I tried my best to struggle free but couldn't. The whole thing must have lasted around ten seconds but it felt a lot longer at the time. When I was released, I took a gasp for air, swung a fist around me like a hammer while rolling onto my back but struck nothing. Silverdale was standing just a foot or two from the bed, looking real calm at what was unfolding. I'd never seen the guy beside him before. Big guy, looked like a biker. Leather gloves and a pistol sticking out from his waistline. The sight was enough for me to involuntarily release a small stream of hot piss without the slightest bit of warning - thankfully not enough to seep through the sheet and let either one of them know just how much they had scared me.

"I could have him beat the tar clean out of you," Silverdale said, "right now, and he would do it without the slightest trace of mercy. Man owes me. I could even have him shoot you, right between the eyes."

The biker's hand was already too close to that pistol for my liking and I didn't want him to see how nervous I was feeling so I scratched at an itch that wasn't even there just so I would have an excuse to move. "You'd have done it already if you thought I was worth the jail time," I said, hoping he put the unsteady sound of my voice down to just waking.

"No," Silverdale grinned. "I wouldn't have him shoot you here - it's too nice, too clean... I'd have him shoot you when you least expected it, have you bleeding away in a no-good part of town - a place where a man like you deserves to die. Cops won't ever dream of looking into me," he bragged, "You know what would happen - and this is if you're lucky? You'll be another Hollywood mystery to be brought up in niche books by poor writers focusing on this part of the world every couple of years. Depending on how Tiffany Lily uses your death to further her career," he said, "you might just about be worth a couple of sentences at best."

"Look," I told him, "I'm thankful for the little wake-up call because I have a lot of work to be getting on with, but can we get this over and done with? What's all this about?" I asked despite having an idea. I asked simply to try and get him to walk out of here without first deciding to have the shit kicked out of me before breakfast.

"The investigator you went and hired blew a case on me by standing out like a sore fucking thumb!" he snarled. "You think you're the only job I'm working right now? Well," he said to answer his own question, "you will be if Bill Dexter shows up again and I can't afford one fucking job! I threatened the little son of a bitch but he looks desperate enough for the money you're paying to keep turning up and believe me," he warned, "it won't turn out good for any of us - especially your little friend!"

"You think Bill Dexter means anything to me?" I laughed even though I knew angering a man with a psychotic piece of muscle awaiting orders isn't the best move to make. "I went to him hoping - no, *praying* to the fucking gods above - that he would be half as incompetent as you've already made him out to be. You want to beat on him, beat on him. I'll be there with him when he presses charges and I'll pay for his lawyer when he hurls your ass in front of a judge and I'll be outside the D.A.'s office with him when they put your licence through a shredder."

The biker offered Silverdale the briefest of glances, real blink and you'll miss it. The gumshoe stood inanimate for a while and I didn't allow myself to breathe until he had nodded to the man at his side and broke into a smile. "How could it be," he pondered, "that there's more to a two-bit piece of guy-candy like you than meets the eye?"

"I'm a hustler," I told him with a shrug, "you do what you do and learn a lot along the way."

"I can get that," Silverdale nodded. He hinted at some kind of respect, some kind of appreciation, but it was probably nothing more than an attempt to work my own ego against me. "There is something you have to understand," he said, "this is my world, this is my work, and you're judged by how good you did on your last case... You can understand that, surely?"

"Sure," I nodded, "I can dig that."

"If you want me to stop looking for Lee," he said, "you have to get into your old lady's ear and have her call me off - it's that simple. Truth is," he smiled, "it's up to him if he wants to turn his back on all of this luxury and not be found, I can't say I give a true shit either way."

I pointed to the jeans I'd slipped out of during the early hours of the morning and left in a crumpled pile on the floor. "You mind if I get a smoke?"

"Go for it," he said.

I took my time taking the pack from the pocket and took twice as long lighting the first cigarette of the day. "You want me to have Bill Dexter leave you alone, all you got to do is leave *me* alone. We're just two guys trying to make a living out in sunny California, am I right?"

"That all?" he asked. "You don't want me to go drop the search for Lee altogether?"

"Lee can take care of his own problems," I said, "he's caused me enough trouble with you already. You back away from me and you stay clear of the people I talk to and as far as I'm concerned, we have an understanding. But if I think for one minute I'm being followed by someone on your orders," I warned him, "I won't just send Bill Dexter straight up your ass but any and every friend he has made in the business."

Silverdale laughed. "That's twice I've seriously misjudged you," he said.

"And you really don't want to do it a third time," I told him, overcome with confidence. Even the biker looked confused at how things were running. "Do we have a deal here or what?"

"Sure," he said, "we have a deal," and he turned and made his way out of the bedroom without stopping to look back. He waited until he was halfway down the stairs before he called the biker to follow.

PART 3

NIGHTCRAWLER

1

WHEN I ANSWERED the call to Pate I prepared myself to have my ass torn clean off of me. I had been panicking for a good twenty-four hours because he hadn't been answering my calls and now, early in the morning and out of the fucking blue, he was calling me. Now, he was probably ready to let loose at me; to accuse me of running out on his friend during a night on the town.

"Cole," he said, his voice filled with light and free of care, "are you presentable?"

I wondered if it was a trick, if he was just luring me into a false sense of security. I took the bait anyway and resigned myself to taking the worst - glanced down at myself in just a pair of underpants and Tiffany's bathrobe. "I could be in twenty minutes," I told him.

"Make it ten," he said, "there's somebody I want you to talk with," and then he ended the call. I took the quickest of showers, put on the nearest clothes I could reach without taking much of an interest in them and headed out onto the street. He wasn't parked outside so I sprinted toward the gates at the end of the road and saw a limousine parked just beyond them. Two guys were doubling as security. I vaguely recognised one of them. He looked at me and said, "We invited him in but he said he would be fine right here."

"Don't worry about it," I said as the gates electronically opened wide. I squeezed between them as soon as I could, opened the back passenger door and saw Pate sitting there with an open book on his lap. I saw it was cheap-looking science fiction when he closed the cover over and looked at me. "Cole," he smiled, "it's good to see you again. Jump in and we can be going."

"Thank you," I said, closing the door behind me while claiming a little room for myself. The driver was the same as last time - an unhealthily good-looking specimen. He started the car without waiting to be asked, reversed onto the main road at the back of us without delay.

"So, how have you been?"

"A little worried," I admitted. "You heard from Nate Leonardi at all?"

"Nate?" Pate laughed, "Of course I have! He feels awful about leaving you without a word the other night - said he took a little too much to drink and stumbled out of some club without even checking you were following."

"That's good," I laughed, "I had no idea where he had gotten to."

"My fault," Pate smiled, "I should have told you about his bad habits when you agreed to hit the town with him. But have I missed anything else?" he asked. "Any calls from Tiffany?"

"Not yet," I said.

"Fuck her," he said, "she was probably laughing like an old witch every time you tried calling her."

"I can imagine that," I sighed. "But who is it you want me to meet?"

"Anthony," he said like that was enough. "Very blue and very crass," he added, "but a very old friend of mine and he knows the right people so he will be very useful to you. After all," he grinned, "he is Ezekiel Bircham's uncle."

"I thought nobody could know the kid we're writing about is based on him?" I asked, a little confused.

"They can't," Pate told me, "that's why you're going to be extra careful while we're all talking."

"Fuck," I said, "I don't know if you should trust me on this one..."

"Please," Pate smiled, "he's easily one of my best friends in this business but he's still a moron! You could dance around him all night with that brain of yours."

2

It was yet another exclusive restaurant with bar area, this one hidden way up high in a tall building; every wall a window to give the diner a panoramic view of Los Angeles regardless of where they happened to be sitting and - if you wanted to get closer to one of the windows - the insignificant people far below. Pate was immediately recognised and we were led to a table to sit four people. "A pleasure to see you as always, Mr Pate," the employee announced, easing a chair out from beneath the table for him to sit whereas I was left to see to my own, "Mr Leonardi is already here but your guest is still to arrive."

"Thank you," Pate said on sitting down, "what can you recommend?"

"The steak is twenty-one days matured-"

"Please," Pate grinned, "I'm thirsty in this heat - it's choking me - I need to know what you'd suggest to drink."

"Forgive me," the waiter smiled, "but the Mojito is especially pleasant today; we have a new mixologist on duty and his cocktails are the best in town."

"Then bring me a pitcher," Pate said, "with four chilled glasses."

"Right away," the waiter said with a bow before leaving and he was replaced by Nate Leonardi almost immediately after, the latter appearing more than a little flustered. "Scott," he said, shaking his friend's hand, "good to see you. Cole," he nodded to me, lowering himself down into the opposite chair, "I know I had a good time with you because I remember next to nothing about it."

"Cole was worried he would be in trouble for losing you," Pate smiled softly, "I had to put his mind at ease. But how about you?" he asked. "You look a little troubled."

"It's that same old son of a bitch as always," he said, "the stupid old Jew is going to put me in an early grave... Man's only making threats of sending Boston's finest knuckle-dragger in my direction!"

"Rather him than the psycho from Texas," Pate reasoned with a relaxed shrug.

"That's true," Leonardi said in agreement, "at least you can try and reason with him."

I wanted to ask who exactly these people were and what was happening but knew I shouldn't. The reason for this meeting was to get a little extra information on Ezekiel Bircham and not those I was already with. Fortunately for me, Pate's old associate and cocaine fiend moved us on to other topics before the idea of opening my mouth became too difficult to ignore. "Will you look at us?" he smiled at me. "Two old farts living a lifestyle because we're too old, too accustomed to it, to come close to changing it - and here you are - one of the new bloods of the new day, and you're forced to endure us."

"Please," I blushed, "I'm just thankful for being here."

"Well how about we find real reason to be thankful," he grinned - speaking in a hushed tone on leaning closer, "by getting a couple of girls to celebrate once we're done here?"

"That's one of his answers to almost anything!" Pate laughed. "Come on," he said, "don't go getting the boy into too many bad habits or he'll lose the motivation to write."

"Like Tiffany Lily hasn't had him do worse," Leonardi shrugged. "I like to think we got to young Cole here just in time, before he had his talent and his soul ripped away from him, and we're going to lead him to better days."

3

Anthony Bircham looked like a spoiled fat man going out on safari once he finally had his fill of the buffet spread. He wore beige khaki trousers with sand-coloured loafers and a cream shirt with the sleeves rolled up to show the gold chains and expensive watch. He didn't say a thing on first arriving; he nodded, sat down alongside us and dabbed at his mouth with a napkin he had taken from the table. "Hope I didn't keep you waiting too long," he said, finally speaking, "I have had a day and then some."

He finally appeared to notice me, leaned over across the table and shook my hand. His grip was stronger than it had any need to be. The sensation of his skin wasn't too different than that of a chicken fresh out of the refrigerator. "I don't think we've met," he said. "I'm Anthony and I've had the great misfortune of knowing these two guys for a very long time."

"Cole," I answered with a smile, "I guess I'm the new arrival to the circle."

"Cole," he said back to Pate, "that old witch's prisoner?" and the question he asked stole the wind from my sails because it left me doubting there was a single person working out in Hollywood that hadn't heard of me and my arrangement with Tiffany Lily.

"Now," Pate quickly said - looking more than a little embarrassed, "I'm confident that my good friend Cole here could answer any question you had for him - if only we didn't have better, more polite things to discuss at the table."

"You're right," Bircham said and he looked to me and added, "he's right... In all the years I've been lucky enough to count Scott Pate as a friend, I can't remember a time he has ever been wrong. I apologise if I was a little off right now, it's just today has been hectic. I'd appreciate it if you could just rewind the film back a minute or so and record over it... Give us the opportunity to start afresh?"

"Cole doesn't have a problem with that," Leonardi responded for me and with a bright smile, "he's one of us, aren't you?"

"Speak freely and openly in front of him," Pate included, "because I can vouch he really is one of the pack."

Bircham smiled at me. "One of us?" he said, raising his eyebrows as if in appreciation. "You talked old Lily into putting the money forward for a project of yours?"

"Why would people like us line her purse any more than we need to and for a moment longer?" Pate said, "Cole here has found a place under my wing... His writing is phenomenal... Phenomenal! I'm guiding this man to the stars and he's going to guide me even farther."

"I'm impressed," Bircham said, "very impressed... It's not often I hear young talent being spoken of so highly when they haven't the resume to back it up. So, tell me," he asked, "what's the idea you're pitching?"

"It's in the early stages," I answered a little nervously, "and anything and everything could change depending on how the wind blows, but it's focusing on characters around college age and a little younger because I think we could pull a large audience in once we offer them a show worth looking away from their social media accounts and games consoles for."

"I don't know," Bircham shrugged, "many have tried and failed when it comes to that age group."

"They haven't tried my idea yet," I shitted him, "I'm talking a brutal representation here - no barring or cuts. I'm talking drink and drugs and promiscuous sex."

"HBO could be your only hope," Bircham said, "what's going to have them feel they can't risk losing a shot at this production?"

"Don't underestimate the content of my scripts," I told him, "I'm talking boys fucking dudes that want to be girls; I'm talking more dangerous drugs and alcohol out of the downtown shit-holes than you can imagine - people from every walk of life doing their thing. I tell you - record numbers of viewers will be tuning in just so they can complain to congress about it after each episode. And to top it all off," I said just to convince him it was about a lot more than people like his nephew in particular, "I'm talking about a healthy addition of really creepy science fiction and fantasy being revealed piece by piece. The bigger picture is going to blow every fucker clean out of the water."

The fat man stared at me for a couple of seconds before turning to Pate with a smile. "Okay," he said, "I'm sold - what do I have to fuck to see my name attached to this?"

"I hate to have to tell you this but we're not looking for any more names to come aboard at this moment in time," Pate said, "I'm just making sure Cole gets to know the right people so he won't be taken over to the dark side whenever I happen to be out of town."

"Ha!" Bircham said, "You dangled that carrot right in front of my face and then you went and hit me with it! Well," he shrugged, "maybe circumstances somewhere down the line will change your mind for you but until that day comes, let's eat and let's talk about the things men like us talk about best."

4

BIRCHAM DROVE A Hummer; a chariot large enough to sit a god and hungry enough to drain Iraq dry. It was a symbol favoured by many men of wealth out in Los Angeles.

He even told me about the security features he'd added - door handles that could electrocute anybody foolish enough to try and force their way inside were the latest trend; bullet proof glass and a tracking device that could also be used to make direct contact with a private security firm. Despite all of these things, I didn't feel heading into one of the roughest parts of town was a good idea, but we did it anyway.

A Latino crew stood beneath a streetlight on one corner, gathered around a burning trash can. They only lifted their heads ever so slightly to watch us passing by, like they were scared they would miss some great reveal in the light of the fire if they looked away from it for too long. Less than a block away we saw a group of skinheads sitting on a stoop. They jumped up to their feet on seeing us, hurled bottles of beer alongside obscenities and gave us the finger - one walking out into the road, beating his chest in challenge as we left him behind. I wondered which gang would be the first to get on the phone to some boys they knew, let them know about the flash car heading their way.

And then the road became worse. It became so bad even the suspension of the tank we were sitting in struggled to give us a smooth journey. The eyes of a dozen bums inhabiting the darkness covering the wasteland behind an iron link fence penetrated the hardened glass and infected my pores.

When Bircham pulled the car to a stop outside a twenty-four hour mini market on Old Thomas Drive, I felt he was asking for trouble. He was already out of the car - slamming the driver's door shut - when I turned to Pate and asked, "What're we stopping here for?"

"We're going in."

"What the fuck for?" I asked, "Nachos?"

My response was Leonardi's cue to laugh. "We own the place," he said, "well, the apartment upstairs."

Pate got out next. I followed suit - looked to the second floor of the building, to the glass windows with only darkness behind them - and just couldn't believe it. "Why would you want an apartment out here?" I asked.

"*Real* people reside in places like this," Leonardi said, putting an arm over my shoulders so he could pull me close. "The moment a creator is somewhere too comfortable, too quiet and only for him, is the moment a creator is working too hard on his dialogue to try and make it memorable."

Pate took a bunch of keys from his coat pocket as we headed around the side of the building; a red door that didn't appear even slightly out of place.

"What about the car?" I said, "We really leaving it out here?"

"Well it isn't going to fit through the fucking door! Don't worry," Leonardi told me, "we know what we're doing - we do it the world over. No one will touch that car, and do you know why? We provide the dealers with a hell of a lot of business in this area; if it isn't us it's the A-lister we've loaned the apartment to so he can get high and screw a couple of whores.

"People know who we are in neighbourhoods like this one," he assured me, "and if they fuck with us, they're fucking with the people we're keeping in nice clothes or they're fucking with the private security boys over at the studios who are always looking for an easy bit of cash-in-hand work."

The other side of the door was reinforced steel. A locked gate stood in front of the door at the top of the stairs. Leonardi must have known the reveal had me doubt everything he had told me outside because he turned to me and said, "Every couple of years, the cops and the feds start targeting people in our line of work. My lawyer's job is to let me know the second some bastard starts discussing warrants and I'll have one of my people rush over, secure the place and get rid of anything that could see me facing charges. Last thing a man in my profession needs is a lawyer's bill for possession."

Pate unlocked the gate, pulled it open and unlocked the door behind it. The whole thing was mind-blowing to me, a whole group of explorers and the secret discovery kind of vibe. "Open Sesame," I muttered to myself as he pushed the door of the apartment open. Somewhere within an extractor fan kicked into life.

5

THE HALLWAY WAS larger than most bedrooms. There was a closed door to the left and an open archway partly revealing a dining area straight ahead. A large painting of Marlon Brando as Don Corleone was on one wall, a blown-up poster advertising a Chinese or Japanese children's show was on the other - filled with indecipherable autographs. "Bedrooms and study and work areas are through there," Pate said for my benefit as he pointed to the closed door, "we go straight on when it comes to putting the world to rights."

He led us through the archway and revealed the beyond without the appreciation it deserved. A spacious and modern kitchen area joining onto the dining area had been kept out of sight from where we had entered; the dining area joined onto a living area with couches the size of decent beds. All high-tech appliances and no dust, the walls spotless and white and holding more framed items of interest.

A black and white photograph of Al Pacino and Francis Ford Coppola sharing a joke on the set of The Godfather II, signed by both men.

A promotional poster for Easy Rider, signed by Dennis Hopper.

A large picture of a young Warren Beatty (I think...) and a pretty blonde, the two dressed like it was the 1920s/30s, both directly facing the camera - Beatty pointing a gun at it, to be precise - signed. The title was in some foreign mark or other but I didn't want to show my ignorance by asking what the movie was.

"I know," Leonardi said into my ear, pulling me back into the room - having me realise how Pate and Bircham were already raiding the refrigerator and I hadn't even noticed them making their way over there, "it can be a little too much to take first time, am I right? But this and everything like it is so easy to achieve if you do your work and you work with the right people - don't let any snot-nosed cunt tell you any different, you hear?"

"This," I muttered, "this seems so out of place..."

"Because of what's outside?" Leonardi grinned with pride. "This is L.A. and we're the magicians," he said, "we bring far off lands from other realms to wherever we want them to be. The difference between us and some bum struggling to keep a roof over his head is we know the world is just another set! Look at the quality of the walls - I bet you can't tell where we left them how we found them, to where we had new ones built! Sit down," he said as he gently shoved me toward the nearest couch, "I'll put some music on."

The sound system was the only thing that didn't belong here, the one thing to show just how these men were of their age and not really of the modern times; it was a CD player. It looked expensive and there was no doubt in my mind the tiny speakers hidden away were high quality but for me it showed these men could not have been all they were cracked up to be and it made me confident I could outsmart them if ever needed.

"What music do you like?" Leonardi asked, his finger already hovering over *play* so I knew my answer wouldn't have been too important to him anyway. "Somebody was trying to get me interested in a drama set during the Vietnam War and they gave me this to listen to. I like it," he said as Creedence Clearwater Revival burst into life. "Every track just makes me want to dance."

The sound of the rotating steel blades within a powerful blender came unexpectedly and from behind. I looked back to see Pate and Bircham laughing like the best of friends in the kitchen, a collection of alcoholic drinks and fresh fruit claiming most of the nearby worktop.

"You want a smoke?" Leonardi asked. I looked back to him, saw he already had a cigarette hanging from his mouth and was holding an open pack out for me to notice.

"Is it allowed in here?"

"Is it allowed," he laughed. "You want to stay young, you want to stay in the game," he advised, "you need to push the boundaries instead of waiting for it to become the norm," and with that he tossed a cigarette and a matchbook claimed from a strip-joint I'd never visited onto my lap.

"We have the refreshments if you have the thirst!" Bircham called, walking a step ahead of Pate as the two finally joined us. Pate was carrying a tray holding four tall glasses - the contents of each glass didn't look a million miles away from the slush that collects around a car tyre following a long drive in the snow. "To the talent of tomorrow," he said with a laugh and he took two glasses, dropped into the space beside me and handed me a drink I reluctantly accepted. I thought he was going to try speaking with me - going to try poaching my talent - but he turned his attention back around to Pate soon enough.

Leonardi took a mouthful of his drink, winced ever-so-slightly, and continued directing his full attention to me for the moment. "I was too young to serve," he said, "and soundtracks like this always make me kind of sad about it. You imagine it?" he asked before pausing to take a long drag on his cigarette. "Whole experience could have been like a cool movie! I'd have made a better film about it all than Oliver Stone did, I can tell you! JFK was good," he said, "I've got to give him that - but every man on the planet has to have at least one good idea."

Pate looked to me from the opposite seat and threw me a bemused look before turning his attention to Leonardi. "What about Roland Emmerich? You can't tell me he's had a good idea."

"Sure he has," Leonardi answered him, "his idea was to make a lot of money."

6

OFF IN THE distance, the skies above were holding traces of pink as the light of early morning began to increase and so spread. The silence had long been broken; the sound of car engines somewhere nearby carried along by the breeze of a new day. Occasionally, the sirens of patrol cars or paramedics were also audible.

Pate had already retreated to one of the bedrooms and I had been relieved because it meant no more of his drinks that tasted of little other than bitter lemons and gasoline. Bircham had fallen asleep beside me, his head on my shoulder. Leonardi and I were the last men going but we were both too fucked to move, it was just too much of an effort regardless of how much of his coke we had done. The air was nothing but the stench of stale cigarette smoke.

And the music was still playing in the background. Occasionally I would hear it, picture myself sitting there as people watched me on the big screen.

Leonardi rubbed at bloodshot eyes and looked at me like he had only just realised we were sharing a room - still going strong. "What's your writing method like?" he asked.

"My writing method?" I said back to him. It's a bad habit of mine - repeating something back to the person that had said it - and it only intensifies when I'm tired or super fucked.

"What is it?" he wanted to know, lighting a cigarette I wouldn't have believed he wanted going by the look on his face as he did it. He weakly tossed a second cigarette in my direction - said, "You have set times to write or a word count or what? I'd honestly like to know. My own motto used to be: *When it's light, you write.*"

I nodded, took a deep breath and lit the cigarette he had given me before answering. I didn't want him to know how often I struggled to write; didn't want to lie and have him expecting me to knock a page out of the park within minutes. "The bones of an idea can come at the strangest of times," I told him, "like when I'm in the shower or taking a shit or even doing a little gardening... That trace of an idea will just pop into my head and I'll keep thinking about it during the day. But I write at night," I claimed, "because there's nobody around to disturb me, I've no errands to run, and the temperature nearly always seems to be just right."

"Another nightcrawler," he said in understanding and I was so fucked off my face at that moment in time I didn't understand what he had meant - in fact I wondered what the fuck the blue guy from the Uncanny X-Men had to do with what we were discussing.

"A lot of writers I've met work best at night," he continued. "It's a habit made from working nine to five for so long. They're used to planning some of their writing during the workday in a dead-end job and getting to work writing it down once they've got home and taken a shower and had a bite to eat.

"Those writers that made it pretty successful," he went on with a smile, "first thing they did on quitting the day job was buy a humongous writing desk and swear they would now write nine to five, five days a week, without fail because it was now they're *real* job. It's as good as impossible to find one that managed to do it. I don't know," he shrugged, "the idea of quitting for the day once they had put a thousand words down was too ingrained in their routine. If I was you," he advised me, "I'd stick to what works and never try to change it."

Bircham's legs began to twitch. We both looked at them in complete silence, both of us suspecting he was having a dream that saw him rushing someplace or another but we didn't say it - we just watched his legs like they were the most fascinating thing in the world. When Leonardi decided to bring the silence we shared to an end he did so by asking me, "What do you think of Los Angeles?"

"I think it's a fucking dump if I tell you the truth," I told him. "Even the clean parts are dirty."

"Yeah," he sighed, "I'd have to agree with you. Don't get me wrong," he said, "I love the place with all my heart but the Los Angeles they show you on the screen just doesn't exist. If they started giving a realistic portrayal of how it is, nobody would recognise the place.

"I remember when I was young," he laughed, "watching all these Westerns filmed out in Spain and places like that... Well," he said, "I always figured they were filmed in Texas, because that's where you think of when you think of cowboys - you know? I still remember the first time I went out to Texas. Man," he grinned, "trees and grass and just so... *suburban*. Blew my mind," he said. "I couldn't figure out for the life of me how they had made it all look so different in the movies."

I nodded, remembered the cigarette I was holding and took a long drag on it. "I used to dream about people telling me that my life would change once I reached Texas."

"That where you're hoping to end up," he asked, "Texas?"

"No," I said. "I haven't got one reason to go near there. Plus," I laughed, "somebody once told me that if you live in Texas, you can shoot a man for approaching your front door. That moment he sets foot on your yard, you can take his life away from him."

"And that," Leonardi observed, "is how the West was won. And by god," he said to himself, "I sure wish somebody would want to make a decent Western again..."

"I could give you a Western," I said easily, "I could get the whole fucking genre really out there."

"Yeah?" Leonardi asked me, "Who'd you have in the lead?"

"I don't know," I said, "maybe someone who nobody would recognise... Man's the sole survivor of his town, because it's been ravaged by disease, and he goes looking for his brother. His brother," I told him, "he's the A-list actor, has one short flashback scene right at the start of the movie... You see him explaining how he's going looking for another town, a place with medical supplies or something? But the true protagonist goes looking for him after burying their mother, because now he has no reason to stay behind. He gets to a town way off on the horizon," I finished, "place is corrupt as they come and he finds out the bastards tortured and killed his brother a few nights earlier... Nailed his brother to a cross and set it on fire, even."

Leonardi took a deep draw on his cigarette and slowly released the smoke. "That," he said, "is the best idea I have heard in a very long time," and he moved a finger like he was poking each and every word he spoke out of the air the second he said it. "We have to find the time to make this happen."

Bircham jumped onto his feet and gasped for breath like somebody had just shoved a cattle prod way up of his ass. "I don't know where it is," he said, "but I have to go to a meeting so for the love of god, find it already!"

And with that he made his exit.

7

PATE WAS SITTING opposite me when I woke up, wearing a cotton bathrobe he'd taken little attempt to close properly so I saw his chest of sagging skin with its rug of dull black hair and the purple cotton briefs he was close to spilling out of. In his defence he looked as fucked as I was feeling. The half drank glass of juice in his hand was clearly doing little to help him recover.

"Good morning," he said to me in broken tones. "How are we feeling today?" he smiled.

Leonardi wasn't there. I wondered where he was. For a moment I even wondered where Bircham was but then I remembered him leaving some time earlier. Hours? Minutes?

"Like crap," I told him. "Where's Nate?"

"I heard him stumbling into one of the bedrooms a couple of hours ago. I did try getting back to sleep," he smiled weakly, "but the head is too sore and I don't like taking aspirin for a hangover, so here I am. Did you enjoy yourself last night?"

"Yeah," I nodded. "But I don't think I got much to use on Bircham's nephew."

"But he knows you now," Pate smiled, "he'll open up around you a lot easier because of it. You mention the script he thinks you're working on and he'll drop a little information on Ezekiel. He won't find any of it to be particularly relevant but for a man of your talent, it will be."

"Here's hoping," I said.

"No," Pate said, raising his glass in a toast, "here's *knowing.*"

I smiled weakly and tried rubbing the throbbing sensation from the back of my eyes but it was no use. Sleep felt to me like the best option, but it wasn't going to be made available; Pate was awake, having grabbed an early night, and he was wanting somebody to talk to.

"Where do you see yourself when all of this works out?" he

asked. "Are you wanting your own place up on the hills? You moving to London and rubbing shoulders with the so-called auteurs?"

"Berlin, most likely," I sighed. "Go the places David Bowie went to and hang out with Anton Newcombe."

"I had a friend who lived there," Pate said, "and I stayed with him a couple of months during my travels around Europe. This was a good fifteen or so years gone but I can't imagine the place has changed all too much."

"How'd you find it?"

"Berlin itself is a wonderful place," he said, "it's just I had the misfortune of being there during the soccer season and the place was overrun with Spaniards. You ever encountered a Spanish citizen? They're ruder than you could imagine - pushing into queues, pushing you out of their way on the street, you name it and they'll do it. And so racist," he added, "you should have heard them whenever a black guy took the ball! Can you imagine that," he asked me, "having such a problem with somebody because of the colour of their skin?

"You try talking with them about their behaviour and they pretend they can't speak English until you give up and walk away. The irony is," he finished, "is they behave like gentlemen on their own soil."

"Do you travel a lot?"

"I have money," he smiled, "I've made it my mission in life to see every corner of the world at least once."

"Any place you recommend?"

"You probably assume Amsterdam has everything for a man of your age and interests," Pate answered, "but Prague is much better if you ask me. The beer is strong and cheap and the women look like supermodels - even the ones selling themselves on street corners. When you get a little older and a little wiser," he said, "there is always Vienna."

I yawned, nodded slowly and scratched at a developing itch on my elbow. "I think I'm going to have to make tracks in a minute," I told him, "get some decent sleep in a bed I recognise."

"Hold on a couple of hours and I'll let you share a limo with me."

"Thanks," I said, "but I'll catch a train and a couple of buses before jumping a cab."

"Quite a mission," Pate said with a smile, "it won't be easy and it certainly won't be fast."

"I need to sweat," I said. "I need to feel like hell and then getting into bed will make it all worthwhile. It'll help me with my writing when I get out of bed in the early hours."

"All great men should know what it means to suffer for their art," Pate said and he toasted me for a second time.

8

I MADE IT back to the house in time to see two removal vans parked outside; skinny guys in white overalls were coming from the house carrying open boxes and guys carrying sealed boxes were heading into the house. It was something I wasn't prepared to see and my mind jumped to all of the worst possible conclusions because of it. Was Tiffany throwing me out or was this a debt being collected?

I ran as best as I could given the circumstances, almost knocking one guy to the ground, running inside. Nothing looked to have been taken away. The guys in the overalls were all heading upstairs or coming down them. Chambers was standing close to the kitchen door, seemingly overlooking it all, biting down on a thumbnail as a burning cigarette went to waste between his fingers.

"The hell is going on?" I asked him.

"You," he said - clicking his fingers at me like I was a trained dog, "this way."

He led me out back. Tiffany was sat in a wheelchair with her back to the pool. I knew it was Tiffany despite the fact her face was hidden away behind tight white bandages, her eyes hidden from view by expensive sunglasses. She was in a white robe, hooked up to an I.V. on a stand with a young doctor stood at either side of her.

"Tiffany," Chambers said, "I found him."

He gave me a look of pity. The two doctors gave me a look of both mild curiosity and pity between them.

"Won't somebody here tell me what the hell is happening already?"

"I'm Dr Remond," one said and the other said, "and I'm Dr Flitch," immediately after him. It was a choreographed routine practiced and timed to perfection.

"And you are Cole, yes?" Flitch said. I was expecting Remond to open his mouth again but he allowed his partner to continue for them both. "It is our sworn duty not to offer just peace of body but also peace of mind," he claimed, and his statement provided the briefest trace of a smile. "Miss Lily is our latest patient and so we shall be residing here during her recovery."

"Right," I said, lighting a cigarette. "I bet you're getting paid well during her recovery, am I right? It's no skin off my nose," I sighed, "it's good to finally know where you have been and why you haven't been returning my calls but I'm busy so if you'll excuse me-"

"If you can delay your departure for but one moment," Remond intervened, "it would do Miss Lily's recovery a great deal of good. All scars must be given the care they need to heal," he said.

"Fine," I said to Tiffany, "what is it?"

She didn't answer me right away; she lifted her chin a couple of millimetres, softly tilted her head to one side and just looked at me for a second. It was all drama for the scene and without her expressionless face on show, it almost worked.

"You son of a bitch," she said, sounding like somebody was pinching her cheeks far too tight, "you give a hint of happiness and then you take it all away. You're the most self-centred individual I have ever met and believe me - I have met a lot in my line of work. You manipulate and you abuse and yet you still portray yourself as the wronged soul."

"I'm happy to have been of service," I said quickly, "now that this session is-"

"I'm not done with you," she said, "not yet," and she took tight hold of the arms of the wheelchair and trembled, pulling herself up with both doctors offering minimal assistance, Chambers ready to pounce for fear of her dropping to the ground and breaking into hundreds of pieces.

"Come on, Tiffany, what more could you have to say? You want to strip away the subtlety and call me a bastard? Then do it already!" I shouted and I brought a fist to my chest in a show of power.

Tiffany took a deep breath - released it and said, "Look at

what you made me do... Just know that *you* will never get this again," and she lifted her hospital-issue dress to show large and tight panties combined with surgical dressing; what looked to be a plastic tube some two inches long sticking out from a hole in the crotch.

"The fuck," I muttered in both horror and confusion, "what the fuck is that? The fuck have you done?"

"Vaginal remodelling," Remond answered for her.

"A complicated procedure," Flitch claimed, "but one proven to improve mental recovery following physical trauma."

"And expensive," I said, "I'd bet anything you wanted it's expensive."

"You've nothing to bet with," Tiffany was only all too happy and willing to remind me, lowering her dress before she lowered herself back into the chair. "Everything here - you included - belongs to me," she said, "and I'm only keeping you here now so you can see my transformation and feel yourself slipping away into obscurity while I continue to ascend *and* transcend."

"Ascend and transcend," I nodded, "let me guess - the brochure these two bozos gave you is filled with slogans like that, am I right? Well, boys," I said, "congratulations on a job well done but now, if you are all ready to excuse me-"

"GO," Tiffany screeched as well as her overly-tightened lips would allow her to scream, "go run on to your drug dealers and your junkie friends and your pusher whores! Go crawl into the gutters where you know you belong!"

"Enjoy the rest of your life, Tiffany."

"Mr Cole," Remond called after me, "I look forward to speaking with you during our sessions."

"I won't be back here," I told him.

I made my way back after two days with a blocked nose and a pounding headache.

9

WE MET IN Knewman's at short notice. I was a train-wreck and I knew it; didn't even try hiding it because I thought it could go well with a tortured artist routine that I could develop. But that wasn't the only reason for me to arrive with bags under my eyes, dishevelled and dressed like a bum... I was hoping Pate would take one good look at me and make promises of all kinds of assistance in my time of need.

Instead he provided me with a dry laugh as he leaned in close across the table and asked in a hushed whisper, "You drove her to have work done on her pussy?"

"No," I told him defensively, "I'm not having this one on me... This is all on the doctors she went out to see during her little disappearing act."

"Let me guess," he grinned, "one of the doctors is named Troy? I can't remember the partner's name - sounds Irish - but he'll fuck anything in a skirt that goes into their surgery. Those two are the go-to-guys of the minute, from what I hear."

"No," I said, "those aren't the names. It's Remond and Flitch. The sons of bitches are with us now - they apparently provide various counselling and life coaching sessions alongside the recovery process. It must be costing a fucking fortune," I sighed, "because they're living with us and we constantly have people in white jackets turning up to supposedly check on her. I walked in on them draining excess fluid from her cunt this morning."

Pate laughed again, covered his hand with his mouth and sent away the approaching waiter with a soft hand movement that even a cat would have barely noticed.

"How," he looked to take great delight in asking, "are you even coping?"

"I'm up all night," I told him with a shrug, "and I claim the bed once she's up so we're not having to really see each other - although I did get to see her without the bandages a little earlier.

146

She isn't too badly bruised but the cheeks are sure swollen and the eyes have been pulled a little too tight."

"This is wonderful," Pate laughed, "this is truly all that we could have hoped for! You do know she is scheduled for shooting in the next three days? Her appearance could mean filming has to be delayed and, if it comes down to it, scripts having to be rewritten. Even Tiffany Lily's popularity isn't enough to spare her the wrath of the studio if that happens."

"Like I told you - I've no idea what she has coming up in the foreseeable."

Pate smiled, traced a small circle across the tablecloth using his pinkie and looked up at me from under his eyebrows. "One day you'll look back on this time of your life and struggle to understand how you ever managed."

"I'm not managing," I desperately said, "Tiffany has put a limit on the cards; after all the years I've been at her side, putting up with all the shit like some dumb little pet or employee of hers, she's placing the pressure down on my back like loyalty means nothing to her. She's out to make me suffer," I told him, "she's cutting me out of the picture piece by piece."

He made another subtle motion of the wrist and the very same waiter he had previously held back came rushing over to the table. "Just focus on your writing and keep gritting your teeth - that's the only advice I can give you."

"But can you help me out while I'm writing?" I asked him, "Can't you and Nate agree on some kind of salary or even a loan between the two of you while I'm working for you?"

"We'll discuss that if and when we really need to," Pate said - straightening his posture and speaking a little more clearly as the waiter stopped beside us and just like that, the current line of conversation was over.

10

"You would be amazed if I told you how many of our clients come to us with skin problems caused by the sun."

I opened my eyes and struggled to keep them open because of the bright morning light. The previous night had seen me unable to find the laptop that I had been working on and its disappearance had caused me to be overcome with rage. I'd screamed at white coats- accusing them of being med students addicted to prescription drugs, accused them of lifting my laptop to fund an easy score and told each and every one of them to get the fuck out of the house before I really lost my temper.

Tiffany was not home, conveniently. She had gone to a meeting but who she was meeting and why was a mystery to me because we still weren't talking, and it had been almost a week since I had last spoken to either Pate or Leonardi. But the important thing is Tiffany was off the premises along with both of her most recent of surgeons and I had helped myself to the alcohol we had lying around the place and used the last of the cocaine that had been within my budget for the previous few days.

The moment Flitch woke me, pulled me from my state of peace upon the sun lounger next to the pool, I knew that I had stormed back inside of the house more than a couple of times to continue screaming at the hired hands but I couldn't remember any of It - not a thing. What I had said and to who was a complete unknown.

The surgeon smiled at me and tilted his head to appear completely straight in my line of vision. The smile was one you'd give an idiot whose trust you were out to gain. Even the way he had repositioned himself as if for my benefit was fucking patronising.

"I know you aren't involved in the business but you'd be

surprised how many people come to us with issues a little sun lotion could have prevented. You're a handsome man, but that complexion isn't guaranteed to last in these conditions," he said with the smile remaining in place. "You can't tell me that it's your ambition to one day resemble an alligator handbag, can you?"

"Is that the reason you're here," I asked him, "to find more business?"

He smiled. "No," he said, "not at all. Why improve the body if you will only leave the mind to waste, and vice versa?"

"Oh," I told him, "there isn't a thing wrong with my mind, believe me."

He nodded, looked out to the pool for a moment and looked back at me. "I heard you got yourself pretty worked-up last night... almost put your foot clean through one of the doors."

"I don't remember that last part," I shrugged, "but it could have happened."

"And what was it over again," he said, "a misplaced laptop?"

"Not misplaced," I corrected him, "*stolen*."

"Not stolen," he said with his Hollywood smile, "more, *relocated*. You would have found it in no time if you had checked the media room."

I knew the room he meant; the room where Tiffany had cabinets and shelving units filled with video cassettes and DVDs of her TV performances and appearances, a couple of things tied to people in the industry she knew, and a home computer she never used. There was a couch in there, too. She had seduced me on that very couch and, more recently, Lee also.

"The fuck is it doing in there?"

"Dr Remond and I thought it would be a good idea to place it there," he said, "to encourage you and Tiffany to share both private space and personal interests... To have your own place away from the world and the distractions of others, where you could discuss your dreams and your plans for the future."

"You have no right to touch any of my fucking things. If Tiffany wants to pay you two grifters to hang around here and help yourself, well that's on her, but your being here should have a minimal impact on my day-to-day life."

"How have you been sleeping?"

"For the love of... Is it selective hearing with assholes like you or what?"

"Has anybody else ever implied you have a very short fuse? I have worked with a lot of people over the years and you are up there with the best when it comes to snapping at any given moment in time."

"Let me guess - next thing you want to know about is how me and my mother got along, am I right?"

"You can tell me anything you would like and I won't breathe a word," he said. "With that in mind - would you say you and your mother had a *healthy* relationship?"

I laughed right in his face and got out of there.

11

I SAID, "IT was like a fucking intervention... I walked in and everybody - hired hands I hardly ever saw, a guard from the gates - was sitting in a little circle with Tiffany and the two quacks waiting for me and I had to sit there with them because I was desperate for a little money. Every one of them," I continued, "took a shot at me and this wasn't just your everyday character assassination; they took my character out into the fucking parking lot and gave it a beating for the whole world to see."

I'd met Pate and Leonardi in a 1950s-themed fast food joint one of them was interested in buying into. It looked nice but that was just about it... too many details prevented you from believing you may have possibly just stumbled back in time.

There was no segregation. The manager, a retired stuntman named Kelley G. Willridge that Pate had worked with in the past, was even black.

Smoking was not permitted. You wanted a smoke, you had to walk out back and stand amongst the trash cans.

Don't get me started on how the prices differed to those of the 1950s.

The two wealthiest contacts I had access to didn't use the information that I had given them as a source for pity but as a cause for laughter. Pate said, "I have to hand it to Tiffany and her agent - they're a lot smarter than I have ever given them credit."

Despite the surgery she had recently gone through, Tiffany had kept her role on the daytime TV show; her swollen face being explained by the character she played having suffered an allergic reaction to peanuts or shellfish off-camera. Pate had sworn he had been ready to can her, but Chambers released a book Tiffany had supposedly written at just the right time alongside an interview in a glossy magazine in which she flaunted her surgical "improvements". The public went wild for the interview, for Tiffany's carefully scripted responses and anecdotes. She came across as a rebel; a woman not only giving the finger to age but to the industry she was desperate to remain a part of and the ratings increased enough overnight because of it. It had led to Pate declaring he had found a worthy opponent in both of them, but all who dared oppose him supposedly became smoking ash to be scattered by the winds of time.

His words.

"You two have got to help me out," I begged, "I'm fucking broke; the bitch has as good as got me living on thin air out here."

Leonardi took a sip of his milkshake before asking, "What is it you would you have us do, Cole?"

"I need something of a regular income, or some kind of loan to help me out while I'm writing for you," I said, "and I know I've discussed it before with at least one of you, so can you help me out here?"

The two exchanged a look. Leonardi turned back to me and said, "Unless you're a union member, we'd be taken up the ass for helping you out like that and the decent unions won't have you until work of yours has been aired or regularly performed on the stage. I hate to tell you this but there is nothing we can do for you right now."

"So what the fuck am I supposed to do?"

"We might be able to help you out," Pate said with a shrug and a look of mild pity. "Get you some paid work as a background actor on shows here and there."

"You want me to be an extra? I don't know," I said, "even the two of you are always saying how most of the shows on TV are complete bullshit and I don't want to be on one of those cheesy TV shows airing footage of somebody who would become famous a couple of years down the line, playing a burns victim or something just as embarrassing."

Pate looked to Leonardi, laughed, then turned around to look at me. "Cole," he said, "do you think this business is nothing but picking the best projects for yourself and leaving the garbage for somebody that doesn't know any better? Let me tell you -

you've no idea how many things I have been and will be tied to that I'd rather have avoided."

"He's speaking the truth," Leonardi said with a nod.

"You want to survive here," Pate said, "you get used to bending over and taking a good hold of your socks whilst somebody takes you up the ass! You play your cards right and you'll give it a lot more than you are forced to take it but this is Hollywood and one thing with a lot more importance over quality out here is the financial return."

Willridge returned to our table for what must have been the twelfth, maybe thirteenth time - still smiling like a lunatic. He had the build of a heavyweight boxer but the hair looked to have been modelled on Little Richard's. Pate had told me it was a wig; said the guy's head was filled with scars from a car stunt gone wrong. It was the car stunt and following coma that had him settle on a change of career. "Still here," he observed with pride, "I just knew you would appreciate this place because there is nowhere else quite like it in the whole of California. Top up your bottomless coffees?"

"For the price you're charging," Leonardi said, "they had sure better be bottomless."

"You're paying for the quality of the coffee," Willridge said to defend the pricing. "Are you really going to tell me the coffee you're drinking right now hasn't surpassed all of your expectations? You," he said to me, "I've never seen you before and I sure don't recognise you but you're with these two fine gentlemen so I'm going to hazard a guess that you are Joe Public moving on up in the world - am I right?"

"Come on, Kel," Leonardi groaned, "leave the boy out of it."

"I'm not pressuring him any," he said, "just think of this as a customer satisfaction survey, why don't you? So here I am, conducting my survey, and I would like to know because of it - if that is one of the best, if not the best, cup of coffee you have ever had out in Los Angeles."

"It is a good cup of coffee," I said to Pate and Leonardi with a nod, "you got to give him that."

"Boom!" Willridge cheered, bringing his hands together in

celebration. "The kid knows what's good. Let me tell you all something," he said, "the coffee here is so good I should be charging a lot more for the flavour you get out of my beans."

"You keep your dark old beans the hell away from my cup," Leonardi grinned.

"And now we know why your name isn't associated with comedies," Willridge said in response. "But what do you think, honestly," he asked me, "isn't this the kind of place you could see yourself in over and over again?"

"The guy's got a nice place."

"You see that?" Willridge excitedly asked. "He's young but he knows that places like this are the best places to invest in! Let me tell you something," he said to me personally, "a lot of people say you should invest in land because there's only so much of it. And that's fine," he shrugged, "if you're happy with the idea of only making so much return on your investment. But there are two things people will always want; food and a story."

Leonardi snorted with finding Willridge's statement humorous.

"Come on," the retired stuntman said, "you know it's true, even more so out in this part of the world."

"Okay," Leonardi said, "what's the story here? Don't answer - let me finish. This," he continued, "is half an act. You should have people thinking they have really been transported back in time to the 1950s instead of just reminding them of Happy Days or pictures from a history book."

"He's onto something," Pate said and the three words had Willridge look to Leonardi with a new sense of interest.

"What you really should do," Leonardi advised him, "is pick a particular year in the 1950s instead of being *generic* 1950s. You have each and every day you are open running like it really was that point in time; have old radio news and sports broadcasts interrupt the songs on the jukebox and the waiting staff react to it like it is really happening. Knock up some old newspapers and leave them on a table here and there."

Willridge thought it over for a second but eventually laughed. "You're crazy," he said, "you want me out hiring a whole load of method actors to wait on tables?"

"Kelley," Pate grinned, "at a guess I would say at least three quarters of your staff are already struggling actors!"

Leonardi joined in with the grinning, leaned back and held his hands out. "You see? You would be providing the paying public with an art performance - a real piece of drama and escapism - and every meal would be all the better because they realise at the end it isn't going to come with a nuclear holocaust."

"I don't know," Willridge said in the manner of the eternal pessimist, "it can be difficult enough just getting the staff here to seem cheery throughout a shift. What about you," he asked, "you sold on this idea of theirs?"

"You need a couple of waitresses on roller-skates," I said, "it'd make the place feel dynamic."

12

Tiffany had continued to strip back the amount of cash I had access to and it was fucking torture, like she was peeling one layer of skin from me at a time. I'd used to sit out by the pool to nurse a hangover or simply kill a little time, but it had become the norm for me to sit there just because there was nothing else readily available to me.

Remond came out to talk with me on his last day at the house. Him and his business partner and all of the drones they had running around after them were finally moving on, out to fleece some other sucker and no doubt about it.

"Another beautiful day out in Los Angeles," he said, stepping beside me, eyes on the horizon. He was pretentious enough to smoke a pipe and not particularly heavy; just enough to keep the tobacco burning. Appearance means more to people like him than anybody else and with good reason - it was his bread and butter. "Even the air feels a little fresher today, doesn't it?" he added.

"If you say so," I sighed, expecting him to drop a few more suggestions that I would benefit from a little surgery - a nip and a tuck here and there...

The moment word he was moving on had found me, I *knew* it was because no one under Tiffany's control had approached the two surgeons for their help. I mean, sure - the two would have been getting money for sticking around to listen to her bitch and moan, but that must have been small change compared to what they would be paid for sucking the fat from some old girl's ass or putting silicone implants behind some aspiring model's beestings. And of course, more than anything, I was looking forward to watching the sons of bitches leave because without them around, I figured Tiffany could be sweet-talked into letting me have just a little more money.

"I suppose you're looking forward to seeing us leave," he

smiled at me, "particularly myself and Dr Flitch?"

Dozens of potential responses ranging from dry and witty to plain old aggressive were on my tongue but I didn't want him to know how much he had pissed me off so I took my time in answering, easing a cigarette from the pack I had swiped from one of the cleaners earlier that morning to try and see me through until I could get a pack of my own.

"I don't know," I finally responded with a shrug. "It's her money you're helping yourself to, not mine. You're just a bunch of ghosts to me if you must know."

He smiled, took a couple of faint puffs on his pipe and surveyed the pool. "I am sorry that I couldn't improve things between you and Tiffany," he finally said. "I know she's very interested in what you are writing."

I hadn't been writing at all. The laptop was still in her media room and I spent a lot of time sitting in front of it but the motivation had been drained from me alongside every bit of money Tiffany refused me. It's easy for you to say how I should have kept writing because it could have seen me getting paid in the near future, but it's hard when your mind is being pulled to countless problems in need of solving.

"That a fact?" I sighed.

The cigarette didn't have enough nicotine in it for my liking and on top of that it was cheap, and you knew it was by the taste alone. A discount brand where they sweep the tobacco that has spilled from the conveyer belt from the ground and wrap it in recycled newspaper.

"It is," he said with a nod and a smile. "Maybe the two of you could run through the dialogue together - let you see how it rolls when it's off the page?"

"Yeah," I told him, "I can't see that happening."

"Things won't improve unless you start making a little effort," he advised, "and I mean both of you - working together."

"Why do you care? Whether we start talking or not," I said, "she'll still go back to you in a year or less for a little more surgery. You think of talking about that kind of shit with her," I asked him, "maybe bringing an end to the facelifts and the peels and whatever else she feels she has to do?"

"Is it the surgery that bothers you? Do you feel that - every time she undergoes a procedure - a little bit more of the Tiffany you know is replaced?"

"Well fuck me, Dr Remond - you've cracked it! That must be it," I said sarcastically, "and now you have revealed it to me, I know that everything in the world is going to be just divine."

He smiled, looked to see if the tobacco in the bowl of his pipe was still burning and looked back to the pool. "Are you aware of how defensive you become as soon as somebody makes a suggestion as to why your life is going the way it is?"

"I wouldn't say that... It's just stupidity," I told him, "I'm surrounded by it out here... It's all just stupidity and lies. You want honesty? I lie in my own way," I said, "I lie in the way everybody in the world does; I act the way I feel I should in my situation and I fucking dream of the day when I'll be able to act truthful to myself - to just tell so many people to go fuck themselves and to be able to quit worrying about hurting the feelings of the people I wouldn't even make any effort to see if things were going differently."

"It sounds to me that you long to rid yourself of your conscience."

"Exactly," I smirked, "I want to be exactly where you are."

13

It was a nice watch Tiffany had bought it for me. As soon as the guy in the pawn store asked if I had proof of purchase, I knew he was out to screw me over. He went on pretending to examine it even after I told him that, no, I did not have proof of purchase; talked about the *fluidity of motion* being a little off and how he would have to spend some of his own money to get it right again. When he offered a couple of hundred bucks I was more than happy to accept it and get out of there.

Tiffany had finally restricted every dime she had to her name and despite the fact I had seen it coming, it was still a shock to the system - finding myself with no money, especially after I had been itching to make a decent score for the best part of a week. The last times I had been by Albert's place I had bummed from him like a man without a trace of shame and although you could think he surely owed me something for all the money that I had handed him over the years, he was just a man out to run his own business and I had no right to jeopardise it like that so I pawned a fucking beautiful watch and headed straight to his place with the money in my back pocket.

Matt was already at the door and it wasn't the Confederate Flag tattoo on his scalp that stood out for a change but the black eye he had. The left eye looked like it had been replaced with an 8 ball and the right had a noticeable scab over it.

"Matt," I said, "the fuck has happened to you?"

"Nothing too bad," he said, "bunch of niggers dropped by, shouting about Albert ripping them off. They left - I thought I had handled the situation well - and then they come back with pool cues and lead pipes."

"Jesus," I said.

"Oh," he laughed, "Jesus sided with *me* that day! Look at me," he said, "one of them popped me with a set of brass knucks but I kept standing, kept fighting, and I'm still standing here proud and tall after those assholes went racing out of here in their car."

"You asking for a raise?" I asked, only half joking.

"You pulling my chain?" he laughed. "Jew will probably start talking about tax thresholds or some such bullshit. You here to see him, anyway?"

"Thought I'd pick up while I was in the neighbourhood."

"Go on up," Matt said, opening the door for me, "he isn't doing anything too important."

"Thanks," I said and I walked on in. The hallway was quiet, devoid of life, and not a single soul passed me as I made my way up the stairs. The door was ajar so I could hear Albert talking, assumed he was on the telephone and knocked at the door.

"Cole," he said - answering my call with pale skin and bloodshot eyes, "I was wondering when you'd next come by! Come in," he said, "grab yourself a pew."

"Thanks," I said, walking towards the couch he rarely chose to sit on. He had music playing so low it took me a moment to even notice it and another to recognise who it was. Faith No More. Post - Angel Dust, so not really my scene.

"How's the writing going?" he said the moment I sat down. "That's the only reason I could think of for you not being here."

"It's getting there," I smiled. "The problem is that getting there doesn't pay the bills."

"I can bet," he grinned, "I can bet. You just make sure you send all those stars you have working for you to me, okay?"

"Sure," I laughed, "I'll do that."

"Appreciated. But what do you want," Albert said, "are you here to pick up or do you want to get high?"

I almost fainted with relief on hearing those words because they meant I could get reasonably fucked here and for free but also leave the place with some produce. If Albert stayed in a good mood, I'd even score a decent discount.

"Buying," I said, "but I'm in no real rush, so I suppose I could stay here a while."

"Right on," Albert said and he took a wooden jewellery box out from underneath the couch, opened it to reveal the treasures stored within; a little grass, papers, shit like that. "I'm going to have to come down a bit first before I can join you," he said, "because I'm as good as touching the stars right now."

The bathroom toilet flushed and I was reminded of how I had heard Albert talking to someone before I entered. It was far from uncommon for him to be entertaining a guest but for some reason on this occasion, I started to feel a little nervous - a little scared - at not knowing who it could be. When a guy in his early to mid-thirties, dressed like he worked in a bank or a jewellery store, came stumbling out in the process of fastening his carefully pressed trousers, it did little to make me feel better. "Oh," he said - clearly surprised to find somebody else had now joined the party, "didn't hear you arrive. I'm Marnell," he said by way of introduction, offering a hand I could only hope he had remembered to wash.

"Cole," I said, accepting it. "Good to meet you."

"Good to meet you," he said before moaning as he lowered himself down beside Albert. "So what's this," he asked, "we dropping the volume here a little?"

"Just trying to get back onto equal footing with my friend here," Albert said, rolling a fat and untidy joint.

"I haven't seen you around," Marnell said to me. "You just out of jail or something?"

"Definitely something," I laughed. "I'm here or I'm not," I told him, "I'm one extreme or the other."

"Well you missed all the recent excitement," he said, "you get a good look at Matty's eye?"

"Fuck," I said to Albert, "I'd forgotten all about that! It must have been some trouble out on the street last night."

"Dangers of the job," Albert shrugged, "he knows the risks and he knows he's paid for taking them but I wouldn't be surprised if he starts expecting more money because of it. You imagine that?" he laughed. "It would be like me asking the big bastard to tickle my balls every time he has some whore give him head on the stairwell - which I know he does."

"He's a big guy - loyal as an ox," Marnell observed, "and I know for a fact that people like that are hard to come by... Whatever it is you're paying him," he said, "you really should be sure it's enough."

"Remember this guy," Albert said to me with a smile, "there's a chance you'll be working with him one day," and he turned to Marnell to add, "Cole is buddying up with a couple of producers."

Marnell looked over to me and laughed. "Don't fall for it," he said, "he's poking fun at me."

"I'm not," Albert insisted, "Cole might just be behind your next commercial. Have you seen it?" he asked me. "Guy's face is being shown all over the TV."

I asked, "What is it you're selling?"

Marnell laughed, took a pack of Marlboros from his trouser pocket but struggled to locate a light. "Peace of mind," he grinned. "I work for a place that's just moved into a new building, so we're trying to get as many new clients through the door as we can right now."

I nodded. "You're a psychiatrist?"

"Psychiatrist," he laughed, "psychologist... Counsellor, life coach..."

"You should see all the certificates this guy has," Albert said, "holograms on them and everything!"

"Extensive training courses," Marnell laughed right as Albert got his joint burning and the all too familiar smell claimed the clean air. "I came out of college and couldn't find work and my folks started pulling strings to get me where I'm now stuck for the foreseeable. But funnily enough," he said, "I have had a couple of famous faces coming to me with their problems."

"What kind of problems? Anything interesting?"

"Well," he said, "it's more the studios sending them as some form of damage control. You could have an actor who went and forced himself on an actress or went with a minor. The studio will do their best to make the girl agree to keep quiet. Offer her anything and everything," he shrugged, "and they tell her how the man is seeking professional help for his problem... for his *illness*. If the girl in question won't make a deal, or he does it again and it makes the press, the studio has a folder proving the man is doing his best to become a better person and he should be pitied... Maybe even applauded. And if it isn't that," he concluded, "it's directors or whatever claiming stress. It's to try and not be sued as much for falling behind a schedule."

"Shit," I said, "you telling me that happens?"

"It happens," Albert said with a nod, the guy who supposedly knew everything. He took a drag on his freshly packed grass and said, "It's the foundations of the industry, corrupting anything that grows there."

My legs trembled once I was back on my feet, the backs of my knees nothing more than jelly. The urge to let go, to fall back onto the couch and stay there screamed out at me and was almost possible to ignore but Albert had got talking about wanting a burger and it had got all of us wanting one. All three of us had sat there talking about how badly we each wanted a burger for fifteen or more minutes and in the end, it was just too much to ignore; it was a craving that would last the night and beyond if it really had to.

"I'm going for my damn burger," I announced defiantly, "who wants what?"

Albert's eyes lit up as he asked, "Where you going?"

"There's a McDonald's a couple of blocks from here."

"Fuck the corporate clown," Albert said, "the deli is better and almost as close."

Marnell looked to his dealer and said, "Did you get me that double burger with the jalapenos inside it from the deli?"

"Sure did," Albert told him.

"Fuck McDonald's," Marnell said, "the deli gets my vote."

"Two to one," Albert smiled.

"Fine," I said, "fine, I'm easy. Who's having what?"

"What was that burger you got me again?"

"You had the Wildfire Inferno with extra relish."

"You get me one of those?" Marnell said, "With a diet coke?"

"Same here," Albert added, "and one for yourself. Three large Wildfire Inferno specials and I'll give you the money when you get back."

14

THE NIGHT AIR seemed colder than usual and my legs were unsteady and weak, but I made it all the way to the deli where warm air was produced en masse thanks to the flame grill and deep fat fryers. The only bad thing about the place was the lighting in there; exposed tubes on the ceiling of a sickly yellow colour. The place was deserted, bar a lone black guy with a cotton hat pulled down tight over his head. He looked away from the wrap he was eating the moment I entered and kept his eyes on me even when I had my back to him... I could feel his eyes on me.

"Yes," the man behind the counter asked me in a manner that seemed far more challenging than welcoming, "what are you having?"

"Two large Wildfire Inferno Meals," I said, looking over the menu on the boards at his back, "and a cheeseburger meal with an added hash brown."

"Drink?"

"Diet cokes with the Infernos," I said, "and I'll take a Sprite."

The guy nodded, took three raw burgers wrapped in greasy paper from the refrigerator and prepared them for the grill. For a moment I wondered if it would bother Albert - my not getting a Wildfire Inferno meal - but my concern was replaced when I heard the black guy sat behind me say, "Hey."

The guy behind the counter glanced up, saw it wasn't his attention being sought and went back to preparing the latest order. Hoping the black guy would leave me be if I chose to ignore him, I simply started counting in my head with the belief that he would lose all interest in me if I hadn't responded come the time I reached seventeen seconds.

"Hey," he repeated just as I reached twelve. I swallowed, closed my eyes tight for a moment and willed my body to grow into that of an imposing figure. He was still sitting there when I

164

finally turned to face him, his eyes still on me. They had never even left.

"Hey," I said back to him with a smile, hoping he wouldn't have it in him to beat on someone so full of joy and innocence.

"I thought it was you," he smiled, and the smile grew as he realised I had no idea who the fuck he was. "It's me," he said, "Kelley! From the diner!" he eventually included in an attempt at jogging my memory.

"Willridge? The stuntman?" I laughed, approaching his table with a newfound sense of ease.

"That's me," he laughed, "the stuntman! It's Cole, right? What the hell are you doing out here so late?"

"Picking up a couple burgers," I shrugged. "You?"

"My niece lives down the street," he said, "I'm just grabbing a bite to eat before I pay her a visit."

"Good to know. So how are things?" I asked him.

"Not too bad," he said, "not too bad at all. How about you? You seen anything of Scott and Nate?"

"Not lately," I told him, "we're all pretty busy right now."

"All have our own jobs to do," he said with a smile and an understanding nod of the head.

"Isn't that the truth! But how about this place - how do you rate the competition?"

"It's exactly what you expect on a street like this; there's nothing here that lures you in - you come in purely out of habit and because you know what you're going to get. Still," he shrugged, "there's a strip joint just down the street so you don't have too far to go for dessert," and on saying that he threw his head back and laughed as if his own remark was the funniest he had ever heard.

"Salt on your fries?" the guy behind the counter snapped at my back, coming across as a man annoyed at how I'd found somebody to speak with.

"Please," I said to him and he started to shake the container over the three bags of fries until they were covered with a red dust. "Wait a minute," I said in a panic, "I thought you asked if I wanted salt!"

"Salt and paprika," he said, "nowhere else does that around here."

"Trust me," Willridge said, "it's the best thing about this place. Shame you got to go back to your friends," he added, pointing at the meals being prepared, "you could have came back to my place for a couple of beers, traded a couple of war stories."

"Some other time," I said with a weary smile.

"You bet," he said with a smile of his own, "I have a lot of fun tales to tell about the business you're involved in - thought about writing my biography a couple of times-"

"Autobiography," I corrected him.

"What's the difference?"

"You write the story of your life and it's an autobiography; you write the story of somebody else's and it's a biography."

"Editor would fix all that," he shrugged, "but the stories I can tell! Only thing stopping me is the number of people who'd be out to sue me or worse for it. Sometimes I think of writing it down under a pretend name, claim it's nothing but fiction, but I'd know," he laughed. "Oh," he said, "you just wouldn't believe the stories I could tell about my time working in Hollywood."

Golden flames danced around the raw burgers on the grill, the dripping fat only acting to encourage their movement.

15

WHEN PATE GOT in touch to see if I was able to meet him and Leonardi on the down-low, I as good as tore his hand from the wrist. The only problem I had was how to get to them, because I had used all of the money I had made on the watch, so I took a couple of crumpled bills from Tiffany's purse when she wasn't around.

She was doing it on purpose - cutting me off and leaving me with no other option than to lift it from her. She knew what I was doing, I have no doubt about it; it was all a power trip to the old bitch. "Where are you going?" she asked, thumbing through a gossip magazine as I was making my way to the door.

"Meeting a couple of friends," I told her, stopping to stand there in clothes I felt smart yet casual in and wearing the cologne still to disappear from my collection like the rest of them had done already.

"Are you sure you want to go out like that?"

"What do you mean?"

"That shirt makes you look a little chunky," she said. "It isn't very flattering on your frame."

"Go fuck yourself," I said.

"If you don't want people to talk about your love handles," she called after me, "do something about them."

The boys on the gate went a couple of seconds pretending they were too busy discussing a sports article to let me out. They exchanged cock-sucking smirks with one another when they finally let me through and I wondered if they would even let me back in later and if it would necessarily be a bad thing if they didn't. I was annoyed at what Tiffany had said, annoyed at how she was treating me and making me live. It was enough to have me start hating on Lee, because everything I was experiencing could be traced back to his little disappearing act.

"Fuck every last one of them," I cursed.

16

I HAD TO meet Pate and Leonardi at a studio lot where they were watching some joint production of theirs being filmed but no buses stopped that close to the place and I didn't have money to spend on cabs so I jumped a bus and then struggled to jog the rest of the way. As always, a man in a phony cop's uniform was guarding the entrance.

"I'm here to see Scott Pate and Nate Leonardi," I struggled to tell him without revealing how desperate I was for air, "they're expecting me. Name's Cole."

"Hold on a second," he said and turned to the side to speak into the little walkie-talkie fastened to his shirt as if it was enough to keep me from hearing what he said into it. "I have a visitor named Cole here for Mr Pate and Mr Leonardi; name's Cole and he believes they are expecting him."

He got his response and turned back to me - fishing a laminated card with VISITOR stamped across it in bold green letters for me to wear around my neck from a nearby drawer. "Here you go, sir," he said, "just follow the signs until you reach the Hitchcock Stage."

"Thanks for your help," I said, "you'll be seeing a lot more of me in the near future."

"I'm sure I will," he said.

"I ask you something?" I stopped to ask, "Did Hitchcock ever shoot here? In this studio?"

"You're asking the wrong guy," he shrugged, "I wasn't working here back then."

The grounds of the studio was a small city unto itself; large hangars in place of houses on designated streets named after them like the aforementioned Hitchcock Stage being on Hitchcock Close or Grant Place or even Lucas Avenue. When I got onto Hitchcock Close - off Edison Way and Keaton Drive - the place had been made to look like a high street in New

York or some instantly recognisable place like that. The only difference was that from eight or so feet upwards, the stores were obviously no longer solid walls and glass but wooden frames and panel boards. No shooting was taking place, but cameramen remained beside their trusted machines, boom-mic operators walked back and forth in conversation with guys rushing about with megaphones in their possession. The performers, directors and everybody else appeared to be waiting on the far side of the lot - waiting for something to happen before they could begin. And I kid you not - I watched one guy (a set designer, most likely) strategically placing litter around a toppled trashcan but the trashcan itself wasn't real, it was a prop; it looked like a trashcan spilling waste but the waste in question was built into it - it was one solid structure.

"You," a short black guy wearing lime green eyeliner and a ruby-red bandana asked, rushing toward me, "are you here to replace the fans? Please tell me you're here to fix the fans and you had best have a good reason for running so late."

"I'm not here about the fans," I said, "Scott Pate and Nate Leonardi are here to discuss a project with me."

The guy swallowed loudly and lost his confidence where he was standing. "I'm sorry, sir," he said, "they're in the coffee house."

"Where's that?"

"Right there," he said, pointing across the pretend street and to a pretend coffee house. Through the large front window, I spotted them both sitting at a table, laughing over coffee. They hadn't noticed me.

"Thanks," I said, making my way over.

"Let me know if you need anything," the black guy called out to me, "you can always depend on Daniel J. Jackman."

The place smelled and felt like a real coffee shop - the girl in uniform behind the counter even had the *can't give a fuck any longer* expression like a real barista.

"Cole," Leonardi said with a smile to show teeth recently whitened within an inch of their life, "have a seat. Sophia," he called to the girl, "get Cole here a large vanilla latte, would you?

That's her speciality," he added for my benefit.

Sophia stepped forward and went to work on my vanilla latte - the machines in front of her were real.

"He's impressed," Pate laughed. "You weren't expecting that to happen, were you? Sophia is a background actress," he said, "but she works most of her days in a Starbucks out in the projects."

Leonardi moved in closer to me - said, "Remember all the bullshit about David Copperfield making the Statue of Liberty disappear? Well that's all it was - bullshit. Any cocksucker can make something disappear," he assured me, "all he needs to do is open his mouth wide enough and have a handle on his gag-reflex! But making things appear," he smiled, "that's real magic. Look at this," he grinned on sniffing his latte, "we've made a city inhabited by people with their own jobs and stories. Even God left that kind of tricky shit for man to sort all by himself."

"Here's your latte," Sophia said, lowering my drink down on the table.

"Sophia," Leonardi said - arm shooting up so he could stroke her lower back, "you're too good to be working with misfits filled by delusions of grandeur. How about we get you your very own business?" he asked while his hand fell down her back with ease and squeezed at her ass. "I can get you a stake in a franchise with no trouble at all. Fuck it," he said, "you can be your own franchise!"

And she just stood there, acting like she had no idea of how he was grabbing at her. Truth of the matter is it made me feel uncomfortable.

"Can I get you anything else?" she asked without emotion.

"You've done more than enough," Pate told her with a kind smile, "go back into position, darling, we'll be ready to roll in a minute."

Sophia nodded, sighed, and turned to make her way back behind the counter.

"You have no idea how hard it is proving to get a fan capable of blowing garbage at the correct speed and force," Pate told me in a hushed tone. "We didn't make all of what you see right now possible, just for discarded newspapers to be blown unrealistically down the street!"

"It's the Irish director," Leonardi grumbled, "we heard good things and he was cheap and it turned out he really was too good to be true."

"Enough of our problems," Pate said as he patted the back of my hand. "How's your work for our own secret project coming along? Are you still writing?"

"Things aren't going too good if I'm honest," I said, "I can't get my research online anymore because Tiffany has put a fucking password lock on the internet connection."

The two producers looked to one another and smirked. "Like a child safety lock?" Leonardi laughed.

"It's not funny," I said, laughing despite myself. "It's not just the research - or lack of it - keeping me from writing, it's everything else... The bitch has completely cut me off financially. It's hard to write when you can't do anything else than worry about how you're going to buy essentials."

Pate took a deep breath and slowly released it, leaning back in his chair, taking his time surveying me. "This bothers me," he said, "and it could bother our project and our long-term goals in doing so. Luckily for us all," he added, "Nate and I have been discussing your reluctance in appearing on film and how you should be rewarded for working for us - off the books, if you will."

"And?" I asked hopefully.

"It's like this," Leonardi said, "we're going to secure you regular work as a background actor; speaking parts, because the pay is extra. It's just the scenes you are in will be cut from the finished product - to spare your modesty."

My fucking heart swelled for joy and they hadn't even finished yet.

"And as long as we receive regular work from you," Leonardi continued, "we're thinking at least twenty pages per month, you will receive loans from us that you repay once you've found your feet. But we can't stress this enough," he said, "you can't tell anybody about how we're helping you out here or the unions really will take us out of the picture. *Pictures*," he grinned.

"I don't know what to say," I beamed, feeling more joy than I had ever imagined possible.

"Say very little," Pate advised me. "Tiffany can't know about what we have going here or she'll only ruin everything, so you have to convince her you're getting the regular work from a casting agency. And we mean it," he said, "we expect twenty pages or more each and every month; it doesn't matter how rough they are, just provide us with something – anything - we can get to work with."

"I will," I promised, "you had better believe I won't let you down on this."

PART 4

BACK AND FORTH

1

I HAD TO go downstairs in my underwear because Tiffany had hidden her robe in an attempt at annoying me and with barely any nicotine in my system, it worked like a motherfucker. It worked but I kept it hidden from her as best I could. She was downstairs, in the living room, looking through a script as a studio lackey – Dolores - applied her makeup for her. I was a little curious to why Dolores was here, but not curious enough to ask for an explanation.

"Oh," Tiffany sarcastically announced, "what have we here? If it isn't Cole, up and about at an hour he mustn't have known existed! To what do we owe the pleasure?" she smiled, taking the pack of cigarettes placed near her. "This has got to be the most unexpected event of the year."

"You're real funny sometimes, Tiffany."

"Ha! Don't put yourself down like that," she said, "getting up this early is a big achievement for you! What's the matter," she grinned, "you wet the bed? Did the little baby have an accident?"

"If you must know," I told her, "I have to be somewhere before they can start filming."

Even Dolores stopped working on hearing that one. Tiffany stopped breathing for a second. The two exchanged a glance. Dolores got back to work once Tiffany had looked her in the eye and smiled but her hand was trembling.

"Is that so?" Tiffany said through a smile as delicate as wet paper, "I'm sorry, it's just no one told me they were making a documentary on struggling drug addicts."

"It's not a documentary, Tiffany," I said, heading out to the kitchen, "it's a movie."

I opened the refrigerator door, looked inside. The door was slammed shut and Tiffany was suddenly standing in front of it, blocking its contents from me, and showing a face only half prepared for the working day ahead but full of rage.

"What are you really up to?" she snapped.

"I told you," I said, "I've got to be somewhere for shooting."

She was still holding her pack of cigarettes so I took them from her, slipped one free and returned the pack over to her. If I'd been wearing absolutely anything with pockets, I'd have slipped them in there.

"So what," Tiffany said, "all of a sudden, you've decided you're going to be an actor?"

"I wouldn't say that - it's more acting chose me. And I have to tell you," I said, "it's just so fucking easy, isn't it? I've walked straight into a job here without even trying."

She took a step back and looked me up and down, intending to spot a tell the second I provided her with one.

"What's the project?" she asked.

"There isn't a lot I can give away," I answered, taking the time to enjoy a momentary break from her interrogation by stopping to light the cigarette on the stove. "I can tell you it is the pilot for a new drama."

"Who's involved? Does the director of your big show have a name?"

"I don't think I can tell you that," I smiled, "I'm sorry but it's all being kept under wraps. I'm sure you'll understand."

Pate and Leonardi had told me to keep the names of the directors from Tiffany because they knew them, indirectly at the very least, and neither man wanted Tiffany to even suspect they were involved.

Tiffany lit a cigarette of her own. "Do I know him?"

"What makes you so sure it's a guy?"

Of course it was a guy; I just wanted her to start worrying over the thought of me screwing somebody else.

She took a long drag on her cigarette and asked, "Did I introduce you to them at a party? Is it thanks to me you know these people? Thanks to me you got this role... if it even exists!"

"Tiffany," Dolores cautiously said, entering the kitchen, "we really can't have too long a delay if we're going to make it on time."

"Jesus H. Christ, Dolores!" Tiffany shrieked, her face turning bright red as veins in her neck almost broke clear of the surface, "If you really can't do as you're told and just wait in another room, then I really can't see you lasting much longer in this industry!"

"I'm sorry," Dolores said, retreating, "I just thought you'd like to know," and she was out of sight, back to waiting in the other room.

"Nice girl," I said, "somebody had to remind us we're not in charge of today's schedule, right?"

Tiffany span back around and pointed a sharp finger at my throat. "I don't know what you are playing at, mister," she warned, "but things tend to change out here at the drop of a hat."

"You're absolutely right," I smiled.

"Go on then!" she said - her voice filled with spite, "go and master a profession it can take years just to find your feet in; I'm sure a college-drop out like you will be a big star in no time at all! Who knows," she challenged, "maybe you'll finally be able to start paying back all the money I've loaned you over the years!"

I resisted the bait, didn't bring up how she had never told me the money I had taken over the years would one day have to be paid back in full. Not only did I resist the bait but I helped myself to a little money from her purse before heading out.

2

THEY WERE SHOOTING in a long-forgotten warehouse kitted out to look like a nightclub. The majority of background actors were guys and girls around my age or slightly younger, each and every one dressed like they were ready for a wild night on the town. I spotted a couple of faces I recognised, the almost-named stars amongst us having appeared in small roles across various TV movies or short-lived dramas.

Of course, they were kept away from us whenever possible. Word was one background actor had already been sent home for daring approach one of the key players for an autograph. And of course, they had access to a spread of smoked salmon and fine cuisine spread out on clean tables whereas myself and the others in my position had to make do with the occasional offer of a store-bought sandwich along with a cup of lukewarm coffee.

I was given no preferential treatment; Pate and Leonardi had told me to expect this. They told me the director and his assistant would know who I was, of what the deal was, but to everybody else it had to remain hidden. I was playing the role of a background actor looking for that big break and when the time came, I acted surprised when the director picked me for a speaking part as if at random. The looks I received off some of the others immediately afterward were unbelievable! They acted like they were happy for me but you just knew they were pissed; knew they were sure it was a mistake and it should have been them in the speaking role. I imagined how happy they would be once the production hit the TV screens and the scene I was in had been removed during the editing process... Imagined how happy they would feel, thinking I'd be saddened to have been left on the cutting room floor. It was all such petty bullshit but it was money in my pocket and doing something that I told myself I would never have to do again.

So, I was playing a bartender of all things, looking out at a group of less than twenty people all packed together to be filmed at an angle that would fool the audience at home into believing they were inside a busy nightclub. I had to make out like I had just finished serving another background actor, then turn to one of the stars of the show - an actor with an obvious coke problem who had found fame as a child on one of those Nickelodeon shows. That whole simple motion of turning from one person to face him? It must have taken several takes; they just kept redoing it from one angle to the next. Sometimes they'd have me hand the other actor some loose change, sometimes they'd have me start wiping the bar down in between serving the big talent, but each and every time would have me turn to him and ask, "What'll it be?" and he'd place a twenty dollar bill down on the counter - push it towards me and say, "Get me a shot, a brew and a word with the big man," in response.

And you have to hand it to him - for a guy so clearly in need to rush back to his little trailer for another line of coke, he did his best each and every time. The poor sap had no idea the scene wouldn't be used, that what he was saying was of no importance whatsoever, and he would probably take it as a personal blow once he watched the finished product and saw that this vital scene hadn't been so vital after all.

3

WHAT LOOKED LIKE a brand new, top of the range Jaguar was parked outside the house when I got back - a black guy built like a footballer was standing beside it, all gold chains and rings and it was him who looked at me like I was the one out of place.

"How's it going?" I asked, passing him. He grunted but that was all.

Chambers walked past me as I entered the place, talking quickly into his cell on turning to head up the stairs. It didn't bother me, his paying me so little attention, because we had always been that way with one another. Finally, I stumbled across Tiffany, wearing a new bikini as she lay back on a sun lounger with a drink on the floor beside her. Her eyes were on the guy pulling himself out of the pool; body carved from marble, some form of tribal design tattooed under his right shoulder. He was wearing a pair of my black shorts, legs rolled up to make them more like tight-fitting underwear.

"Hey," he said, noticing me, "what's up?"

Tiffany looked back and smiled, seeing that it was me. "Cole," she said, "you're back from filming already? I wasn't expecting you to be back so soon. This is Eddie," she added as my physical superior dived back into the pool, "he's a professional actor; very talented, very dedicated. Did you know he's committed to the Scientologists for over one thousand years?"

"No," I said, "I didn't know that at all. Fascinating."

"He knows Scott," she added as he surfaced, shook a little water from his hair and took to doing lengths of the pool. "Scott's confident he could be the next big thing."

"Scott Pate? So does Eddie here dabble in writing?" I asked, watching him move through the water with ease, speed and grace.

"Eddie, an occasional writer? Ha!" Tiffany said, "You think somebody with his looks and talent should be sat behind a desk in this business? That's always been your problem, Cole, you just can't see what's right in front of you. I bet you struggle to see your own coke-ravaged nose."

Eddie climbed out of the pool, moved his hands over his head to brush his hair back. Slow, deliberate movements; he walked over to us like he was in an aftershave commercial.

"Eddie," Tiffany laughed, "Cole just asked if you were a writer! Can you believe that?"

"A writer," he smirked, taking a hand towel from the free lounger and dabbing at his chest. "Maybe if I weighed an extra hundred or so pounds and my hair was thinning..."

Tiffany laughed at that - her fake, unconvincing actor's laugh. She put too much effort into it for the laugh to ever come across as genuine.

"So, Tiffany tells me you know Scott Pate," I said, talking over her noise.

"Sure," he said, "almost everybody working out here knows him."

"It was Scott that cast Eddie here for the show," Tiffany took a lot of pride in announcing, "he said the onscreen chemistry between us is remarkable, it's electric, and so it should be if we're going to be playing lovers. We'll be seeing a lot of each other, won't we, Eddie? You may as well pack your things and move in right now," she laughed.

4

PATE LOOKED TO me and said, "We needed someone to attract a younger audience and Eddie Shure was the ideal candidate because he already has a following from that sitcom he started up in. Guys want to have a beer with him, girls want to marry him," he shrugged, "and of course, his knowing the *right* people helped him to secure the role a great deal."

We'd met in Willridge's diner but the man himself wasn't here. He might have been playing it cool, I don't know, but Pate was holding a lot of meetings in the place. Maybe he was seriously considering freeing the old stuntman's hands of the establishment, maybe he just wanted Willridge to think he was and enjoyed teasing him, I can't tell you for sure. Leonardi had said he was going to meet us here but had cancelled at the last minute due to problems on set somewhere or other.

"So, you didn't get him the job because he's a Scientologist?"

Pate pulled a mildly confused expression and asked, "What does his personal beliefs have to do with anything?"

"I don't know," I said, "I thought you guys stuck together... Helped each other out."

"Hold on a minute," Pate grinned. "You think I'm a Scientologist?"

"You are, aren't you?"

"No," he laughed, "no, no, no, no, no! I can't believe that's still following me after all these years," he said, "after all this time!" and he took a napkin from the table to dab the invisible tears from the corners of his eyes. "Years back," he explained, "probably before you were a twinkle behind your old man's eyes, there was an actor on the verge of becoming a huge star. Gigantic, even. And I wanted him to appear in a movie I had a small connection with for all the obvious reasons that you can imagine.

"Now at the time," he continued, "this guy had just gotten

involved with Scientology and you know what it's like, right, when somebody suddenly takes to believing in something? Well he was like that - well and truly obsessed. Him and his agent wanted me to attend a lot of functions with them to see what it was all about, to meet the people he was meeting and to try and have me donate my hard earned alongside them, all of that nonsense. Now the press obviously wanted pictures of him at these events, I was in the background in a couple of them, and a lot of people got the idea that I had got him into Scientology... That I'd told him to join if he wanted to further his career. I never corrected anybody," he shrugged, "it was no big issue from where I was sitting. If anything, it's helped me secure a few names for roles because they assume I have buried memories of being tossed into a volcano in another life or whatever crazy bullshit it is they claim to believe. But let me tell you this," he grinned, "I've secured just as many others by ordering food from the kosher menu, you understand?"

"Sure," I nodded, smiling and relieved. "I thought you were hoping on the two getting together - if you get what I mean..."

"Ha! You think Eddie would take a second look at Tiffany if he wasn't working with her? No," he said, "I'll give him the big parts when I need to but in the end, it will all benefit me just as much as it does him and his friends. You know the two are going to end up as onscreen lovers?" Pate smiled. "All those fans of his will turn on her because of it. Her own fans will turn on her because of the age difference and because of their own jealousy. I'll use it to my advantage because in this world you use anything and everything you can to improve your position in life. Tiffany Lily will not last much longer on my show."

"As long as you know what you're doing," I said. "I still don't like how much time he's spending at the house," I admitted anyway.

"Eddie is a professional," Pate said matter-of-factly, "he's just taking the time to try and find something to like about her because they're going to have a *lot* of screen-time together."

5

IT WAS SOME form of *Buffy the Vampire Slayer*-style TV show and it was a long day of filming; most of us were there for a little after seven in the morning and they carted us all off to our own little section of the studio where we couldn't bother the 'stars' of the show. They didn't offer us breakfast, but weak coffee was made readily available. Some of the people already knew each other from other shows and they sat together, started conversations about how close they were to getting their big break. Some must have known this kind of day could be expected and so they sat alone with a book they had brought along with them or they sat listening to music with their eyes closed. I hadn't brought a thing with me to occupy my mind but I had no desire to talk with any of these people so I sat back, got comfortable and closed my eyes to have them think I was all one with Zen or some kind of bullshit.

Filming got underway a little after nine in a part of the studio lot made up to look like a high school and the adjoining grounds. The central characters of the show - two supposed cheerleaders and a bookworm who were played by professional actors with a combined age of around one hundred - sat talking at an outdoor table while we background actors either stood in groups or walked back and forth. I made out like I was checking my cellphone, even stopped a couple of times to wave to somebody that wasn't there and tried not to think too hard about whether I would pass as a student or a professor.

The director half-turned to his assistant and quietly said something to her. The assistant rose to her feet at record speed and brought that section of filming to a sudden end. The cast regulars lit up cigarettes and headed in separate directions with barely a nod to their co-stars, some looking pissed whereas others looked like they felt the show was beneath them. We silent heroes of the background just stood around, as good as glued to where we had been standing and awaited further instructions.

"Okay, everybody," the assistant director yelled loud and clear, "we're about to bring this week's big bad on so can everybody please get to the far wall over there?" she said on pointing to her left and like herded sheep we made our way over to the wall without complaint as a truck slowly reversed to hand. "A lot of the buzz around this show is the surprise," she continued, lighting a cigarette, "so please keep what you see here today to yourself if you haven't been told to already."

A crew of middle-aged men with spreading guts and thinning hair pulled a puppet to be operated by at least four people from the back of the van; it looked a lot like a giant caterpillar with deformed human arms and the face of a man twisted in pain and torment. Someone behind me turned to the nearest person and muttered, "What the fuck is that supposed to be, man? It looks like a dick with a bad dose of the clap!"

The director said something into his assistant's ear; she looked at me, nodded and walked over pretending to look us all over with consideration before asking me, "You think you're up to a speaking part? Won't be more than a sentence but it's an integral part of the show."

"Sure," I said, "I could do that."

"Okay," she said, "go have the makeup department get you ready and then go straight over to wardrobe and wait for somebody to come and bring you back here. You get to be the school janitor."

"Thank you," I said but she was already heading elsewhere, shouting commands to the lighting operator.

"Hey," another extra said with a smile as he took a tight hold of my elbow, "you must be pretty pumped, right?"

"You heard what she said," I shrugged, "it's only a line."

"Don't you watch the show?" he asked in astonishment. "You're the janitor," he grinned from ear to ear, "they've *never* shown the janitor before but he's mentioned in every single episode! People online are going to go crazy over you! This could even become a recurring role!"

"Let's take it one step at a time."

6

THE COFFEE WAS guaranteed to taste burned or dull and the doughnuts were a whisker away from officially being stale but there was an internet cafe I now favoured above all others. I'd go there with my laptop and email a couple of scenes or musings for a scene to Pate and Leonardi (fucking Tiffany still had me locked out of the internet at her place); sometimes I'd print a couple of short scenes off and write a couple of random notes here and there before handing them over to Pate in my attempt to look like somebody putting real thought into what he was writing.

If my thoughts weren't on how to try and get a little extra money from the two producers because I'd already wasted the latest loan, they were on the waitress who had me returning to the cafe where she worked despite her inability to pour a decent cup of coffee or prepare a fresh batch of doughnuts.

She was an angel, she really was. All brightly coloured ink or her forearms and a lot of earrings and hair cut at sharp angles and dyed a new and brighter colour almost every weekend. She was talking to a customer once and I heard her say she was in a band called *The Uptight Cats* or something and it only had her appeal to me all the more because I'm a heterosexual guy and a heterosexual guy can't help but be all the more attracted to an attractive babe the second he finds out she can play a musical instrument.

And I like to think that things would have been different, that I'd have talked to her or something, if the place where she worked only had a policy of employees having to wear a name-badge like every other place does. I would have worked my magic all over her ass if it wasn't for the lack of a name-badge and if it wasn't for *him*.

It was raining. Light rain with winds becoming increasingly heavy; darkening clouds spreading overhead. It had to be like that. The scene could only possibly work if it was a day like that; a day with a sense of brooding, a sense of forewarning lowering close to the ground of Los Angeles.

Okay, so I had been looking over Ezekiel Bircham's social media profiles on a regular basis and I had been struggling to keep count of the number of times he had said he would be taking a break from these very same profiles, because that's what he did; he said things/people were depressing him, personal issues were dragging him down, and only a break from his online activities would help him get back to a good place. He'd say it and post something moronic within an hour, a still from an obscure movie or an indie comic book, no doubt as he tried to deal with his disappointment at having not a single soul publically bombard him with pleas to just hang in there and look for a brighter dawn. I'd never met him and he was bugging the shit out of me... I just wanted to slap him across the face and tell him to stop trying to make problems out of thin air, to stop trying to become this angst-ridden martyr...

And on this one occasion I realised I'd long stopped thinking about him, had long stopped thinking about *anything*, and was simply staring at the angel working the counter. I could have been staring at her for hours but it didn't bother me. If she had noticed she hadn't complained, so I just kept staring and watching her easy, fluid movements. She was pretty crappy at her job but she looked good doing it. She looked so good doing it I suddenly realised how I was getting onto my feet, preparing to walk right over to her and ask if she would like to see a movie or something that weekend. She liked music and I liked music. I was creative and she was creative. The gods themselves had brought us together.

I was as good as fully standing when I saw him walk by outside - Father Doyle himself.

"What the *actual* fuck?" I muttered.

His hair had been cut down a lot shorter than I had ever seen it during my time with him - pretty much right down to the bone. It looked a lot darker because of it.

The off-white clerical collar was still at his throat. The scuffed black boots looked to be the same he had been wearing on the day we first met but the black jeans and shirt looked like they could have belonged to Lee once.

I rushed out of the cafe, caught sight of him from behind in a moving sea of people and went to follow the tide but remembered my laptop at the last minute. "Shit," I said, rushing back into the cafe to retrieve it before some son of a bitch went in there and lifted it.

I had it shut down within seconds, was packing it all away at desperate speed when it dawned on me just what I was doing and what good could possibly come from it. Behind the counter, my potential soul mate was preparing a batch of beans to be ground. She hadn't noticed my rushing out and immediate return. She was unaware of the decision I had been presented with.

I told myself to quit being so dramatic, told myself to quit being a little queen like Ezekiel Bircham, and I took my laptop and headed back out onto the street to try and calmly find Doyle.

7

I HAD HIM a matter of paces ahead of me in less than a minute. He didn't seem aware of the fact that he was being followed. I still kept at least three to four people between us anyway. Three to four people because I had no idea how he would respond to becoming aware of me after all this time.

Doyle guided a cigarette to his lips. He was wearing his black leather gloves. They were worn to keep most people from seeing the ink beneath each finger. When Doyle put his fists side by side, the word REDEEMER was made. I tried to remember the tattoos beneath his black shirt but all my memories could evoke was blurred patches of skin with zero detail. A lot of tattoos he must have done with a friend when he was a lot younger mixed with prison-issue tattoos; random and tribal markings he would occasionally laugh about.

Father Doyle, walking on ahead of me on the streets of Los Angeles like it was the most natural thing to occur. I realised at some point, I too had lit up a cigarette.

And I kept tailing him, never blinking, never taking my eyes off him. I managed to move down the street without really paying attention to my surroundings but I stepped aside whenever I had to give somebody room to pass or to avoid stepping in dog shit. The adrenaline, the excitement, it all had me feeling lightheaded but it didn't stop me, didn't cause me to drop my pace or turn back. Thoughts of following Doyle, of wondering just how I would react when Lee stepped out from a shop doorway and dropped in line beside him, kept me moving. They also encouraged me to ignore the fact Doyle wasn't the only one of us being followed for longer than it should have.

I finally paid heed to that niggling voice hidden away at the back of my skull and swallowed. Somebody was following me, I just knew it... I could feel it.

Resisting the desperate urge to look back over my shoulder I kept on Doyle, glanced at a shop window on passing under the pretence of checking my appearance when really I was trying to get a good look at the people behind me. No one I recognised but nowhere near enough time to take a proper look.

Taking a drag on my cigarette, a burning stone of ash stung my fingers because I'd smoked it right down to the filter. I shook the sensation from my hand as good as I could manage whilst flicking the cigarette into the gutter. Doyle - still to look back at me - made his way to stone steps leading to the subway, black glove taking the handrail for support. Another handrail drunks probably thought it hysterical to piss on during the early hours. And I wanted to go down there, to join him in the crowded tunnel system of artificial lighting and bodies reluctant to be placed too close to another, but I closed my eyes and took a deep breath - kept on walking to keep whoever was following me from inadvertently following the street preacher himself.

8

I PICTURED AN unknown figure in Tiffany's employ breaking free from the flood of people to drive a blade into my heart before disappearing just as efficiently as I bled-out on the sidewalk... A loner with no real connection to his surroundings having picked me at random stepping forward and letting me catch a glimpse of the gun in his hand before he blew my brains out... Of the girl from the internet cafe revealing years later how a popular b-side her band recorded was inspired by my untimely murder on that fateful day.

People grumbled, muttered curses because I had turned back on myself and was unexpectedly heading toward them and we had to do that awkward little dance that comes when trying to avoid walking into fellow members of the public. Each one of them looked at me, shot me a cruel look due to this grand inconvenience I had cast down onto them, but the gazes never lasted and I knew these people hadn't been following me because of it.

When the guy stopped just a few paces ahead of me, he smiled without blinking and held his arms out to his side like he was beckoning me in for a hug. I knew it was his gaze that had followed me so far beneath the sun.

Hair dyed as black as ink was pushed back, close to his scalp because of an overuse of gel or wax, and a carefully trimmed and maintained goatee beard. A smart and reasonably expensive charcoal suit with black belt, white shirt open at the collar and a blue tie recently loosened. Black shoes that shone like they were fresh from a store window.

"Come on," he said in a voice that only acted to make him appear instantly recognisable, "you can admit it - you're impressed, aren't you?"

"Dexter?" I asked because it just seemed so implausible. "Bill Dexter?"

The private investigator who slipped his cheaply-produced business cards into the back of crime magazines. The very same I had hired just to get Hollis Silverdale from my back via his clear incompetence.

"The very same," he replied and, clearly impatient, he moved forward and threw his arms around me so he could pull me in close. He smelled of cologne and cigarettes. The whole encounter just felt so completely unexpected, completely out of the ordinary, that all I could do to respond was just stand there and go on letting him embrace me like a once forgotten relative come home to roost. People complained at our taking up space, threw more bitter looks on passing for the fraction of a second we were adding to their travel time. Still taken aback, I didn't have the slightest idea of how to respond.

"Look at you," he smiled, finally holding me at arm's length. "Surprise is written all over your face! I wish I could take a picture!" he laughed.

"Right," I nodded, "it's good to see you too... So what the hell do you want, Bill?"

"Don't look so nervous," he laughed, "I'm not looking into your private business or anything! I saw it was you and thought I'd see how long I could follow you, before you noticed. It's the boss," he grinned, "he says I don't observe naturally... Always telling me I just need to relax more."

"You have a boss? Who's your boss?"

"You won't know, will you!" he said and he couldn't keep the smile from reclaiming his facial features - didn't even try fighting it. "I work for Mr Silverdale now!"

"Hollis Silverdale? You're working for the guy I paid you to tail?"

"It's a funny old world, isn't it?" he laughed. "I'm not complaining," he said, "work is regular and the pay is a lot better... Only downside is I don't get to choose my own hours anymore. But yeah," he nodded, "quite a world we're in."

"You sure he hasn't put you up to following me?"

"No," he insisted, "it isn't that at all! I swear," he said, "I had just left an insurance company we have dealings with and I spotted you - thought I'd let you in on how things were going for me."

"I believe you," I smiled, "but plenty of others wouldn't.2

"Look at this face," he said with a smile of his own, "does this look like the face of a liar? Anyway - I have plenty of time at my disposal right now, so are you interested in grabbing a coffee?"

"Some other time," I said, "I'm a little busy right now."

"Definitely," Dexter said with a nod, "soon as there's a time that suits us both, am I right?"

"Get in touch with my people and have them arrange something," I joked, turning to make my exit, "we'll do lunch."

9

Tiffany wasn't home when I got back. The whole place was empty, quiet; a mausoleum long forgotten by the continuing bloodline. But the air was a little stuffy, the thermostat left a notch too high. There was a packet of cigarettes and a box of matches on the kitchen worktop so I took them outside and lit a cigarette near the pool. A couple of leaves were floating along the surface of the water, some had already settled on the bottom. I wondered if Tiffany would allow the pool to rot, just so I wouldn't have anything nice to laze around in front of, or whether she would get it cleaned first thing the following morning - just to encourage the young and able Eddie Shure to take another dip.

And I remembered the times me and Lee had spent standing out there, just talking and enjoying our own company... The last time I spoke to him, right there, in the early hours of the morning and when I woke up he was gone and Tiffany was shouting and screaming, claiming I was somehow to blame for it all.

He wasn't with Doyle... Doyle had been walking the streets alone. Was that a good sign or the complete opposite? During my time with the preacher, I'd kept right at his side. I'd followed his every word, tried to think like him and tried to move like him and tried to be like him because he managed to make everything look so much easier. The preacher was looking a little tired now, a little more worn around the edges, but it still seemed improbable - the idea of him being gone long before California had been consumed by wildfires or swallowed by the ground on which it now stood during an earthquake.

Yet I had never seen Doyle appear so visibly mortal and if Lee wasn't at his side right now, where was he?

Sometimes the only available option is to pretend you don't care how someone is doing because wherever they may be is where they *chose* to be, so I dropped my cigarette to the ground and stepped down on it before heading back inside. The realisation of my very own mortality planted a flag at the front of my thoughts and everything just seemed so trivial, so petty, and it was more than enough to have me head upstairs in search of Tiffany; to see if she was maybe having a nap or even going over her lines in her media room, her personal church of self-worship.

Tiffany wasn't in the bedroom. The sheets had been changed, the pillows fluffed and there was a faint trace of vanilla in the air so I knew the maids had visited at some point during the day. Resisting the urge to light another cigarette I made my way to Tiffany's private room, even calling out for her before entering. She wasn't practising her lines, wasn't watching an old recording of herself on a long-forgotten TV show - the place was empty. It would have been more than enough for me to step back out onto the landing, close the door behind me and find something else to do if it wasn't for but *one* thing.

I could see the safe wasn't locked.

The safe she usually kept hidden from view and locked immediately after she had placed something inside it or retrieved something from it. You could see the open door of black metal with the numbered buttons on the front, clear as fucking day. It was just so unexpected that I couldn't help but stare at it for a while, like I was waiting for my brain to realise it was picking up the wrong information from my eyes and it would be not only locked but hidden from my sight in the blink of an eye.

The safe remained in view and open even as I started making my way towards it... Remained unlocked as I opened the door a little wider and had a look inside. A black tin with lock (keys in the fucking lock...) sat atop of a printed script. The script was of no interest to me at all; I ignored the script like it was yesterday's news and opened the tin, admiring the neat piles of fifty and twenty dollar bills unexpectedly made available to me.

10

Via his Myspace profile page, Ezekiel Bircham had made the whole world aware of his intentions of attending a gay night at a club. I found out about it at a twenty-four hour internet cafe, showered and smartly dressed with a wad of bills in my wallet but no plans other than a trip to Albert's for some supplies. Filled with confidence I left the cafe and walked into the convenience store next door, browsing the aisles with no direction; just to take up a little time before I'd stop at the counter for some cigarettes and jump a cab once the transaction was completed here.

The music magazines weren't produced for people like me. I took the time to look over them anyway, just to feel superior over the morons with a genuine interest in this shit; the idiots I would never encounter, let alone talk to.

Shock-rocker Tony Warr was on the cover of one magazine but the makeup to have him look like a man who slept through the day and celebrated the light of the moon was missing, as were the coloured contact lenses and the lipstick and bright colouring around his eyes. If his name hadn't been placed directly across the image of him, I doubt even a fan would recognise him. But Warr was back with a new record and from the quotes taken from the interview within, plans of a directorial debut based on a novel of his due to be published by a major publishing house. Just in case that wasn't enough to draw a fan or curious member of the public in, there was another quote beneath it - this one drawing attention to a less than flattering opinion he held on fellow artists allowing TV shows they had no interest in to use their music. I flicked through the magazine regardless, finding an article on how Neil Young went all crazy Republican during the 1980s which was interesting if not out of place and far too brief. The token four or so pages on the latest cinema and DVD releases were largely dedicated to shit blockbusters and violent offerings you'd never heard of. It was all enough to make me even more determined to be a vital part of the next big counter-culture revolution that was long overdue.

The cashier was a Mexican and I got the impression he had an issue with me the second we made eye contact. When I told him my brand he just turned, took them from the shelf and scanned the barcode; he didn't even tell me how much they were, he left me to go by the reading on the cash register. As he handed me my change he said without any other emotion than boredom, "There's a public library down the street if you want to read stuff for free." It was so unexpected it made me laugh but it wasn't enough for me to say something back to him.

I took myself to Willridge's business of burgers and nostalgia with hopes of finding Pate and Leonardi there but there was no sign of them. I ate there anyway, just to take up some time, and had the Original Rock n' Roll meal with a sundae for dessert. The place looked busy until you noticed how a lot of the people had long stopped eating but were still at their tables, staring off into the distance or reading a newspaper in a desperate attempt to waste some time. It started making me feel down so I headed to a nearby bar, took it easy with a few drinks and finally headed on to the club that the Bircham boy was planning on going to later that same night.

11

THE GAY NIGHT was as big a nightmare as you should always expect; shit music and rainbow flags, drag queens and plain queens and women currently in the process of piling on the beef and trying to keep their hair short and like a man's. And it was a huge success for the club in question because of it, you could practically smell the pink dollars it was that busy. After smiling at every slender girl with long hair who might have just been there for a good time whilst personally still being groped by my fellow man more times than I would care to admit, I tallied the night as a loss and made my way back out onto the street - taking a quick glance over the smokers outside. There was no sign of Ezekiel Bircham amongst them and even if he was inside, the odds of my spotting him were single figures if I'm being generous. Lighting a cigarette of my own to take up the wait until the glow of a cab's light came down the quiet road, I tried to imagine what his Myspace or Facebook pages would be all about the following afternoon. At a guess I had it at two to three days before he started openly worrying about his chances of having contracted AIDS.

"You have a spare light?" a cautious voice asked from my back. I turned to see a guy who would definitely have been asked to show his drivers' licence on arrival and envied his hair a little. It looked a little messy, a little carefree, but it must have taken him a long time to get it just right.

"Sure," I said with a nod and I handed him my lighter.

"Thanks," he said, accepting it. The glow of the flame lit up his face as he used it to get his cigarette burning. His forehead wasn't too smooth under close inspection and I put it down to the gel or whatever he used - spilling onto the skin and causing untimely breakouts. "You waiting for somebody or just getting some air?" he asked, handing me back the light, smoke from his mouth immediately being pulled away by the breeze out on the street.

"Waiting for a cab," I told him.

"Shame," he said, "I was just about to buy you a drink."

He tried to sound confident but his voice had trembled a little at some point during the claim he made.

"Trust me," I told him with a smile, "there's someone in there desperate to buy *you* a drink."

"I have rush," he blurted out, "and I don't have any preference..."

A cab turned the corner at the top of the street, started crawling towards us, and it felt wrong to just leave the boy out in a place like this while he was saying shit like that... Somebody could really take advantage of him, really hurt him. But I really wanted to get that cab before it was gone...

"How old are you?" I asked him.

"Old enough to keep you from getting into any trouble," he said back to me without hesitation.

"Listen," I said - stepping out into the road to signal the approaching cab, "just stick with your friends and have a good time, okay? Don't do anything you might regret."

"My friends have bailed," he said, "can't I share a ride with you?"

The driver stopped nearby, waiting for me to hop into the back, and I stared at the kid and wondered if he was telling the truth here or just trying to con his way back home with a stranger. "Now that is something you'd regret," I said, "just take one last look for your friends and grab the next taxi if you have to," and I climbed into the back seat and slammed the door shut behind me.

12

IT WAS RAINING heavily come the time I had the taxi stop outside Albert's place - cold rain with occasional gusts of colder winds; the kind of weather that leads to a migraine if you're outside in it for too long. Puddles in the gutter became lagoons that crept up onto the sidewalk to sweep us all away. Matt was still manning the door, the padded coat he was wearing being the only sign he had noticed how bad the night was becoming. He only gave the cab the briefest of glances and then he went back to staring at a building across the street and a few doors down; construction workers had paid it a visit, placed it behind a cage of scaffold like an animal in the zoo. Pneumatic drills had shattered patches of concrete in front of it and traffic cones were in place to keep people from falling over the ruin. It was surprising to me that nobody had lifted those cones yet.

I paid the driver and stood beside Matt as he drove on, looking for another fare. "What's happening?" I asked, joining him in staring at the building.

"Bad news for the Jew," Matt said. "Work on one building will lead to a whole redevelopment of the block. There's no way we'll be here this time next year."

"Maybe they're just tearing it down?"

"Same thing," Matt said and he turned to face me. Rain or not, you couldn't help but notice how his swollen eye was now leaking. "A crew offered me work not too long ago - Asian niggers," he laughed. "It's good money but more work than I do here; I won't just be tossing out the assholes but selling. You imagine that," he grinned, "me, doing all that math?"

"But you're still thinking about it, right?"

"I'm always thinking," he said. "You want to survive in this world you have to be more than muscle - you have to watch shit on the Discovery Channel, get smart. Anyway - you can go right up; nobody's up there with him and you're getting soaked."

"Watch you don't catch a cold out here."

Stepping into the building was like walking right into a refrigerator but I was glad to be out of the wind and rain - you could hear them both knocking at the stone and glass exterior. There was a bum crashed-out on the stairs between the second and third floors; his face was black with dirt like he had been working down in the mines all day. He didn't even notice me until I was struggling to step over him. "Got a light?" he asked and he held an open hand out for a lighter or loose change or both.

"Sorry, I don't," I said.

"Got a light?" he asked again. I turned to look back over my shoulder, expecting somebody else to be heading up the stairs behind me, but there wasn't; the guy had turned his head, asked me the same question from over his shoulder. I apologised again and carried on.

The door to Albert's apartment wasn't just closed over but locked from the inside. I had to knock, stand there waiting for him to answer and when he finally did he didn't look too good. The slick sheen covering his skin made it look like he hadn't just turned the heating onto full but also sat in front of an open fire and the whites of his eyes were a deep shade of pink. Whether the tennis racket he kept tight hold of was intended to be used as a weapon or not, I can't tell you.

"Cole," he finally said, "good to see you... Come on in."

I stepped into the apartment. The air was too hot now, almost as if it wanted to push me back outside. The windows were closed, blinds shut. I noticed the song he was playing right as he was closing the door behind me - it was Mazzy Star's *Fade Into You* of all songs and I had to keep it from pulling me back in time, back to a road journey that didn't end well.

"You see what they're doing?" he asked from my back. "They let this neighbourhood rot for years and now they've decided to get it ready for the yuppies. You wait and see," he said, "all kinds of landlords and owners who hadn't thought of the place for years will come crawling out of the woodwork now. All the small businesses and the people that've lived here all their lives will be getting forced out, like a fucking exodus!

"Not that it'll matter to me in the long run," he grumbled, wiping his nose across the back of his wrist. "I'm surprised you're even here," he said. "You remember Julius Caesar? Well I have Brutus manning the door outside," he smirked. "He thinks I'm as dumb as he is," he continued, locking the door, "you expect me to believe a bunch of *blasians* offered him work with them and he's only just bringing it up? Bullshit," he said, claiming one of many free seats, "he's been planning this with them for fucking years and now they have the perfect opportunity waiting right in front of them, I'm telling you!"

I should have given it no attention, paid for what I had come for and got out of there but I didn't. Instead of being intelligent I sat on the chair opposite him and asked, "Who's planning what?"

"Fucking Judas out there!" he yelled. "He's always hated working for a skinny Jew and now that we could have shit going down - just for *being* here - he's gone and made some tight connections with the fucking black gooks! You watch," he said, "he'll start by letting all kinds of trouble go down here - just so people are reluctant to come back - and then he'll start talking about these other dealers he knows... Dealers with a cosy setup where nobody even raises their voice or looks at you funny! And if it isn't that," he claimed, clumsily lighting a cigarette, "he'll look the other direction as his friends pull over and start selling whatever they happen to have in the glove box, undercutting my ass."

I sat right back in the chair to get comfortable while lighting a cigarette of my own. "Come on," I reasoned, "how long have you known Matt? And look at his face," I said, "that big bug-eye he has right now shows you he's chasing the right people away from the place, am I right?"

"That's what he wants you to think," Albert said, "but it's all a part of what I was just saying - about making the place look bad... It has to be!"

There was silence in the background for somewhere between two and three seconds as the previous song finished and another began; Mazzy Star gone and replaced by an old Johnny Cash song. I tried to picture the Man in Black, young and out of his mind in a place like this, but couldn't.

"I have plenty of my own blacks working for me," he sneered, "I have my own suppliers and they have their own connections and they won't just sit by and watch me get pushed out of the picture. If the sons of bitches want a fucking turf war, I'll give them a fucking turf war and I'll fucking win."

"I don't know," I said with a shrug, "you could be worrying over nothing. Sleep it off and it'll all look better in the morning, right?"

"Son of a bitch has gotten to you," he said with a shake of the head, "playing it dumb on the door, big old white Uncle Tom act has you thinking he would never do something to benefit himself at my expense... He's one move away from having me pull the trigger on his bald ass."

The situation, the whole feeling was way off and I knew it would be a dumb idea to stay there any longer than I had to. Being there could only drive Albert further and further into his state of paranoia with him having somebody to pour his thoughts onto and the last thing I wanted was for him to get to his feet and storm downstairs to confront Matt out on the street so I took the wallet from my pocket and said, "I'm sure it'll all work out for you... I don't suppose you have anything left over to sell, do you?" knowing full well that he would.

"Don't worry about it," he said with a wave of the hand, "I've been chewing your ear off like an asshole - just chill here with me; my way of setting it right."

"I'd love to," I lied, "and you know I normally would, but I have to get to a club before they stop letting people in. I'm meeting a couple of the producers I've been working with."

"Right on," he grinned and his head rolled across his shoulders for a second like it was ready to detach itself from the neck. "I'm fucking happy that everything is working out so well for you," he said, getting to his feet to grab some supplies from the adjoining room. "You ever need anything for the big stars you'll be working with, I'll give you good prices. Fuck," he smirked, "you never know - this fucking neighbourhood redevelopment could mean I have to take up law again! You ever need somebody to get you out of a tight spot, you come to me. So how much are you hoping to buy, anyway?"

The rain wasn't so heavy anymore out on the street but the wind was still there. Matt was still on the stoop, the loyal pit-bull surveying the very same building he had been when I went on in. It was like he was expecting to see workmen suddenly arrive and get back to work in the dead of night. "Any developments?" I asked him, just to let him know that I was leaving.

"No," he said. "Can't even see any lights on over there... You'd think they'd have security watching over the place, wouldn't you?"

"Maybe it's not worth it," I suggested, "maybe they're bringing the whole building down to make way for a new one?"

"That'd cost too much money," he said, "no one would invest in that - not unless there was already a success story to encourage them."

"Whatever it is," I said, "I'm sure we'll see it soon enough. Anyway... I'm getting out of here."

"See you around."

The lights were off when I got back and there was the smell of alcohol and cigarette smoke in the air. Tiffany had entertained guests; five glasses and ashtrays littered around the room with an empty bottle of beer here and there. Whatever the cause for a celebration was, she would have worked hard to guarantee all attention was on her.

More bottles of drink, ashtrays and dirty plates were scattered around the kitchen. First, I noticed how the doors to the back weren't fully closed, then I saw the silhouette standing before the pool and my heart took one single bound to lodge itself at the back of my throat. It had to be Lee. Only Lee's return would be reason for such an unplanned party.

13

I LIT A cigarette to get my cool on before stepping back outside. He had his back to me; stood out in the wind and rain like it didn't bother him even though all he looked to be wearing was Tiffany's bathrobe. He had either heard the door or my stepping out, one of the two, and it was all the invitation he needed to turn and take a look at who was joining him.

It wasn't Lee. Eddie Shure, out in the wind and rain in his co-star's bathrobe. He looked at me and smiled. It wasn't the kind of smile you like to see; it's the smile you give somebody when you truly see them for what they are and the sight disgusts you.

"Cole," he said, "you missed quite a night."

"I was busy," I said moving forward to stand at his side, placed in front of the pool in the wind and the rain despite longing to be inside where it was warm and dry. "Went for a little something to eat, met a few friends for a few drinks... Got to remember to step away from all of this from time to time and enjoy life."

"I bet," he smiled. "So, were you blowing through your acting money?"

"No," I said like I didn't see the shot he had thrown, "I haven't touched that - have no need to. I'm rich, you dig? One of my ancestors was the emperor of an advanced alien empire and he left me a fucking fortune in space gold."

It wasn't subtle but I hadn't wanted it to be. He grinned, nodded, looked to his bare feet and finally looked out to the rain disturbing the surface of the pool.

"One day," Eddie said, "somebody will be able to heal you of all your dependencies."

"Ha! Come on," I said, turning to look at him, "let it all out, sport - what dependencies are you worried about?"

He turned to face me without losing the challenging smile. "I'm sorry," he said, "I didn't want to mislead you right there but I really, really couldn't give a shit about your issues. It's no hassle of mine… *dude*," he added mockingly, like *dude* was my corporate logo or some shit like that.

"One day," I said calmly and with a smile, "somebody may be able to heal you of all the brainwashing you've endured at the hands of a cult founded by a writer of god-awful science fiction."

He laughed and repeated the action of nodding and looking to his feet but this time his eyes rose to mine in place of looking over the pool. I'd known him for all of ten minutes and already it was clear for me to see how poor a choice of movement it was to make. The nod and look to the feet offered more than enough time to land a shot on the asshole's jaw if you wanted to take it.

"I really think some counselling through a charitable organisation would do you good," he said. "Just to help you get your head in the right place and to learn to accept each and every one of your many faults could work wonders."

"I think the same could apply to you," I said, tossing my wet and ruined cigarette out at the pool. "Look at you - you must think you're fucking big and you've made it and everything is exactly how you want it to be, but just stop for one fucking minute and really look at the picture you've become a part of... You're on a fucking soap opera and you're fucking the elderly has-been you work with. You're standing out in the rain, right now," I laughed, "wearing her fucking bathrobe! Can you really tell me that *this* was your lifelong dream?"

"Let me tell you something," he said and he placed one hand on my shoulder and started to lean in close; it's most likely he wanted to say something right into my ear but it's just as likely he was planning to take a bite out of my neck but either way, the whole movement was too patronising for me so I took the only action suitable given the circumstances...

I landed an uppercut to the side of his jaw and watched him topple into the pool.

"Eddie!" I heard Tiffany shriek and it made me jump because it was so unexpected and I had no idea where she was until I finally spotted her, leaning out of an open upstairs window. She disappeared from view, desperate to rush down the stairs and out here before her young piece of ass had the chance to drown.

14

THE WIND HAD died down but the rain was still falling. I had the cab driver stop a few streets early and jumped out, hoping the rain would have me looking all dishevelled and worn. The scratches Tiffany had put to my cheek felt bad in the cold and a lot worse than they really did look. It felt as if somebody was cutting at my face with a needle.

Matt was still manning the door, still going strong. He was looking up and down the street now, the nearby building soon to be undergoing major surgery was no longer capable of keeping his full attention. The padded jacket he had been wearing earlier was now gone, missing from sight.

He saw me coming but didn't give me a nod of the head or a faint smile. He glanced in my direction, turned to face the other way almost immediately after.

"Long night," I said to him with a smile, longing for him to inquire about the dramatic change in my appearance.

"Cole," he said sounding more than a little tired, "where are you going to?"

"Just thought I'd come here and speak with Albert."

"I can't let that happen," he said.

"Right," I grinned, certain he was joking. "He up there?"

"He's up there," Matt nodded, "man's sleeping."

I'd never actually imagined Albert having to sleep. Sure, I was in the habit of contacting him nine times out of ten instead of just turning up, but I'd never actually thought of him having a need to sleep. That could be the reason why I decided to push on despite the big man's talk.

"You mind if I go up? I won't try and wake him if he's sleeping, I'll just crash on the couch or the floor or wherever... The stairs, if I have to."

"This isn't a hostel," Matt told me, "this is a place of business and I'm the 'Do Not Disturb' sign on the manager's door right now. You want a bed? Find a motel. You want to get high? Jew has enough guys taking care of the streets."

I smiled at him even though it may not have been the best idea. I was torn, still trying to figure out if he was joking right now or whether Albert had been casting accurate prophecies a little earlier; when he had talked of Matt turning away business so he could venture out alongside somebody else.

"Come on, Matt," I grinned, "how long have you known me?"

"I've been asked that hundreds of times in the last hour and every time I've said it doesn't matter shit," he said. "Now if you don't mind - fuck off until the store reopens or hang around until you see me heading home."

"Nice try," I said, laughing while taking my first step closer to the door. Matt lunged forward with impossible speed for a man of his size, took hold of me and spun me round as he pulled my left arm high up my back. Electrified pokers pierced what I had for a bicep.

"Listen to me, you fucking little prick," he growled into my ear as he marched me toward the kerb, "when I tell you the store is closed, you fucking take note that the store is closed! Now get the fuck out of here," he said and he pushed me into the gutter. Ice cold water claimed one side of my body. It was a big enough shock to the system to have my body outright ignore my demands of getting back onto my feet and for a second or more I just stayed there, looking at my hand submerged in filthy water. That same hand felt even colder once the air hit it. Getting onto my feet, I turned and looked at Matt. He was back in his place, almost shaking he was that angry, but back to looking up and down the street.

"What the fuck is your problem?" I yelled.

"You wanting round two, motherfucker?" he shouted at me in response, strides in my direction deliberately slow to give me the time to start making my quick exit. "You won't be getting back up if I put you back down on the canvas," he warned.

"You're fucking crazy," I said, trying my best not to look the coward while making a hasty departure. "You need to have your doctor prescribe you something, I'm fucking serious here."

<h1 style="text-align:center">15</h1>

Pate didn't answer my call, but I thought it pretty understandable given the hour. I tried to imagine how he and Leonardi would react on hearing I punched Eddie Shure and faced Tiffany's wrath as the young actor with his sex appeal pulled himself from the pool, coughing and spluttering with his dick on show, and imagined the two of them laughing their asses off. A twenty-four hour liquor store handed over a bottle of Jim Beam, twenty cigarettes and a disposable lighter in exchange for bills difficult to separate because of how much water had reached them.

It didn't seem so bad, walking along with a drink and cigarettes, even if the wet clothes only encouraged the cold feeling to increase. I saw the familiar sight of bums crowding around a fire held in place by a lifted trashcan on a couple of occasions but ignored the urge to seek warmth there because they would expect me to share my supplies in return. I just walked on, desperate to forget how uncomfortable I was feeling - eventually laughing as I imagined how this night would seem in retrospect, a couple of years down the line when I was financially better than the majority of people out in Los Angeles... Out in the whole of California.

The cold claimed the centre of my bones and the Beam became harder and harder to drink. Smoking only made me gag. I thought of turning back and handing over what remained of the bottle and the cigarettes in exchange for the warmth of a fire but kept on walking. You might think there's this feeling of respect and solidarity between all bums out on the street because of what the TV dramas show you but you'd be fucking wrong.

I should have gone back with the young fag when I had the chance.

16

I WITNESSED THE rain coming to an end and the dawn of a whole new day out in Los Angeles as the sun crept out onto the skyline on tippy-toes and although it felt like I hadn't slept at all, I knew I had at some point. It was a lot harder to sleep rough than I ever could have remembered or imagined. An underpass allowed the cold winds to enter but never to leave; a dumpster was like a coffin. Because of this I had walked on and on before my body ached and there was no other option than to claim a park bench and allow the elements to do their worst.

The Jim Beam had become undrinkable but I didn't want to toss it into the air or leave it abandoned; that would be too much of a waste. So I pissed into the open neck, acid diluting the alcohol, and left it leaning against a wall for another down and out to eventually find.

Cars began to claim the roads; slowly at first but once they were there, they were fucking there. Then pedestrians filled the sidewalks. I lit a cigarette, resisted the urge to barf and watched them. My cell began to ring after a while. It was Pate. I smiled, thought about how funny it would be to tell him what had gone down with me and the kid actor and the older woman he had maybe just nailed for the first time. Before answering I took a good lungful of smoke and held it a while, knowing my voice was destined to sound rough as hell anyway but this would only encourage it and have me sound all the more rock n roll on answering to Pate's call.

"I was wondering when you'd call," I answered with the sound of my cocky grin travelling down the line.

"What the fuck are you fucking doing to me?" Pate screamed down the line. I jumped a little, straightened my posture in alarm as my heart moved like the wings of a hummingbird. This was *not* how I had been expecting things to run.

"Are you out of your fucking mind?" he yelled. "Are you really so fucking stupid? Well?" he cried, "Are you going to answer me or not?"

"Scott," I said.

"Don't you *Scott* me!" he screamed, a voice of pure rage to have you sink right back into your chair like an altar boy facing the wrath of a violent priest. "At what point did breaking Eddie Shure's nose seem like a good idea?"

"I never touched his nose!"

"You broke," Pate cried, "Eddie Shure's nose! Do you have any idea how much filming is going to be delayed because of you? How much money that is going to cost the studio? His looks are everything!"

"Just write it into a scene," I recommended out of desperation, remembering how they had done the exact same thing for a post-operation Tiffany.

"Don't you dare talk to me like I'm some studio drone, you little prick! Who the hell do you even think you are talking to? We're on a big storyline and on an even tighter schedule and you think you can just go around, breaking the noses of the talent we rely on to attract a new and bigger audience? Fuck you, Cole! Fuck you!"

"Listen," I pleaded, "he came at me first! He-"

"He could have come at you with a smile on his face and a lubed-up boner in his hand for all I care, it doesn't mean you can hit him in the fucking face! And Tiffany," he growled, "Tiffany is too distressed to film any of her scenes! She isn't leaving his side, won't listen to anybody!"

"Come on," I said, "you're making it sound like I'd beaten him half to death!"

"Who the fuck do you think you are? Who the fuck do you think you are talking to right now? You think this conversation is your time to step up?" He asked, "You think this is a game where one tells the other to go fuck themselves? Well how's this for a *go fuck yourself*... Any business arrangement or verbal agreement we had is officially over!"

I was fired from a cannon, projected way out into space and lost of gravity.

"Scott-" I started but never got the chance to finish.

"You can't play the game so I'm not offering you the chance," he said, "take your writing and shove it up your fucking ass already, because your name is trouble before you've even made one for yourself! And don't even think about reaching out to Nate," he warned, "because I've talked with him already and he can't believe how fucking stupid you've proven yourself to be!"

"Scott-"

"We offered you the fucking world and you rode on our asses like we were whores, but no more! You want to make it as a writer, go pull the wool over some other sap's eyes, you filthy son of a bitch! But just you remember," he warned, "if I ever hear of your involvement with any production, I will bury it deep in the ground with all the power I have."

He hung up on me.

I felt like crying. I felt like jumping into the path of a speeding train. I didn't recognise the land I was walking on.

Tiffany.

The only hope I had was of winning back Tiffany's favour, and quick.

17

One of the guards manning the gates saw me coming from the shelter of his little hut and the sight of me gave him cause to grin or sneer or both. He got up, walked to the entrance with his hands at his hips and his partner falling in beside him - like something straight out of a Western, the posse of two coming together to confront me. And I just kept on walking with my head up high, knowing I had nothing to lose if I could get beyond these two clowns and back into Tiffany's jurisdiction.

The first one to have spotted me hocked up some phlegm like he was removing chewing tobacco from the back of his mouth, stepping up into the role of gunslinger as best he could. When he looked back at me he said, "I don't think you have any business around here, son."

These assholes, these arrogant sons of bitches, they'd been waiting a long time to talk to me like I was beneath them. Let them, I thought, shrugging it off, this will be their one and only time and then I would sure enjoy making them kiss my ass for a long time.

"You going to let me through or what?"

"I think I'm going to have to say... '*What*," he said and his work buddy sniggered into his shoulder, looking away like he was no part of this at all.

"Just let me in already."

"No can do, padre," he smiled. "You've had your hall pass revoked. We are under strict orders to send you away from this place."

"Go call through to Tiffany," I said, "and tell her to just give me five minutes, it's all I ask."

"It's Miss Lily's orders I'm following," he smirked. "Obviously, if it was up to me then I would let you in - but she pays my bills..."

"How much for you to look the other way?" I asked, defeated

and slipping a hand into my wallet.

"I can't accept any bribe," he grinned. "Now please, sir, move along."

"Come on," I pleaded, "just get her out here for five minutes or let me go on in there for three... You know who I am."

"I do," he nodded. "So beat it before we have to call the cops to have you removed."

"Why waste everybody's time like that?" I asked him.

"Sir," he said as he began to ease the can of pepper spray he was carrying from its holster, "I'm not going to ask you again."

"Okay," I said with my hands in the air for a sign of my admitted defeat, "just let me go in and grab a few things, would you? Tell Tiffany I'll be in and out in no time at all."

"No," he said, "you won't be going in there at all. Now keep walking," he said, "with your back to me. This is your last warning... Don't push me on this one."

"Enjoy this," I said with a grin, "savour the fucking moment because you *know* I'll be back in here within a couple of days. Hours, even."

18

It was a train ride and a long, long walk to get to Willridge's place. I took all the time in the world for two reasons; the first to give Tiffany time to realise she was missing me or even build up enough anger to call me (let her hiss and cuss, I was confident I could sweet-talk her if she just gave me the opportunity to open my mouth) and the second to give Pate and Leonardi time to head there for a little brunch or an early lunch. Of course, the two weren't there but Willridge himself was - with his Little Richard wig and uniform starched to cutting point.

"Cole," he excitedly said, stepping out from behind the counter, "good to see you, good to see you! What're you doing here?" he asked with a smile. "You meeting with Scott and Nate?"

The small number of customers went on examining their menus. A girl behind the counter merely glanced over before continuing with her work.

"Just me dining here today," I said and although Willridge attempted to hide the disappointment he felt on hearing that, it was too much for him to fully cover.

"Well, take a seat," he said, ushering me into a booth. "Are you hungry? What do you want to eat? It's on the house," he added, convinced I could help encourage Pate and Leonardi to buy into the place. I wondered if he would be half as considerate to me if he knew how I'd gotten on the wrong side of the two.

"You look like you had one memorable night!" he laughed. "You just sit back there and I'll grab you a newspaper and make you the best and biggest breakfast you'll ever have."

"I don't know if I can stomach much," I warned him.

"Trust me," he smiled, "what I'm going to get you right now will make you feel like a whole new man," and with that he headed back for the counter, the sound of each step he took on the tiled floor having him sound like a tap-dancer long out of his prime.

My cell began to ring again while I was still eating my free meal. I didn't recognise the number. All hopes were on this being Tiffany calling from the studio. The battery was almost completely gone but I was confident of my ability to sweet-talk her.

"Tiffany?" I answered.

"No," the man on the line said, "is that you, Cole?"

"Who is this?"

"It's Tony," he said, "Tony Bircham."

When had I given him my number? It was difficult to remember with my attention being pulled in so many different directions... I wondered how would I cope on the streets if Tiffany didn't contact me, whether Pate or Leonardi would find forgiveness with my name on it and my biggest regret wasn't the fact I had apparently broken some punk's nose but abandoning a bottle of Jim Beam - even if I had used it for a toilet.

"Hey," I said - feeling a little confused. "How're things?"

"Cole," he said, "I just heard what happened last night and if it means anything, I think Scott and Nate Leonardi are overreacting to the whole situation."

For the first time in hours, I felt relief. Bircham was on my side, maybe he could win the other two guys back over for me...

"From what I've been told," he continued, "Ed has admitted he was getting up in your face, so what would they rather you do - just lay back and take it? No way," he said, "that's not how any man with respect would have reacted! If you ask me, you should be given a medal for not being intimidated by the little asshole!"

"Tony," I sighed, "I'm sure glad to have you in my corner."

"Of course I'm in your corner," he said, "and I'm not just saying that because I believe you could have quite a career in the industry. But how are you, anyway? Are you okay?"

"Not really," I laughed, "I'm pretty fucked right now from what I can see."

"Well where are you staying?"

"I slept on the fucking streets last night," I said, then voiced a silent apology to a young woman who turned and gave me a disapproving look for my language.

"Are you serious? Where are you now? I'm sending somebody to pick you up and we're going to put our heads together and work something out, okay?"

19

The guy turned up in a silver Mustang that attracted the eyes of every man, woman and child in the immediate vicinity. The driver looked like yet another advanced cyborg residing in the state because of all the injections he had taken to the face to keep wrinkles at bay; sunglasses kept frozen eyes hidden from the world. "Cole?"

"You must be Corsoe," I said, climbing in beside him, "thanks for coming to pick me up."

"Don't thank me," he said, feeding the engine a lot of gas, "I only do what Mr Bircham tells me to do," and with that the car raced on. He swerved around the other cars on the road like an experienced stuntman, ignoring the blaring horns of infuriated drivers who had slammed down on the brakes long after he had left them eating dust. I was desperate to beg him to slow down a little but thought this could be his way of testing me and, for some reason, I felt it important that I pass.

"How long have you worked for him?"

"Who?"

"Who? Anthony Bircham," I said to clarify.

"Officially," he said, "I don't. It's easier that way and a whole lot cleaner."

He ran a red light, cutting clean through approaching traffic without skipping a heartbeat. To steady my nerves I lit myself a cigarette and went for the safer option of not offering him one from the pack because it could mean his removing a hand from the wheel.

"You're going to get pulled over," I said like it was no skin off my nose but it may be a wise idea for him to slow down.

"I'll be long gone before they even notice me," Corsoe grinned. "You look like shit and if you don't mind my saying," he said, "you smell little better. Where'd you sleep last night," he laughed, "the morgue?"

"If Bircham didn't tell you," I said as cool as I could, "it mustn't be any of your concern."

"No," he agreed, "I guess it isn't."

A couple of minutes crawled by before I finally decided to try a little conversation again.

"So where you taking me," I asked, "one of the studios?"

"Not that I'm aware," he said. "He was celebrating last night. One of the apples of his eye got off to a shaky start but has been renewed for a second season, so he did what any other man in his position would do; he took a few people for a meal and a couple of drinks, visited a couple of clubs, a couple of strip joints, gathered some tail for a private party and took it back to a hotel he knows will never tip-off the press or plant recording equipment in his room."

"Sounds like a good night," I said.

"It was. Now listen," he said to advise me on running another red light, "he could still have a couple of guests up in his room for all I know right now and like I've already told you - his night wasn't suitable for broadcast, if you understand where I'm coming from. You see any young beaver prancing around his room, you don't start drooling on the rug and tugging at your dick - you understand? The man is a professional and he is meeting you as a professional."

"Sure," I said with a nod of the head, "I understand."

"You keep your breathing steady and your eyes on him for as long as you can. California is full of people dreaming they had half the say he does while claiming that they do," he mused, "so you treat him with respect and you do as he asks and everything will come out better than you would ever have dreamed it could."

"I got you."

"Let's hope you do," he said, "because if you miss out on an act of kindness from Mr Anthony Bircham, you will regret it for as long as you live... If you can call what follows *living*. All the guy wants is for his friends to have a fat wallet and to swim in an ocean of clean pussy."

He was driving much more safely come the time we reached

the hotel. I jumped out of the Mustang to follow his lead, watched him toss the keys into the gloved hand of a waiting valet. "Put a little air in the back tyres for me, would you?" he said to the valet but he was walking through the automatic doors before an answer had been given with me close behind. The foyer carpet was white but didn't have a single stain on it. "It's a nice place, isn't it?" he asked like a man thinking aloud because of how much space there was between us, no matter how desperately I tried to gain distance on his heels. "People are always talking about places that have been around for a hundred years or more but I'm a contemporary kind of guy. Antique furniture bugs the hell out of me and the beds... How many sweating, naked bodies have been in those beds when you stop and think about it? You can boil those sheets until they turn see-through for all I care, that shit is still nasty."

He stopped at the elevator doors, pressed the button to call them and finally granted me the necessary moment to catch up with him on doing so. If he was out of breath from how quickly he had been moving, he hid it well. "You like snowballs?" he asked me. "It's Advocaat with lime juice and lemonade over ice - sometimes a splash of vodka. If he offers you a snowball it's a sign you're in and he's going to help you out like no other man can," he said. "You turn down his offer and it's like you've gone slapped him across the face after you've just readjusted your clammy junk right in front of him."

20

THE BUTTON WITH *P/house* beside it had pride of place atop the rest; the angel looking down upon the Christmas tree. Corsoe took a specially produced key - a slender piece of square-shaped plastic - from his pocket and pressed it into the slot at the side. The button lit up immediately. Corsoe pressed it in, pulled his magic key out and smiled as the elevator doors closed silently. "Keeps out the bottom feeders," he said.

"What if somebody had gotten in with us and refused to get out?" I asked.

"I'd fuck them up," he said, leaning back against the wall. "I carry a Taser with me at all times. Small and easy to hide but it'll take someone down whenever you need to. Or want to," he added.

"I'll try to remember."

The elevator stopped in a room that looked to be T shaped; the doors revealed a small corridor that opened out to a much larger room split into two areas - bedroom with queen-sized bed and bedside cabinet, living room with large couch, recliner and flatscreen TV with a mini refrigerator standing beneath it. An open door beside the bed obviously led into the bathroom. Floor to ceiling windows offered a view guaranteed to take your breath away. Even with the empty bottles scattered about the room and the choking smell of old smoke, the room and everything it had to offer was still enough to make you want to own it, if only for a moment.

"What do you think?" Corsoe asked with a smirk, pointing to a latex glove covering a smoke alarm on the high ceiling. "That was my idea. Looks don't last as long as intelligence."

"You must be incredibly proud," I told him.

The bathroom door opened and Bircham stepped out into the bedroom area. He was wearing a pale blue bathrobe that stopped a matter of inches from the hips. So tight it was clearly meant for women to wear. The producer seemed a little surprised on first spotting us. From his back came the sound of a toilet bowl silently refilling.

"You found him okay?" he said to Corsoe.

"Yes sir," Corsoe replied, straightening his back while simultaneously bringing his heels together like a private showing his general the due respect. "Right where you told me to go, Mr Bircham."

"Good work," he said and he took a crocodile skin wallet from the safety of a bedside drawer, opened it up and took out a handful of bills. "Take the rest of the day off; take in a movie or treat your mother to a day spa or something, you hear?"

"Sir," Corsoe blushed on taking the cash, "you need anything else, you call me right away."

"Nah" Bircham insisted, "you switch your phone off and wait until I call you first thing tomorrow morning, okay? Just leave the key on top of the radiator by the elevator doors, would you?"

"Of course," he said with a smile, slowly moving backward. "Glad to be of service," he added and he tenderly placed his special key atop of the sparklingly clean radiator and left in the very elevator we had arrived in.

Bircham looked to me, nodded and turned to head back to the bedroom area. "Take a seat on the couch," he said and he returned the wallet to the bedside drawer and brought out a pack of cigars with Zippo to replace it. "The disappointing news for you is that both Scott and Nate are saying they're done with you and they want you to pay back all of the money they've loaned you - with interest," he began as I lowered myself down onto the couch. Once you were on it, you felt like you were sinking right down to the floor. I noticed a discarded pair of panties to the side of the bed, looked away from them as quickly as I could and back at his face. He took his time lighting the cigar, keeping the flame to the end long after it was burning so he could go on puffing thick clouds of blue-grey smoke.

"The *good* news for you," he said, snapping the Zippo shut and tossing it back within the drawer, "is you have me in your corner and as much as I love those two, I have to tell you right now that I am just as influential, just as important - if not more so - as the two men combined. Take in your surroundings," he grinned, "breathe it all in and tell me if either man ever did show you something like this? Oh," he laughed as he made his way to the recliner, "they made a point of showing you a fancy home or two that they bought cheap thanks to the recession and were too tight to replace any of the fixtures. Showed you property they had got dirt cheap because it was above a store in a shitty area and then set designers did it up real nice as a favour... All this is ringing true, am I right? You don't have to answer that," he smiled, "your face says it all. Consider me your Fairy Godmother," he said, "but without the faggot undertones... If you should ask for my help right this minute, right this second, you will find yourself in a better position you were in before you popped Edward Shure in that stupid fish-mouth of his."

I took a breath out of nerves, worried this was all a plan he'd cooked up with his two friends to lure me into a false sense of security before the two of them jumped out of the bathroom to see the look on my face. "I could really use some help," I admitted.

"It's yours," he grinned, "I'll pay off your debt in full and I'll see that you get regular work that will help you get by while you're paying me back with instalments so small you'll struggle to notice them. Now let me guess - you want to know what I expect from you in return, am I right?"

"Yeah," I said, "you're right."

Bircham sank his back deeper into the recliner and repositioned himself to get comfortable, placing his left ankle atop his right knee. The position he had gone for revealed shaven balls the colour of radishes left out in a cold field; cock like a chipolata draped lazily across one. He seemed unaware that he had pulled something of a *Basic Instinct* on me so I did my best to act like I hadn't noticed. "They both said good things about your writing," he told me, "so I want you to keep on writing, but for me. It can't be what you were working on with them," he continued, "it has to be something new... Any ideas?"

A writer dreams of somebody with a lot of money and

influence stepping up to offer their full assistance but it turns out when it finally happens, your mind goes completely blank and panic takes hold.

"How about something based on me and Tiffany Lily?" I suggested.

"Impossible," he said without hesitation. "You could change the names, change the location, but too much of it would be recognised by her and she must have had you sign a non-disclosure... You go down that avenue," he warned, "and she'll wear your balls as earrings - once she's taken everything of value from them."

"Science fiction?"

"I like it! What's the story?"

"Let me think about it," I said, taking my cell from my pocket to try and buy a little time and also see if Tiffany had been in touch. She hadn't. All I saw was how close to death my battery was. "Shit," I said, "battery is almost gone."

"And let me guess - you left the charger at Tiffany's?"

"Sure did," I said with a sigh.

"Use mine - it's in the drawer over there. I'll loan you a little money to buy a new one today," he added. "But you slept out on the streets last night? Have you found anywhere you can go tonight? Friends you can stay with or something?"

"Sure," I said out of misplaced embarrassment, "I'm comfortable from tonight."

"Well that's good to know, because it's not like I can have somebody with your potential dying of pneumonia, out on the bones of your ass. But let's keep chewing over possible stories to tell," he said, pulling himself up, "see if a little alcohol gets the creative juices running. You ever had a snowball? A lot of people think it's a feminine drink but it tastes good and it gets the job done..."

21

MATT WASN'T MANNING the door and I was glad of it because I wasn't sure how he would react when our paths crossed again but I really wanted to see Albert. I wanted to tell him of my meeting with the big producer and the money that could be coming my way because of it. Obviously, I wouldn't be telling him how the idea I had pitched was about a smart Jewish kid who had dropped out of college to sell drugs with a neo-Nazi as his bodyguard and was now wondering how and when to break the news to his parents. It would also feature a returning character, a hybrid based on both me and Lee to make it all post modern for the small number of people in the know.

But the door to Albert's building wouldn't budge. I pushed my full weight against it - nothing. All kinds of ideas and scenarios ran through my mind.

Matt had killed Albert, locked the place up to buy time between his getting out of the country and Albert's remains being uncovered.

Matt had killed Albert, been double crossed by the rival dealers who had offered him work, and now both their bodies were being kept hidden from us all.

Matt had gone home to sleep and Albert had barricaded the front door from the inside to stop people from getting in while he fully caught up with his own rest.

The latter was most probably what had occurred but it didn't stop me from pushing at the door again and again, looking up at the windows above to see if I could spot anybody moving around in there.

The next living soul actually appeared at ground level; out on the very same street I was on. A guy in his late teens or early twenties, walking straight for the door with his eyes on the cell phone in his hands. He was holding it all wrong, talking right at it instead of through it. His eyes were like marbles. When he got close enough I saw how the inside of his bottom lip was black and shiny. It was most likely to be dried blood but it looked like it could have been tar. The guy didn't even seem to have noticed me until he pushed at the door and it didn't open for him so he stopped, raised his eyes and looked at the barrier in front of him before turning to face me. I knew the high he was experiencing; the kind that expands in your chest and every breath you take lifts you gently from your feet and pulls you backwards until you finally exhale. Coming here to get something to put on top of that feeling just showed me how he was greedy.

"Do you know what's going on?" he asked.

"The door's locked," I said, "there's no way in."

"The door's locked?" he said like it was news to him, turning back to it and trying to push his way in all over again. "I've just got to see my friend."

"I know how that feels. I guess we'll have to try again later," I said.

He pushed at the door again anyway, his brow twisting to show he was confused and frustrated at this unforeseen event.

"It was good to meet you but I'm going," I told him like it was any of his concern, "I'll see you around."

He hadn't heard what I had said or it just hadn't registered. He just kept trying the door over and over again.

22

My reason for going to Willridge's diner wasn't so much because I was hungry but because I wanted more than anything to bump into Pate and Leonardi. I wanted to give them a cocky grin and tell them how Bircham and me had been kicking a few ideas around and settled on something in no time at all. More than anything I wanted to act like there were no hard feelings. It's just the two weren't to be seen when I arrived - Willridge neither. I ordered a meal and asked, "Is Kelley around?" as the girl punched my order into the system.

"Who?" she said without taking her eyes off the screen.

"Kelley Willridge," I said, "owns the place," I added. Today's target was scoring a free meal.

"He isn't on the rota," she said, "so I guess not. That'll be twelve dollars and fifty-five cents."

I begrudgingly handed her the money, gladly accepted my change and carried my meal over to a quiet booth in the corner. The fries were damp and the burger tasted like they had as good as cremated it but I couldn't stop eating for hunger. Willridge himself arrived while I was down to my soda; not in costume but everyday clothes and with a Rams baseball cap pulled down low. I acted like I hadn't noticed him - like I hadn't even been hoping to see him.

"How're we doing today?" I heard him ask the same girl that had taken my order.

"Max called in sick again," she answered, "says the power in her building went down in the night but we've been coping. Had a steady flow of customers and a real busy hour or two."

"You want me to call around - see if I can get somebody else to come in and help out?"

"We're coping. Oh - there's a guy here, was looking for you," she added and I looked down at the table to make out like I hadn't heard a thing and all the while I watched them both as discreetly as possible from underneath my eyebrows. She said the next part real quiet but I'm sure it was, "I don't know if he's a debt collector or not..."

Willridge stiffened up, slowly looked over his shoulder and almost collapsed over the counter on realising it was only me. "It's nothing to worry about," he was glad to tell her, "he's a friend of mine."

"Cole," he called out, heading in my direction, hips swinging with every step as he moved like a man possessed by 70s disco music. Every person in the place turned to see what the noise was about. I raised my head and acted like it was an unexpected surprise to see him here.

"Hey," I said, "I wasn't expecting to see you today."

"I'm only stopping by for a minute or two," he said, claiming the seat opposite me, "you remember what it's like to have a real job?" he grinned. "You get one day to relax and you end up running around like crazy on that day to put things in order! But how are you doing? You shooting anything yet?"

"Few creases to iron out first," I shrugged, "then it's getting the great American novel underway."

"I've thought of trying that myself a couple of times," he said with a smile, "put the few brain-cells I didn't destroy to some use. Trust me - you can only crash a car or dive through a window so many times before it all starts taking its toll."

"You trying to convince me you'd change a single thing if you could?"

"Sure I would," he said like it was obvious when really his answer knocked the wind clean out of my sails. "I should have used my time as a stuntman to get my foot farther through the door - became a director or something. You know how many directors and producers treated me like garbage? Practically all of them. The whole creative industry is overrun with sharks and sons of bitches," he said, "and I could have been one of the few good ones. I could have been somebody people could rely on; no ulterior motives or backstabbing - just somebody seeing good stories being made available to a large audience."

"You say that," I told him, "but what are the chances of you being able to stick with that outlook if you got the chance to do it all again? You telling me you wouldn't want a different pretty girl sucking your dick most mornings?"

"I'd want a different pretty girl sucking my dick most mornings because they believed I deserved it and not because they thought it would improve their career options. We all face judgement in the end," he said, "and God doesn't give a shit how many Oscar winners you were involved with."

My cell began to ring. I gave Willridge an apologetic look before taking it from my pocket. It was Tiffany. I wanted to answer the call but at the same time, I didn't. Let her chase after me for a while; have some power make its way over to my side of the court by convincing her I didn't give a shit.

"I'll leave you to it," he whispered like I had already answered the call. "But come by any time you want," he added, "you can always count on me."

I gave him a friendly smile, looked away as if it would guarantee my privacy and answered the incoming call. "Tiffany... How are you?"

"You son of a bitch," she said back to me. She wasn't slurring her words exactly but it was easy for me to see she was drunk. "You," she growled, "you complete nothing! No, you're below nothing! No," she said, "I know what you are - you're the devil disguised as a man and let me tell you this for free; it's a poor disguise. It's a piss-poor human disguise. It's almost as poor as your writing."

"So you're doing okay?"

"Look at you," she snapped back at me, "always wanting to say something funny... Always wanting to be memorable. I won't remember you five seconds from now, let alone five years."

I tried to figure out the significance of the number five but she carried on talking and it became too difficult to hear my own thoughts over her ongoing verbal attack.

"That sucker punch you landed on Eddie was just like you... *cheap*," she said and I heard the sound of her knocking back a drink and angrily bringing the now empty tumbler down onto whatever was in front of her with some force.

"You," she laughed, "you were nothing when I found you. You were absolutely nothing. Nothing at all. Then I was stupid enough to let you move in here and you walked around the place like a stray dog, desperate to please so you could keep your place by the fire."

"No," I said to correct her, "you weren't stupid, Tiffany, you weren't stupid at all. You were lonely and you were certainly sexually frustrated but that doesn't make you stupid."

"Always so quick to respond; always ready with a response that makes you at least smile and that's enough for you in that self-centred little world of yours, isn't it? Well think of a fun response for this," she said to challenge me, "you left your records here. Your records, your books, all of your clothes and even your beloved iPod. We're having a barbecue tonight... Just me and a couple of friends. And we're going to build a nice fire to keep us warm after the sun has set, Cole. Do you have any idea what we could toss onto the fire? Do you have any idea at all?

"Let me give you an idea," she was happy to say, "you'll soon be on the path of the Buddha - a life of no possessions."

"Tiffany," I told her, "if this is the last time we ever talk, I just need to know I made you aware of *one* thing..."

"How sorry you are? Fine," she said, "tell me how sorry you are."

"Not that," I said, "I just needed to let you know what you already suspect is true, Tiffany... You have no friends. You have no one. Not really."

"You had better get your sorry ass out of California," she screamed down the line, "you should run and keep running if you want to go on living your sorry little life!"

I laughed on asking, "Is that a threat? Are you threatening me now?"

"Don't think I can't have you taken care of!" Tiffany yelled, "Don't think you won't step out in front of a driver that fails to stop, or robbed at gunpoint by an overexcited mugger on a quiet street! I *know* people!"

"Well those people are about to start working for me," I told her and then I ended the call.

23

THERE HAD BEEN so much excitement, it took a while before each and every one of the additional problems called out for me to hear.

I had bought the phone charger, but I was still to find somewhere I could use it.

Bircham had offered me a golden opportunity but the laptop I had was in Tiffany's possession and it was possible she had taken a hammer to it immediately after our last phone call.

The money I had would be gone in no time at all; it wouldn't last more than a day and that was even if I didn't try and find a cheap motel to blow it all in one go.

And Lee came to mind... I tried to imagine how exactly he could be surviving if he wasn't safe at Doyle's side but couldn't. Where was he now? Was he in a hospital someplace or was he a John Doe sleeping in a refrigerated drawer on the other side of the city? A knife could have found him - or even an illness.

Before I knew it, the day had as good as disappeared without my noticing and I was back on Albert's street. Workmen were dragging all kinds of fixtures from the building they had been working on, well and truly gutting the place. It was none of my concern; at best it was somewhere I could spend the night if I really had to but I'd have to be out of there at the crack of dawn.

Matt wasn't at the door. I pushed it open with ease this time, whatever had prevented me from doing that early in the day was no longer a problem. It was quiet inside. I tried quiet steps and failed; could have been wearing boots of solid concrete. I wondered what would happen if Matt stepped out of one of the abandoned rooms to see who it was and saw it was me... Would he be pissed at me or was all forgiven now it was another working day? But he never stepped out to reveal himself, he wasn't around. The door to Albert's apartment was open, quiet music playing within slowly making its way out to me.

"Holy shit."

That's the only thing I could say on walking in there... *Holy shit.*

24

THERE WAS A shotgun on the coffee table as well as an automatic rifle. A couple of handguns on the floor, what looked like a small machinegun on one of the chairs and a huge rifle of some kind left leaning against another. Albert was looking out onto the street - wearing a pair of sneakers, Nike sweatpants with a crisp white shirt and pale blue tie. He turned to face me and smiled, taking a large pull on the joint he was smoking. His skin was pale, waxy, his eyes bloodshot with dark purple bags beneath them.

"Cole," he excitedly said, "what do you think?"

I thought I could probably be arrested for just standing there with all those guns around me.

"What is this? Are you venturing into gun sales or something?"

"Hell no," he said and he jumped into the chair with the rifle propped against it with such force I expected it to fire. "It's all for my *soldiers* out on the street," he explained, "see how big people wanting to muscle in on my territory feel once they see what we've got! I got grenades and all kinds of swords and daggers in the bedroom."

"Jesus Christ," I said, pushing my hair back with my hands.

Albert smiled, then he nodded like he could dig exactly where I was coming from. "I was exactly the same when I first saw all of this... I mean when it was spread out and I really took it in... And get a load of this!" he added, forcing his hand down the side of the cushion he was sitting on to unearth a small handgun that looked to be made of solid silver. I remembered how he had leapt onto that same cushion and almost barfed on thinking how he could have accidentally blown his cock and balls clean off.

"Classy little beauty, isn't she?" he asked. "Only small but I've been told she packs a real punch."

"Albert," I said, "where the fuck did all this shit come from and what the fuck is going on?"

"Told you already," he shrugged, "see if people still thinks it's a good idea to try and steal business from me when they see what me and my people are carrying."

"But where the fuck did it all come from?"

"Same people that provide me with what I sell," he said like it was no big deal. "I'd been thinking of asking them to take care of the cocksuckers trying to take my business from me but I thought I'd show them some steel and take care of it myself. They were impressed," he bragged, "really fucking impressed... Gave me a number to ring if I ever need backup in a hurry."

"Jesus Christ," I repeated. "Albert - have you even fired a gun before?"

"Sure I have," he laughed, "my dad used to take me out to the shooting range every weekend. A few times I even got loaded at home and took shots at raccoons."

"Man," I said, "I think I'm going to hurl..."

"What - because you can't handle a Jewish guy with a gun? That's real racist, you fucking asshole."

"What the fuck are you on about?"

"You come in here," he said, defensively getting to his feet and marching over to me, "and you see all these lying around and you freak out but if I was a black guy, you wouldn't bat a fucking eyelid and you know it."

"Albert," I told him, "this isn't you. If this is what you feel is necessary right now, maybe it'd be best for you to pack up your shit and get out of here."

"Fuck you, you asshole," he said and he shoved me in the chest but moved forward immediately afterward and embraced me. I could feel his heart pounding against my chest, feel the shape of the gun in his hand flat against my back. "I'm sorry," he said, his voice muffled as he spoke into my shoulder. "I should have known this would be too much for you to take in right away, but we're cool - right?"

"We're cool," I told him and he held me out at arm's length, free hand resting atop of the shoulder he had been talking into. He just looked right into my eyes for a moment, smiling at me like we had made some real progress in a counselling session.

"You're a good friend, you know that? And I'll make sure this is all out of the way when you next come by," he said, "but you don't know the half of it! It's all the work they're starting across the street... I can't have all this fall through! If I get moved on from here, it's all going to go to shit for me and I mean that! They turf me out before I have something in place and it doesn't matter how much hard work I've put into this, I'll lose everything and everyone!

"But what can I do you for?" he asked me, wiping his nose against the back of his wrist, real scene over.

"No," I said, determined not to leave any more money with my fingerprints all over it here. "I just wanted to apologise... I was looking for a place to crash last night and I got on the wrong side of Matt because he told me you were sleeping but I tried to come in anyway and then I tried to come by this morning but the door was locked..."

"Forget it," he said, turning to return to his chair. "You want a smoke? I'm going to have to get ready to meet my mom soon but we can have a quick smoke if you want to."

"No," I said, "just tell Matt I'm sorry, will you?" I asked, retreating.

"Don't worry about him, he'll be cool."

I made my way down the first flight of stairs as calmly as I could manage before breaking into a run, leaping down two to three steps at a time. The air out on the street was cold. It made me notice the sweat covering every inch of my body as I ran, still running even when my lungs were ready to burst. Maybe they would have if my legs hadn't given way from under me. My chest was on fire. I stumbled out onto the road. Car horns blared, continued to assault me even after strong arms yanked me onto the sidewalk. For a couple of seconds all I could manage was to cough and try not to choke on the heavy saliva filling my mouth. My breathing stopped altogether when I finally turned to thank the man who had pulled me from the path of a speeding car.

Father Doyle.

PART 5

BREAKUP

1

THE WHOLE THING just seemed so dreamlike, sitting in an out-of-the-way coffee house with Doyle. And it wasn't just because he had been coming to mind and then all of a sudden I was with him; it was everything that happened after he had pulled me out from the road - or the lack of it. Seriously, I had no idea how we had got to be sitting opposite one another - each man having a coffee of his own on the table that separated us both.

"Got an ingrown hair," he said, digging away beneath his chin. "It's been bugging me for a couple of days. You know they grow three times faster than any other hair, because they're not exposed to the elements? Things can lead to boils or rot away inside you. My dad - my real dad and not that fool I had to grow up with - my dad knew someone from inside who had to have an ingrown hair surgically removed," he finished, "thing was almost a metre long and more like wood than any hair either of us will ever have."

I could smell his breath from across the table. Something inside of him must have been rotting away and an ingrown hair was unlikely to be the cause. Even if it wasn't for the breath, I knew from looking at him that he wasn't at his best. He looked like he'd go ten rounds with a bear whereas he used to have been able to put that bear down someplace between two and four.

"Exfoliating is supposed to help," he said, "but what man

234

would feel comfortable doing that? The word just has you thinking of women getting ready for bed."

"Thanks for saving me back there," I said, "I mean when you pulled me out of the road."

"That was nothing," he shrugged, "anyone else nearby would have done the exact same thing. And I've always hated the sound of a moving car coming into impact with anything," he said. "That sound goes right through me."

Doyle had always known what to say to hurt someone and I wondered if the last statement had been his way of trying to hurt me... I wondered just how much he remembered of what I had told him, even if it was so long ago. He raised the cup to his lips like he was going to drink but thought better of it - lowered it back down onto the table and looked out of the window instead. "Some days I just stare out of the window and wonder how different it would have once looked," he said. "I think of the twenties and thirties, imagine young women from the country - now here in the city with dreams of becoming a star. The forties with men on crutches and missing limbs, fifties with the birth of rock 'n' roll...I don't know," he shrugged again, "I guess only the outfits are changing when you think about it."

"Get to see more and more of the women wearing them," I said.

"Get to see more and more assholes bothering them because of it," he added and this time he took the cup fully to his lips and drank a little.

I blurted out, "Is Lee with you?"

"Lee hasn't been around for a while," he answered, carefully placing his cup back down onto the table. "We've had no real way of being in contact ever since he made tracks with Susan."

"Susan? Who's Susan?"

"Girl from New York," he said like it was something everybody in town knew. "Art curator at the gallery? Surprised he never told you about her."

"No," I said, "he never mentioned anybody called Susan to me."

"He must have been scared it would get back to Tiffany,"

Doyle suggested. "But she was a nice girl and she made him happy, that was something even a blind man could see."

"So what happened to them?" I asked.

"She finished working here and went back to New York," Doyle replied, "he went with her. There's nothing you could do but wish them both all the luck in the world. They made a good couple."

"I can't believe it," I said, "I had no idea he was involved with someone. I mean someone else. He never told me."

"Like I said... he must have thought you'd go running to Tiffany."

"To be honest," I confessed, "I might have, just to see if she could have found a way to stop him from leaving."

"Then he did the right thing," Doyle said and he drank a little more coffee before speaking again. "So, things aren't going too well between you and Miss Lily?"

"Especially since Lee disappeared," I told him. "She had someone looking for him - a private eye called Silverdale... You run into him at all?"

"Silverdale," he said back to me. "The name's news to me."

"He was interested in you," I said, "Tiffany had him looking for you. The morning we first knew Lee was gone," I included, "Tiffany had Mark drive her around for hours - looking for either one of you."

"And what happened," he asked, "in the end, I mean?"

"I encouraged the investigator to lose interest and step away from it all. If Lee didn't want to be found, I didn't want them to find him. He was like a brother to me," I said.

"Sounds to me that you did the right thing on this one."

"Yeah," I said, "for a change, right?"

"I didn't say anything."

"I know," I told him, "I know... But what about you? How have you been getting on?"

2

"THIS IS WHERE you're staying?"

"This is where I'm staying," Doyle said.

It was an elementary school - or *was* an elementary school. Saint Claire's, now abandoned. The windows had boards over them, the boards had graffiti over them. A long crack ran down the centre of the building, from top to just above the entrance, almost halving the building entirely. Those double doors at the front weren't boarded up, weren't locked. Doyle pushed one open and straight away you felt the place really did belong to him.

"How long have you been here?" I asked. The bottles of varying alcohols I carried in four disposable bags gently knocked one another, the sound much louder on stepping into the long and dark corridor. Dark, but not dark enough to cover the slogans painted along the walls or the vandalised lockers with piles of dead leaves that had been blown in along the dusty ground beside them.

"I've been happy here for long enough," he said, lighting a cigarette for himself but not offering me one of my own despite the money I had just spent on drinks for us to share. "Place has working electricity and running water... even gas in the science labs upstairs."

"Are you serious? Why haven't they turned all of that off?"

"I have my suspicions," he said, still leading the way. He stopped outside the door of a forgotten classroom - said, "Wait here," and stepped inside, disappearing into the darkness within. It took a lifetime for something to happen again... I was sure Doyle had stepped into another time and place far removed from here but then light came on within the room - a bedside lamp on the floor beside an old gym mat with a sleeping bag on top of it - and I saw him kneeling down beside it with an open bottle of whisky in his gloveless hand.

Doyle slowly turned to face me, took a drag on his cigarette and beckoned me in. The room was cold when I entered; classroom tables and chairs piled high against the far wall. The smell of damp and mould was strong.

"Cosy," I said. "You have the place to yourself?" I asked. A few paperback books were scattered along the floor, next to the makeshift bed.

"People come and go - you know how it is," he shrugged before drinking whisky from the bottle. In the past, whisky had - more often than not - put the good man in the mood for violence. It was remembering this that had me place the bottles of drink I had down on the floor and walk over to the collection of tables and chairs - pulling a chair free to use for its intended purpose but also keep to hand as a weapon if needed.

"That wasn't there this morning," he said, pointing to writing placed across one of the walls in letters approximately a foot tall. They said:

BAD TIMES MEAN BADDER PEOPLE

"There isn't enough respect for old places like this," he remarked, knocking back a little whisky before fully sitting on the gym mat. I put the chair down when I was a couple of feet from him, sat down and took two chilled bottles of beer from the bags and handed one to him.

"To Lee," I said, taking the bottle cap from my own.

"To Lee," Doyle agreed, "may all of his dreams come to reality," and he removed the bottle cap of his beer and drank next to all of the contents in one easy swoop.

My cell began to ring. Doyle looked to me, surprised at the unexpected interruption. As quickly as I could I took the phone from my pocket with an apology, looked to the screen to see who it was and whether I could ignore it. It was Tiffany.

"I'm sorry," I said again, "but I have to take this," and I rushed out of the room and into the corridor - answering her call while looking in at Doyle through the panel of glass on the door to the classroom. He didn't appear too disturbed by the call; he didn't reach under the gym mat to take a blade or any other weapon to end my life once I walked back in there.

"Tiffany," I said, "what's the matter?"

"What's this?" she laughed and even a dead man would be able to see she was drunk by this stage. "It's a ticket stub for a Brian Jonestown Massacre performance," she said in mock appreciation, "and look! It's signed! I'm sure these are the autographs of the original line-up!"

"I know the one you're talking about," I sighed, knowing full well I would never hold that prized possession in my hands ever again.

"It's a shame you're not here," Tiffany said, "at my barbecue... You should see the fire we're having... You'd be impressed by how fast some things burn."

"Sounds pretty quiet," I said.

"I'm back inside!" she yelled. "Everybody is outside having a whale of a time and I thought I'd give you a call to let you know what you are missing!"

"As long as you're happy," I responded.

"I'm happy," she told me, "I'm a child on Christmas morning! I'm a pig in mud! I'm all different kinds of shades of happiness. But how about you?" and she took much delight in asking, "Have you ever seen what happens to a limited edition vinyl record when it's put on top of a fire? The way it bubbles and melts is oh so majestic."

"I'll give it a try some time. But listen," I told her, "give my love to everybody there, won't you? I'm sorry I can't speak with you for too long but my plane is about to depart."

"You're getting a plane," she laughed. "And where are you going to? Hell?"

"No," I laughed, "I'm flying out to stay with Lee for a while."

Silence. Stone cold, edge of the universe in September silence.

"What did you say?" she asked.

"I'm flying out to stay with Lee," I told her. "Only for a week or two but it'll be good to see him again."

"You don't know where Lee is!" she screamed. "You don't know a thing!"

"I know where Lee is," I said, "and I know exactly who he is with. Now I'm sorry but I really have to go right now... We'll speak again soon."

"Don't you dare-"

I ended the call, turned my cell to silent so she couldn't disturb me again. Inside the discarded classroom, Doyle was already on his third beer. He waited until I had reclaimed my chair and lit a cigarette before asking, "Anything important?" without looking at me.

"No," I said, "it was nothing to worry about."

"Do you see me worrying?"

"No," I smiled weakly, "I guess not... But Lee, right? Happy and settled... He was a hell of a good guy, so I'm glad it's all gone right for him... I can really dig that."

"You still speaking like that?"

"Like what?" I said.

"*That*," Doyle said in response. "All 'dig' and what was that other one of yours - 'word up and down'?"

"Straight up and down."

"Yeah," Doyle said, "that was the one. You were always trying to come across as some cat born in the wrong time but it never paid off. It always sounded so forced with you," he told me, "you always sounded like a fraud."

3

THE GENERAL FEELING of unease eventually disappeared thanks to drinking. Doyle would down a beer, knock back a little more whisky and grab another beer - usually whilst lighting another smoke. When a loud bang ran straight through the building I almost shit my pants but Doyle didn't flinch. "The fuck was that?" I asked in panic.

"There're issues with the heating," he said. "The old girl makes her complaints about everything and anything known, no matter the hour."

I smiled, started to relax a little and lit a cigarette. "You have any problems with cockroaches?"

"Nah," he said, "the rats eat the cockroaches."

"Rats?" I laughed, "Are you serious?"

"They don't tend to come near a room while I'm in it," Doyle said. "They used to; up until I caught a couple, took their heads clean off and left them laying around as a warning. You best believe they paid attention to that."

"I'm sure they did," I said, drinking a little beer. My cell was vibrating inside my pocket; Tiffany, no doubt. If Doyle could hear the incoming calls, he didn't acknowledge them. "But you've really landed on your feet with this place... Running water, heating, gas..."

"The neighbourhood isn't quite what she used to be," Doyle said. "It's the dirt, the scum," he continued, "it's never happy having what it already has... It has to spread. It has to spoil as much land as it can. Even for Los Angeles it's getting to be too much."

"Remember the place that used to be a McDonald's?" I laughed in a desperate attempt to lighten the tone. "Had that stall where you literally had to push shit down the toilet?"

"Yeah," Doyle laughed, "the amount of guests I tricked into using that toilet..."

"They always tried to clean up after themselves," I laughed. "They always knew not to try and take advantage of your kindness!"

"And what about you?" he asked before finishing a bottle of beer. "Would you say you took advantage of my kindness?" he said, reaching for the bottle of whisky.

Fucking whisky... It had always pushed him into the mood for violence...

"Come on, Doyle," I reasoned, "I was a dumb kid... I couldn't survive like this."

"It wasn't my issue," he shrugged, "you just remember you sold your soul for the opening offer," and he drank a little more whisky from the bottle.

"I need to take a leak," I told him, desperately hoping the good feeling would return during my short absence. "Where's the bathroom in this place?"

"Straight down the corridor. You'd best not be running out on me," he said.

"I won't even be five minutes."

4

FOR THE FIRST time in a long time, I dreamed about home.

I moved undetected, an astral projection taking it all in. Mom was in her study, putting the finishing touches on a contract regarding a sale. Dad was out front, fixing a neighbour's car. My brothers played ball with the neighbours' kids, my sister and her friends played with their dolls in her room.

The only thing that had really changed was how all signs of my existence - the way my room had been decorated when I had left it, framed pictures of me around the house - had been removed. You would never have known I had once belonged there.

Mom came out of her study, walked along the landing but stopped on reaching the stairs. Her right hand shot up to the right side of her neck like she had been stung. She threw her head back as her jaw clenched tightly, eyes bulging as her mouth began to foam and then she toppled downwards.

I woke with a start in the old classroom Doyle had granted me permission to sleep in the night before. He was sitting in a chair beside the open door, smoking a cigarette while he looked at me. If it hadn't been for the way I had woken, I'd have pretended to be sleeping.

"Doyle," I said, clearing my throat on sitting up.

"You were talking in your sleep," he said.

"Yeah? Anything interesting?" I asked, glancing at my cell to see 27 missed calls from Tiffany and a further 9 from UNKNOWN.

"Nothing worth reporting," he said. "You know I could have really hurt you last night... Don't you ever make me regret not doing it."

I swallowed, took a deep breath and lit my first cigarette of the day. "So, nothing has changed between us?"

Doyle said, "Not a thing."

"So what am I going to do now?"

"It isn't any of my concern."

"I'm on my feet," I told him, "I'm coming into some money... I could take you along for the ride."

"I'm not interested in going where you're going. It was interesting to see you, Cole, but get the hell out of here and don't ever let me see you again. You see me on the street," he warned, "you'd best turn and head the other way."

I nodded in understanding, groaned as I got up onto my feet and tried my best to stretch the stiffness out from my joints. "I have to ask you before I go... Is it true what you told me? About Lee and the girl, I mean."

"It's true," he said, "but I wish it wasn't. I miss him more than you could understand."

"One last question," I said. "How come you can forgive him but not me?"

"He was like a son to me."

"And what was I like?"

"What you might have been like isn't important," he said, "not compared to what you become. All you're good at is ruining things, boy. Nothing is good once it has been around you. You turn anything you can lay your hands on to shit."

5

I HAD ABSOLUTELY no one to turn to, no one to even reach out to and contact apart from Bircham. Tiffany hated me, Pate had made it crystal clear that both him and Leonardi didn't want a thing to do with me, Doyle had as good as chased me out of his place and Albert... Albert was there for me to approach but I didn't want to - not while his mind was pulling him in all manner of directions and he was surrounded by loaded guns.

So I went through my call list and called Bircham's number the second I found it.

"Fuck," I said the instant it went onto voicemail.

There wasn't even enough money in my back pocket for a coffee someplace. The few cigarettes I had to my name would have to be as luxury items until the sun began to shine on me a little brighter.

After what had felt like an eternity, I checked my cell, saw it had only been ten minutes since I had tried getting in touch with Bircham. I tried calling him again anyway and once more, it went straight to voicemail. "Fuck," I repeated.

It was only early. The day had hour after hour of sunlight to waste but I just started thinking the worst from the start - thinking of the impending struggle to get comfortable in a doorway that night; Bircham remaining out of contact as I fought against tight cramps in a confined space filled by the stench of piss left behind by the previous occupant.

It's early. That was all I could say in a desperate bid at reassuring myself... *It's early*.

Bircham could have been busy filming, could be in a meeting with creative types or sleeping off a hangover - having celebrated the completion of another favoured project, so I swore to wait an hour before calling him again...

It led to me walking for a solid hour, impatiently waiting for lights to turn red and give me the chance to walk again. The hour had been met by the time I reached the public park but I wanted a little extra time to go in my favour - kept telling myself to wait until I reached the statue of a once popular public figure now reduced to an immortal yet nameless stone image of his former glory.

I tried Bircham and it went straight to voicemail. Perfect rage erupted from my soul. Growling like a wolf I tightened my grip on the cell, went to hurl it clear across the park but thought better of it. A young mother pushing her young child nearby witnessed it all but tried to act like she hadn't to avoid capturing the attention of the crazy guy in the park and moved on at good pace.

"Fuck," I said from under my breath, claiming a bench, warming beneath the early sun while lighting a cigarette I really didn't have it in me to spare.

6

I WAS DEEP into the afternoon and still unable to reach Bircham. The warmth of the day itself appeared to be fading away alongside my hopes of finding a place to crash for the night; along with my dreams of Bircham providing me with much-needed salvation. Tiffany or Doyle - which of the two would be wisest to approach, pleading for forgiveness with head bowed and tail between my legs?

The record store was a welcome distraction... An honest-to-God record store for the genuine enthusiast. The giant sign placed in the window really grabbed my attention. It read:

UNDER NEW MANAGEMENT FROM MONDAY
LET IT BURN!

There wasn't the expected sound of a ringing bell when I pushed the door open; instead the hinges made a sound that reminded me of watching R2-D2 on the screen as a young boy with my father beside me. The guy at the counter was too busy reading a magazine to look up. Tape from an old music cassette had been attached to the rotating fan on the ceiling in the centre of the room and to the grille of the bulky AC at the opposite end. It fluttered dreamily in an artificial breeze and had me wonder if the air on the tape produced music that only a dog would ever hear.

And it was such a good store - so full of potential. It didn't have much room for whatever fad of the week was currently in place; it was all serious artists on CD and imported CD and both regular and limited-edition vinyl with music magazines and a collection of autobiographies and biographies along a high shelf running the walls. The place was a temple for the few people (myself included amongst them) that were down with music. If I had only found the place sooner, I could have been the new manager that coming Monday - I could have bought the place myself, convincing Tiffany it would be a good investment. Telling myself I was in an alternate reality running alongside our own did little to lift my spirits.

So much vinyl I had never seen before and now I couldn't afford it. Couldn't afford it and even if I could, I no longer had the means to play it or a place to preserve it for the ages.

Once my initial wonder of the store was enough for me to deal with, I finally noticed music playing in the background - coming from all 360 degrees of my surroundings. Otis Redding performing live; a bootleg recording from the sound of it but somebody had clearly gone to great lengths to boost the sound quality. I was in love - I just had to make my way to the guy at the counter and tell him, "This is quite the place you have here."

"It isn't mine," he told me, "not any more... I'm only here because the new guys are paying me to be - they haven't had the time to turn up yet."

"Well whatever they got the place for - it was a steal."

"You can say that again," he laughed, "I'm robbing them blind! Let me tell you," he explained, "there's no money to be made in records anymore; that goes for the stores and a lot of people recording, because nobody wants a full record now - they just want one or two songs and they can get all of that online for free."

"Too bad," I said, "I've always loved these kind of places."

"Well make the most of them while you can," he grinned, "you better love them before they are gone."

7

THE WARM AIR disappeared alongside the day and I had no place to go. Bircham had been impossible to get hold of. I was desperate to crawl back to Doyle, crawl over broken glass if it was necessary, and I hated myself for it.

The bus station was deserted. A lone ticket seller sat behind a plastic screen with a handwritten note stuck onto the inside reading: NO DERELICTS.

He didn't noticed me head right into the bathroom. There was a faint smell of pine disinfectant in the air, a sheet of paper signed and returned to the plastic wallet stuck to the wall said the place had been cleaned in the last hour and a half. I could feel my stomach eating away at itself on the inside but I sat in a stall anyway and shit what I could. Once I was done there I moved into the next stall, bolted the door shut and tried to get comfortable. It would be a long night.

8

"You're sure there's somebody in there?"

Hushed voices from the other side of the locked door.

"He's in there - I looked underneath when it wouldn't budge, saw his feet."

There was a shooting pain at my right side due to sleeping in a sitting position and leaning to one side, head rested against the wall. It was a miracle I didn't groan out loud on moving.

"Probably another fucking junkie... I hope you have thick gloves to pick up a needle."

"Just hope he isn't spoiling for a fight..."

One of the two men knocked so hard against the stall door that it rattled.

"Open up in there," one of the two said loudly and confidently. "You can't use this place as a hotel!"

"Just a minute," I croaked and I cleared my throat, got to my feet and flushed because flushing seemed like the right thing to do at the time.

"Come on," the other bellowed whilst pounding against the door with newfound confidence, "get on out of there before there has to be trouble!"

The moment the lock was pulled back, the door was pushed open and the station security guard forced his way into the stall alongside me in a desperate attempt to spot drugs paraphernalia or anything else that, like myself, just shouldn't have been there. His friend, the caretaker by the look of him, was stood with his hands at his hips; pretending to be chewing gum as he looked at me with the eyes of another bozo with dreams of being a gunslinger.

"What are you doing here?" the guard wanted to know.

"I don't know," I told him, "my blood-sugar level must have dropped too low and I dozed off or something. I'm diabetic."

"Have you got a medical bracelet?"

"Are you fucking kidding me? You think every diabetic should wear a medical bracelet to prove their condition to people, is that what you're saying? I can think of a guy in Germany who once thought it would be a good idea to make certain people easy to spot!"

"Sir," he said - fearing he'd put a foot out of place and could potentially be facing a disciplinary for showing prejudice to those with a medical condition in the near future, "I'm trying my best to see that you are okay..."

His partner no longer looked so brave but he wasn't fully convinced by my act so I headed out of there - trying not to push my luck as I grumbled just loud enough for the two to make out, "Look at these bozos! This fucking shirt costs more than either one of those guys will make in a week!"

Once I was out on the street, I rushed forward with my head down and my hands in my pockets, walking into heavy winds determined to knock me back. And I didn't look back at the station despite wanting to, because I knew the two employees would be watching me from the door. I kept walking, turned out of sight as soon as I could and broke into a sprint.

9

I CALLED PATE and I called Leonardi but neither man picked up the phone. Huddled behind a dumpster in an alleyway to try and escape both the cold and the eyes of roaming gang members, I left a message on Pate's answering machine that showed just how desperate I had become in so little time.

"Scott," I pleaded, "it's Cole and I'm so sorry and I really want to set things right with you and have the opportunity to work for you again because I have so much respect for you and Nate! Whatever it takes to set this right," I told him, "I'll do it. I'm your number one fucking guy, I'll get my head down and I'll have work ready for you at the drop of a hat if you just give me one last chance. You want me to apologise to Eddie Shure, I'll drop down on my knees for him and beg his fucking forgiveness in your name. Scott," I said, "I just really need someone to offer me a hand and believe in me."

10

From first light to nightfall I asked every and any soul willing to spare me a moment for a little help; from the busiest parts of the day to the increasingly quiet times of the deepening night. Reduced to the role of the beggar, doubling over from hunger and exhaustion so soon. Years of luxury now well and truly ended. My body, my mind, didn't know how to deal with the sudden changes. Catching sight of my reflection, I mistook myself for a junkie and began to understand why so few people were willing to help me because of it.

Remembering how you used to look out onto the pool during the early hours does nothing for you when you're certain you're suffering from hypothermia.

People merry from a few drinks turned quiet on seeing me stumbling in their direction; sped up to pass me by as I staggered on, coughing into the palm of my hand and checking there was no blood to be found there once the coughing fit was over and done with.

Had I really survived like this before - longer and when I was much younger? Had I really got by before Doyle found me and took me in? Before I screwed him over by walking out to screw Tiffany Lily?

Neither Pate nor Leonardi had been in touch and Bircham appeared well and truly unreachable, leaving me to wonder whether he had gone elsewhere to supervise some beloved project or been persuaded by the others to spare himself of some trouble by cutting me loose while he had the chance.

More than anything I wanted to stagger back to Saint Claire's and throw myself at Doyle's mercy - to have him end my fucking misery if he chose to - but I didn't. I kept walking on, keeping silent and to the shadows as I passed Albert's place from across the street to avoid Matt... To avoid venturing in and risk having Albert offer me some irresistible money in exchange for taking a gun in my hand and 'taking care' of one of his new enemies...

The building located just a few doors down was still being torn apart from the inside. The scaffolding was still in place; fencing had been erected around the place at street-level with chains and padlocks keeping it together. The fencing shook wildly as I scaled it no matter how slowly I went but every time I looked back, Matt wasn't paying me any attention. It must have just sounded a lot louder to me than it really was but the thought never crossed my mind at the time... I dropped down onto the other side, stumbled a little and twisted my ankle. The sharp and unexpected pain was a welcome yet brief distraction from the cold... From the weight on my chest and feelings of desperation and despair.

You could smell the dust of shattered stone and the shavings of old wood once you were inside the place. The air was cold. You heard strong winds coming from all directions but it never seemed to find you. A couple of hard hats had been left here and there by workmen intending to return early the following morning. Hard hats and plastic cups that had been crushed and dropped to the ground.

The first stairwell I reached had a sign placed on the wall beside it... They must make signs like this with special inks or something because I managed to read it relatively easy without the help of much light. It said the stairs were *not* safe; said the whole structure could fall down beneath me but to be honest, I was just too fucked to give a fuck and I headed up them anyway. Each step groaned and the wood seemed to sink a little beneath my weight but in my mind I had nothing to lose and plenty to gain. The place was being gutted but there still could have been an unattended bed or two up those stairs.

There wasn't.

I found nothing but walls where the plaster had been torn back to reveal bare stone and wooden slats; floors where tiles and carpets had been removed to show the cracked stone hidden from view for so long. Loose hinges doors had already been forced from.

In a room you'd expect to find in some nameless city buried

far beneath the weight of a long and bloody war, far away from America, I curled into the foetal position and tried to get warm. Tried to stop coughing my lungs up. Everything had well and truly gone to shit and I was left without a trace of light or hope in my world right up until the ringing of my cellphone woke me from a state of sleep I didn't even know had claimed me.

Everything around me was that light shade of blue you find with an impending sunrise. And my cellphone was ringing. Someone was reaching out to me, not giving a shit about how early it was.

My fingers were trembling so much I was scared it would stop me from answering the call.

"Hello," I shuddered.

"Cole, is that you?"

Anthony fucking Bircham, at long last.

"It's me," I said, struggling to sit up as a wave of exhaustion came rushing down on me with all of its weight. "It's me."

"Cole," he asked, "where have you been? I've been trying to get hold of you but nobody seems to know where you are or what you're doing!"

"Jesus," I laughed, "you wouldn't believe me if I told you," and then I took to coughing uncontrollably, certain death would claim me now my rescue was so close.

"Where the hell are you? I'll come and get you right now."

11

My forehead was stuck to the cold glass. Streets of Los Angeles, people of Los Angeles, Los Angles went by. Blink and you will miss it.

It wasn't the glass that was sticky; it was my forehead.

My forehead was pressed against the window. The car I was in went along at a respectable speed. The air conditioning or the heating was on; I wasn't sure which of the two but it had warm air continuously blasting my face. It kept me awake but it made me feel a whole lot worse; made me certain that barfing was inevitable.

I felt too tired to sleep. Tired, sick, sore, hungry - I felt it all.

Corsoe was behind the wheel, talking without stopping for air. Something was playing on the car stereo - a record, not a local radio station. It could have been a record with tracks I knew word for word, recorded by guys whose entire history I could usually tell you straight off the top of my head but now it was just *there*, a noise I couldn't focus on. It didn't stop until Corsoe brought the car to a halt. He climbed out of his door and walked around to assist me onto the street and if the artificial air produced by the car had made me feel bad, the natural air on the street only made me feel worse.

"Come on," Corsoe said into my ear, "pull yourself together - this is a respectable place."

He led me to the revolving doors of a giant hotel where the man on the door looked to me alarmed - not even blinking - up until Corsoe broke his spell by tossing the car keys through the air. The guy's leather-gloved hand instinctively shot out to catch them.

"Park it for me, would you?"

"Right away," the guy said, providing us with a forced smile as he walked away from his spot. My legs were already giving way under me and my lungs were constantly leaping up at my throat. Maybe I felt as bad as I looked, maybe I just wanted to appear so, it's impossible for me to remember given the state that I was in.

"Come on," Corsoe hissed to me as we entered the lobby, "snap out of your leisure seizure, already."

"I'm not high," I told him, "I'm far from fucking high."

"The fuck you are."

It was the kind of place that still employs a guy to wait at the elevator and then ride it with you - just to save you the chore of pressing a couple of buttons. His eyes widened on seeing us approach. I heard the click sound of him swallowing before we even got close.

"Same as usual, sir?" he asked Corsoe.

"Just call it for us, could you? I don't want you losing a couple days of work because of the bug this guy has."

"Thank you, sir," he said and the doors opened as soon as he pressed a button. "I hope he's feeling better in no time," he added once Corsoe had bundled me inside.

"I'll call him a doctor if he needs one."

"Excellent idea, sir."

12

Once more I moved undetected, an astral projection taking it all in. Mom was in her study, putting the finishing touches on a contract regarding a sale. Dad was out front, fixing a neighbour's car. My brothers played ball with the neighbours' kids, my sister and her friends played with their dolls in her room.

The only thing that had really changed was how all signs of my existence - the way my room had been decorated when I had left it, framed pictures of me around the house - had been removed. You would never have known I had once belonged there.

Mom came out of her study, walked along the landing but stopped, reaching the stairs. Her right hand shot up to the right side of her neck like she had been stung. She threw her head back as her jaw clenched tightly, eyes bulging as her mouth began to foam and then she toppled downwards.

I woke with a start, registered the feeling of the needle being eased back from my vein. It was a dark room. I was flat on my back, shirtless, in a large bed. Corsoe was standing at the door, the side of his right fist pressed to his mouth; Bircham was standing at the bottom of the bed, looking over me with interest.

"Ah," the doctor said, "he is awake," and he turned to face Bircham with a smile, asking, "do you see how good my supplies are?"

The doctor spoke in a European accent; strong and clear like that of a henchman from one of the earliest James Bond films.

"A simple injection," he said to me as he pushed a cap down on the needle and slipped it into his breast pocket, "what is more commonly known as a *pick-me-up*. You will rest well and your strength will return as you do so. I will prescribe something for the infection," he said to Bircham, "something good, but you surely understand that *good* has to be expensive..."

I looked desperately to Bircham and said, "I can't afford this."

"Come," Bircham said as he moved forward and put an arm around the doctor, "we'll discuss this in the other room - leave the boy to rest."

It took the last reserves of my energy to sit but I managed. "I don't have a computer," I cried as Bircham led the doctor out of the room and Corsoe moved forward to push me back down, "Anthony - I couldn't write for you right now if I tried!"

"Down, kid," Corsoe said, his hands pressing down onto my chest so hard you wouldn't be surprised if they forced themselves clean out of my back.

"Why is no one listening?" I pleaded as the hands of an invisible giant reached down from the ceiling and lifted me from the bed, "Somebody here has to listen to me!"

Corsoe said to me, "You're not even here," and the last thing I can remember before I was gone is his hand covering my mouth and nose, keeping me from breathing.

THE END

If you enjoyed this book, please consider leaving a review on Amazon or wherever you bought it from . It would mean SO much to us.

www.ingramcontent.com/pod-product-compliance
Lightning Source LLC
Chambersburg PA
CBHW060814190726
48285CB00002B/665